KURT VONNEGUT

Jailbird

PANTHER
Granada Publishing

Panther Books
Granada Publishing Ltd
8 Grafton Street, London W1X 3LA

Published by Panther Books 1981
Reprinted 1982, 1984

First published in Great Britain by
Jonathan Cape Ltd 1979

ISBN 0-586-05195-3

Printed and bound in Great Britain by
Collins, Glasgow

Set in Linotype Plantin

For Benjamin D. Hitz,

Close friend of my youth,
Best man at my wedding.
Ben, you used to tell me about
Wonderful books you had just read,
And then I would imagine that I
Had read them, too.
You read nothing but the best, Ben,
While I studied chemistry.
Long time no see.

Prologue

Yes – Kilgore Trout is back again. He could not make it on the outside. That is no disgrace. A lot of good people can't make it on the outside.

I received a letter this morning (November 16, 1978) from a young stranger named John Figler, of Crown Point, Indiana. Crown Point is notorious for a jailbreak there by the bank robber John Dillinger, during the depths of the Great Depression. Dillinger escaped by threatening his jailor with a pistol made of soap and shoe polish. His jailor was a woman. God rest his soul, and her soul, too. Dillinger was the Robin Hood of my early youth. He is buried near my parents – and near my sister Alice, who admired him even more than I did – in Crown Hill Cemetery in Indianapolis. Also in there, on the top of Crown Hill, the highest point in the city, is James Whitcomb Riley, 'The Hoosier Poet.' When my mother was little, she knew Riley well.

Dillinger was summarily executed by agents of the Federal Bureau of Investigation. He was shot down in a public place, although he was not trying to escape or resist arrest. So there is nothing recent in my lack of respect for the F.B.I.

John Figler is a law-abiding high-school student. He says in his letter that he has read almost everything of mine and is now prepared to state the single idea that lies at the core of my life's work so far. The words are his: 'Love may fail, but courtesy will prevail.'

This seems true to me – and complete. So I am now in the abrashed condition, five days after my fifty-sixth birthday, of realizing that I needn't have bothered to write several books. A seven-word telegram would have done the job.

Seriously.

But young Figler's insight reached me too late. I had nearly finished another book – this one.

In it is a minor character, 'Kenneth Whistler,' Inspired by an Indianapolis man of my father's generation. The inspirer's name was Powers Hapgood (1900–1949). He is sometimes mentioned in histories of American labour for his deeds of derring-do in strikes and at the protests about the executions of Sacco and Vanzetti, and so on.

I met him only once. I had lunch with him and Father and my Uncle Alex, my father's younger brother, in Stegemeier's Restaurant in downtown Indianapolis after I came home from the European part of World War Two. That was in July of 1945. The first atomic bomb had not yet been dropped on Japan. That would happen in about a month. Imagine that.

I was twenty-two and still in uniform – a private first class who had flunked out of Cornell University as a student of chemistry before going to war. My prospects did not look good. There was no family business to go into. My father's architecture firm was defunct. He was broke. I had just gotten engaged to be married anyway, thinking, 'Who but a wife would sleep with me?'

My mother, as I have said *ad nauseam* in other books, had declined to go on living, since she could no longer be what she had been at the time of her marriage – one of the richest women in town.

It was Uncle Alex who had arranged the lunch. He and Powers Hapgood had been at Harvard together. Harvard is all through this book, although I myself never went there. I have since taught there, briefly and without distinction – while my own home was going to pieces.

I confided that to one of my students – that my home was going to pieces.

To which he made this reply: 'It *shows*.'

Uncle Alex was so conservative politically that I do not think he would have eaten lunch with Hapgood gladly if Hapgood had not been a fellow Harvard man. Hapgood was then a labour union officer, a vice-president of the local CIO. His wife Mary had been the Socialist Party's candidate for vice-president of the United States again and again.

In fact, the first time I voted in a national election I voted for Norman Thomas and Mary Hapgood, not even knowing that she was an Indianapolis person. Franklin D. Roosevelt and Harry S. Truman won. I imagined that I was a socialist. I believed that socialism would be good for the common man. As a private first class in the infantry, I was surely a common man.

The meeting with Hapgood came about because I had told Uncle Alex that I might try to get a job with a labour union after the Army let me go. Unions were admirable instruments for extorting something like economic justice from employers then.

Uncle Alex must have thought something like this: 'God help us. Against stupidity even the gods contend in vain. Well – at least there is a Harvard man with whom he can discuss this ridiculous dream.'

(It was Schiller who first said that about stupidity and the gods. This was Nietzsche's reply: 'Against *boredom* even the gods contend in vain.')

So Uncle Alex and I sat down at a front table in Stegemeier's and ordered beers and waited for Father and Hapgood to arrive. They would be coming separately. If they had come together, they would have had nothing to say to each other on the way. Father by then had lost all interest in politics and history and economics and such things. He had taken to saying that people talked too much. Sensations meant more to him than ideas – especially the feel of natural materials at his fingertips. When he was dying about twenty years later, he

9

would say that he wished he had been a potter, making mud pies all day long.

To me that was sad – because he was so well-educated. It seemed to me that he was throwing his knowledge and intelligence away, just as a retreating soldier might throw away his rifle and pack.

Other people found it beautiful. He was a much-beloved man in the city, with wonderfully talented hands. He was invariably courteous and innocent. To him all craftsmen were saints, no matter how mean or stupid they might really be.

Uncle Alex, by the way, could do nothing with his hands. Neither could my mother. She could not even cook a breakfast or sew on a button.

Powers Hapgood could mine coal. That's what he did after he graduated from Harvard, when his classmates were taking jobs in family businesses and brokerages and banks and so on: He mined coal. He believed that a true friend of the working people should be a worker himself – and a good one, too.

So I have to say that my father, when I got to know him, when I myself was something like an adult, was a good man in full retreat from life. My mother had already surrendered and vanished from our table of organization. So an air of defeat has always been a companion of mine. So I have always been enchanted by brave veterans like Powers Hapgood, and some others, who were still eager for information of what was really going on, who were still full of ideas of how victory might yet be snatched from the jaws of defeat. 'If I am going to go on living,' I have thought, 'I had better follow them.'

I tried to write a story about a reunion between my father and myself in heaven one time. An early draft of this book in fact began that way. I hoped in the story to become a really good friend of his. But the story turned out perversely, as stories about real people we have known often do. It seemed that in heaven people could be any age they liked, just so long as they had experienced that age on Earth. Thus, John D. Rockefeller, for example, the founder of Standard Oil, could be any age up to ninety-eight. King Tut could be any age up to nineteen, and so on. As author of the story, I was dismayed that my father in heaven chose to be only nine years old.

I myself had chosen to be forty-four – respectable, but still quite sexy, too. My dismay with Father turned to embarrassment and anger. He was lemurlike as a nine-year-old, all eyes and hands. He had an endless supply of pencils and pads, and was forever tagging after me, drawing pictures of simply everything and insisting that I admire them when they were done. New acquaintances would sometimes ask me who that strange little boy was, and I would have to reply truthfully, since it was impossible to lie in heaven, 'It's my father.'

Bullies liked to torment him, since he was not like other children. He did not enjoy children's talk and children's games. Bullies would chase him and catch him and take off his pants and underpants and throw them down the mouth of hell. The mouth of hell looked like a sort of wishing well, but without a bucket and windlass. You could lean over its rim and hear ever so faintly the screams of Hilter and Nero and Salome and Judas and people like that far, far below. I could imagine Hitler, already experiencing maximum agony, periodically finding his head draped with my father's underpants.

Whenever Father had his pants stolen, he would come running to me, purple with rage. As like as not, I had just made some new friends and was impressing them with my urbanity – and there my father would be, bawling bloody murder and with his little pecker waving in the breeze.

I complained to my mother about him, but she said she knew nothing about him, or about me, either, since she was only sixteen. So I was stuck with him, and all I could do was yell at him from time to time, 'For the love of God, Father, won't you please grow up!'

And so on. It insisted on being a very unfriendly story, so I quit writing it.

And now, in July of 1945, Father came into Stegemeier's Restaurant, still very much alive. He was about the age that I am now, a widower with no interest in ever being married again and with no evident wish for a lover of any kind. He had a moustache like the one I have today. I was clean-shaven then.

A terrible ordeal was ending – a planetary economic collapse followed by a planetary war. Fighting men were starting to come home everywhere. You might think that Father would comment on that, however fleetingly, and on the new era that was being born. He did not.

He told instead, and perfectly charmingly, about an adventure he had had that morning. While driving into the city, he had seen an old house being torn down. He had stopped and taken a closer look at its skeleton. He noticed that the sill under the front door was an unusual wood, which he finally decided was poplar. I gathered that it was about eight inches square and four feet long. He admired it so much that the wreckers gave it to him. He borrowed a hammer from one of them and pulled out all the nails he could see.

Then he took it to a sawmill – to have it ripped into boards. He would decide later what to do with the boards. Mostly, he wanted to see the grain in this unusual wood. He had to promise the mill that there were no nails left in the timber. This he did. But there was still a nail in there. It had lost its head, and so was invisible. There was an earsplitting shriek from the circular saw when it hit the nail. Smoke came from the belt that was trying to spin the stalled saw.

Now Father had to pay for a new sawblade and a new belt, too, and had been told never to come there with used lumber again. He was delighted somehow. The story was a sort of fairy tale, with a moral in it for everyone.

Uncle Alex and I had no very vivid response to the story.

Like all of Father's stories, it was as neatly packaged and self-contained as an egg.

So we ordered more beers. Uncle Alex would later become a cofounder of the Indianapolis chapter of Alcoholics Anonymous, although his wife would say often and pointedly that he himself had never been an alcoholic. He began to talk now about The Columbia Conserve Company, a cannery that Powers Hapgood's father, William, also a Harvard man, had founded in Indianapolis in 1903. It was a famous experiment in industrial democracy, but I had never heard of it before. There was a lot that I had never heard of before.

The Columbia Conserve Company made tomato soup and chili and catsup, and some other things. It was massively dependent on tomatoes. The company did not make a profit until 1916. As soon as it made one, though, Powers Hapgood's father began to give his employees some of the benefits he thought workers everywhere in the world were naturally entitled to. The other principal stockholders were his two brothers, also Harvard men – and they agreed with him.

So he set up a council of seven workers, who were to recommend to the board of directors what the wages and working conditions should be. The board, without any prodding from anybody, had already declared that there would no longer be any seasonal layoffs, even in such a seasonal industry, and that there would be vacations with pay, and that medical care for workers and their dependents would be free, and that there would be sick pay and a retirement plan, and that the ultimate goal of the company was that, through a stock-bonus plan, it became the property of the workers.

'It went bust,' said Uncle Alex, with a certain grim, Darwinian satisfaction.

My father said nothing. He may not have been listening.

I now have at hand a copy of *The Hapgoods, Three Earnest*

Brothers, by Michael D. Marcaccio (The University Press of Virginia, Charlottesville, 1977). The three brothers in the subtitle were William, the founder of Columbia Conserve, and Norman and Hutchins, also Harvard men, who were both socialistically inclined journalists and editors and book writers in and around New York. According to Mr Marcaccio, Columbia Conserve was a quite tidy success until 1931, when the Great Depression hit it murderously. Many workers were let go, and those who were kept on had their pay cut by 50 per cent. A great deal of money was owed to Continental Can, which insisted that the company behave more conventionally toward its employees – even if they were stockholders, which most of them were. The experiment was over. There wasn't any money to pay for it anymore. Those who had received stock through profit sharing now owned bits of a company that was nearly dead.

It did not go completely bust for a while. In fact it still existed when Uncle Alex and Father and Powers Hapgood and I had lunch. But it was just another cannery, paying not one penny more than any other cannery paid. What was left of it was finally sold off to a stronger company in 1953.

Now Powers Hapgood came into the restaurant, an ordinary-looking Middle Western Anglo–Saxon in a cheap business suit. He wore a union badge in his lapel. He was cheerful. He knew my father slightly. He knew Uncle Alex quite well. He apologized for being late. He had been in court that morning, testifying about violence on a picket line some months before. He personally had had nothing to do with the violence. His days of derring-do were behind him. Never again would he fight anybody, or be clubbed to his knees, or be locked up in jail.

He was a talker, with far more wonderful stories than Father or Uncle Alex had ever told. He was thrown into a lunatic asylum after he led the pickets at the execution of Sacco and Vanzetti. He was in fights with organizers for John

L. Lewis's United Mine Workers, which he considered too right wing. In 1936 he was a CIO organizer at a strike against RCA in Camden, New Jersey. He was put in jail. When several thousand strikers surrounded the jail, as a sort of reverse lynch mob, the sheriff thought it best to turn him loose again. And on and on. I have put my recollections of some of the stories he told into the mouth of, as I say, a fictitious character in this book.

It turned out that he had been telling stories all morning in court, too. The judge was fascinated, and almost everybody else in court was, too – presumably by such unselfish high adventures. The judge had encouraged Hapgood, I gathered, to go on and on. Labour history was pornography of a sort in those days, and even more so in these days. In public schools and in the homes of nice people it was and remains pretty much taboo to tell tales of labour's sufferings and derring-do.

I remember the name of the judge. It was Claycomb. I am able to remember it so easily because I had been a high-school classmate of the judge's son, 'Moon.'

Moon Claycomb's father, according to Powers Hapgood, asked him this final question just before lunch: 'Mr Hapgood,' he said, 'why would a man from such a distinguished family and with such a fine education choose to live as you do?'

'Why?' said Hapgood, according to Hapgood. 'Because of the Sermon on the Mount, sir.'

And Moon Claycomb's father said this: 'Court is adjourned until two P.M.'

What, exactly, was the Sermon on the Mount?

It was the prediction by Jesus Christ that the poor in spirit would receive the Kingdom of Heaven; that all who mourned would be comforted; that the meek would inherit the Earth; that those who hungered for righteousness would find it; that the merciful would be treated mercifully; that the pure in heart would see God; that the peacemakers would be called the sons of God; that those who were persecuted for righteousness' sake would also receive the Kingdom of Heaven; and on and on.

The character in this book inspired by Powers Hapgood is unmarried and has problems with alcohol. Powers Hapgood was married and, so far as I know, had no serious problems with alcohol.

There is another minor character, whom I call 'Roy M. Cohn'. He is modelled after the famous anticommunist and lawyer and businessman named, straightforwardly enough, one would have to say, Roy M. Cohn. I include him with his kind permission, given yesterday (January 2, 1979) over the telephone. I promised to do him no harm and to present him as an appallingly effective attorney for either the prosecution or the defence of anyone.

My dear father was silent for a good part of our ride home from that lunch with Powers Hapgood. We were in his Plymouth sedan. He was driving. Some fifteen years later he would be arrested for driving through a red light. It would be discovered that he had not had a driver's licence for twenty years – which means that he was not licensed even on the day we had lunch with Powers Hapgood.

His house was out in the country some. When we got to the edge of the city, he said that if we were lucky we would see a very funny dog. It was a German shepherd, he said, who could hardly stand up because he had been hit so often by automobiles. The dog still came tottering out to chase them, his eyes filled with bravery and rage.

But the dog did not appear that day. He really did exist. I would see him another day, when I was driving alone. He was crouched down on the shoulder of the road, ready to sink his teeth into my right front tyre. But his charge was a pitiful

16

thing to see. His rear end hardly worked at all anymore. He might as well have been dragging a steamer trunk with the power in his front feet alone.

That was the day on which the atomic bomb was dropped on Hiroshima.

But back to the day on which I lunched with Powers Hapgood:

When Father put the car into his garage, he finally said something about the lunch. He was puzzled by the passionate manner in which Hapgood had discussed the Sacco and Vanzetti case, surely one of the most spectacular, most acrimoniously argued miscarriages of justice in American history.

'You know,' said Father, 'I had no idea that there was any question about their guilt.'

That is how purely an artist my father was.

There is mentioned in this book a violent confrontation between strikers and police and soldiers called the Cuyahoga Massacre. It is an invention, a mosaic composed of bits taken from tales of many such riots in not such olden times.

It is a legend in the mind of the leading character in this book, Walter F. Starbuck, whose life was accidentally shaped by the Massacre, even though it took place on Christmas morning in eighteen hundred ninety-four, long before Starbuck was born.

It goes like this:

In October of 1894 Daniel McCone, the founder and owner of the Cuyahoga Bridge and Iron Company, then the largest single employer in Cleveland, Ohio, informed his factory workers through their foremen that they were to accept a 10 per cent cut in pay. There was no union. McCone was a hardbitten and brilliant little mechanical engineer, self-educated, born of working-class parents in Edinburgh, Scotland.

Half his work force, about a thousand men, under the leader-

17

ship of an ordinary foundryman with a gift for oratory, Colin Jarvis, walked out, forcing the plant to shut down. They had found it almost impossible to feed and shelter and clothe their families even without the cut in wages. All of them were white. Most of them were native-born.

Nature sympathized that day. The sky and Lake Erie were identical in colour, the same dead pewter-grey.

The little homes toward which the strikers trudged were near the factory. Many of them were owned, and their neighbourhood grocery stores, too, by Cuyahoga Bridge and Iron.

Among the trudgers, as bitter and dejected as anyone, seemingly, were spies and agents provocateurs secretly employed and paid very well by the Pinkerton Detective Agency. That agency still exists and prospers, and is now a wholly-owned subsidiary of The RAMJAC Corporation.

Daniel McCone had two sons, Alexander Hamilton McCone, then twenty-two, and John, twenty-five. Alexander had graduated without distinction from Harvard in the previous May. He was soft, he was shy, he was a stammerer. John, the elder son and the company's heir apparent, had flunked out of the Massachusetts Institute of Technology in his freshman year, and had been his father's most trusted aide ever since.

The workers to a man, strikers and nonstrikers alike, hated the father and his son John, but acknowledged that they knew more about shaping iron and steel than anybody else in the world. As for young Alexander: They found him girl-like and stupid and too cowardly ever to come near the furnaces and forges and drop hammers, where the most dangerous work was done. Workers would sometimes wave their handkerchiefs at him, as a salute to his futility as a man.

When Walter F. Starbuck, in whose mind this legend is, asked Alexander years later why he had ever gone to work in such an unhospitable place after Harvard, especially since Alexander's father had not insisted on it, he stammered out a reply, which when unscrambled, was this: 'I then believed that a rich man should have some understanding of the place from which his riches came. That was very juvenile of me. Great wealth should be accepted unquestioningly, or not at all.'

About Alexander's stammers before the Cuyahoga Massacre: They were little more than grace notes expressing excessive modesty. Never had one left him mute for more than three seconds, with all his thoughts held prisoner inside.

And he would not have done much talking in the presence of his dynamic father and brother in any event. But his silence came to conceal a secret that was increasingly pleasant with each passing day: He was coming to understand the business as well as they did. Before they announced a decision, he almost always knew what it would be and should be – and why. Nobody else knew it yet, but he, too, by God, was an industrialist and an engineer.

When the strike came in October, he was able to guess many of the things that should be done, even though he had never been through a strike before. Harvard was a million miles away. Nothing he had ever learned there would get the factory going again. But the Pinkerton Agency would, and the police would – and perhaps the National Guard. Before his father and brother said so, Alexander knew that there were plenty of men in other parts of the country who were desperate enough to take a job at almost any wage. When his father and brother did say this, he learned something else about business: There were companies, often pretending to be labour unions, whose sole business was to recruit such men.

By the end of November the chimneys of the factory were belching smoke again. The strikers had no money left for rent or food or fuel. Every large employer within three hundred miles had been sent their names, so he would know what troublemakers they had been. Their nominal leader, Colin

Jarvis, was in jail, awaiting trial on a trumped-up murder charge.

On December fifteenth the wife of Colin Jarvis, called Ma, led a delegation of twenty other strikers' wives to the main gate of the factory, asking to see Daniel McCone. He sent Alexander down to them with a scribbled note, which Alexander found himself able to read out loud to them without any speech impediment at all. It said that Daniel McCone was too busy to give time to strangers who had nothing to do with affairs of the Cuyahoga Bridge and Iron Company anymore. It suggested that they had mistaken the company for a charitable organization. It said that their churches or police precinct stations would be able to give them a list of organizations to which they might more appropriately plead for help – if they really needed help and felt that they deserved it.

Ma Jarvis told Alexander that her own message was even simpler: The strikers would return to work on any terms. Most of them were now being evicted from their homes and had no place to go.

'I am sorry,' said Alexander. 'I can only read my father's note again, if you would like me to.'

Alexander McCone would say many years later that the confrontation did not bother him a bit at the time. He was in fact elated, he said, to find himself such a reliable '... muh-muh-muh-machine.'

A police captain now stepped forward. He warned the women that they were in violation of the law, assembling in such great numbers as to impede traffic and constitute a threat to public safety. He ordered them to disperse at once, in the name of the law.

This they did. They retreated across the vast plaza before the main gate. The façade of the factory had been designed to remind cultivated persons of the Piazza San Marco in

Venice, Italy. The factory's clocktower was a half-scale replica of San Marco's famous campanile.

It was from the belfry of that tower that Alexander and his father and his brother would watch the Cuyahoga Massacre on Christmas morning. Each would have his own binoculars. Each would have his own little revolver, too.

There were no bells in the belfry. Neither were there cafés and shops around the plaza below. The architect had justified the plaza on strictly utilitarian grounds. It provided any amount of room for wagons and buggies and horse-drawn streetcars as they came and went. The architect had also been matter-of-fact about the virtues of the factory as a fort. Any mob meaning to storm the front gate would first have to cross all that open ground.

A single newspaper reporter, from *The Cleveland Plain Dealer*, now a RAMJAC publication, retreated across the plaza with the women. He asked Ma Jarvis what she planned to do next.

There was nothing much that she could do next, of course. The strikers weren't even strikers anymore, but simply unemployed persons being turned out of their homes.

She gave a brave answer anyway: 'We will be back,' she said. What else could she say?

He asked her when they would be back.

Her answer was probably no more than the poetry of hopelessness in Christendom, with winter setting in. 'On Christmas morning,' she said.

This was printed in the paper, whose editors felt that a threatening promise had been made. And the fame of this coming Christmas in Cleveland spread far and wide. Sympathizers with the strikers – preachers, writers, union organizers, populist politicians, and on and on – began to filter into the city as though expecting a miracle of some kind. They were frankly enemies of the economic order as it was constructed then.

A company of National Guard infantrymen was mobilized by Edwin Kincaid, the governor of Ohio, to protect the factory. They were farm boys from the southern part of the state, selected because they had no friends or relatives among the strikers, no reason to see them as anything but unreasonable disturbers of the peace. They represented an American ideal: healthy, cheerful citizen soldiers, who went about their ordinary business until their country suddenly needed an awesome display of weapons and discipline. They were supposed to appear as though from nowhere, to the consternation of America's enemies. When the trouble was over, they would vanish again.

The regular army of the country, which had fought the Indians until the Indians could fight no more, was down to about thirty thousand men. As for the Utopian militias throughout the country: They almost all consisted of farm boys, since the health of the factory workers was so bad and their hours so long. It was about to be discovered, incidentally, in the Spanish-American War, that militiamen were worse than useless on battlefields, they were so poorly trained.

And that was surely the impression young Alexander Hamilton McCone had of the militiamen who arrived at the factory on Christmas Eve: that these were not soldiers. They were brought on a special train to a siding inside the factory's high iron fence. They straggled out of the cars and onto a loading platform as though they were ordinary passengers on various errands. Their uniforms were only partly buttoned, and often mis-buttoned, at that. Several had lost their hats. Almost all carried laughably unmilitary suitcases and parcels.

Their officers? Their captain was the postmaster of Greenfield, Ohio. Their two lieutenants were twin sons of the president of the Greenfield Bank and Trust Company. The postmaster and the banker had both done local favours for the governor. The commissions were their rewards. And the officers, in turn, had rewarded those who had pleased them in some way by making them sergeants or corporals. And the privates, in turn, voters or sons of voters, had it within their power, if they felt like using it, to ruin the lives of their superiors with contempt and ridicule, which could go on for generations.

There on the loading platform at the Cuyahoga Bridge and Iron Company old Daniel McCone finally had to ask one of the many soldiers milling about and eating at the same time, 'Who is in charge here?'

As luck would have it, he had put the question to the captain, who told him this: 'Well – as much as anybody, I guess I am.'

To their credit, and although armed with bayonets and live ammunition, the militiamen would not harm a single soul on the following day.

They were quartered in an idled machine shop. They slept in the aisles. Each one had brought his own food from home. They had hams and roasted chickens and cakes and pies. They ate whatever they pleased and whenever they pleased, and turned the machine shop into a picnic ground. They left the place looking like a village dump. They did not know any better.

Yes, and old Daniel McCone and his two sons spent the night in the factory, too – on camp cots in their offices at the foot of the bell tower, and with loaded revolvers under their pillows. When would they have their Christmas dinner? At three o'clock on the following afternoon. The trouble would surely be over by then. Young Alexander was to make use of his fine education, his father had told him, by composing and delivering an appropriate prayer of thanksgiving before they ate that meal.

Regular company guards, augmented by Pinkerton agents and city policemen, meanwhile took turns patrolling the company fence all night. The company guards, ordinarily armed only with pistols, had rifles, and shotguns, too, borrowed from friends or brought from home.

Four Pinkerton men were allowed to sleep all through the night. They were master craftsmen of a sort. They were sharp-shooters.

It was not bugles that awakened the McCones the next morning. It was the sound of hammering and sawing, which gabbled around the plaza. Carpenters were building a high scaffold by the main gate, just inside the fence. The chief of police of Cleveland was to stand atop it, in plain view of everyone. At an opportune moment he was to read the Ohio Riot Act to the crowd. This public reading was required by law. The act said that any unlawful assembly of twelve persons or more had to disperse within an hour of having the act read to it. If it did not disperse, its members would be guilty of a felony punishable by imprisonment for from ten years to life.

Nature sympathized again – for a gentle snow began to fall.

Yes, and an enclosed carriage drawn by two white horses clattered into the plaza at full speed and stopped by the gate. Into the dawn's early light stepped Colonel George Redfield, the governor's son-in-law, who had been commissioned by the governor, and who had come all the way from Sandusky to take command of the militiamen. He owned a lumber mill and was in the feed and ice businesses besides. He had no military experience, but was costumed as a cavalryman. He wore a sabre, which was a gift from his father-in-law.

He went at once to the machine shop to address his troops.

Soon after that wagons carrying riot police arrived. They were ordinary Cleveland policemen, but armed with wooden shields and blunt lances.

An American flag was flown from the top of the bell tower, and another from the pole by the main gate.

It was to be a pageant, young Alexander supposed. There would be no actual killing or wounding. All would be said by the way men posed. The strikers themselves had sent word that they would have their wives and children with them, and that not one of them would have a gun – or even a knife with a blade more than three inches long.

'We wish only,' said their letter, 'to take one last look at the factory to which we gave the best years of our lives, and to show our faces to all who may care to look upon them, to show them to God Almighty alone, if only He will look, and to ask, as we stand mute and motionless, "Does any American deserve misery and heartbreak such as we now know?"'

Alexander was not insensitive to the beauty of the letter. It had, in fact, been written by the poet Henry Niles Whistler, then in the city to hearten the strikers – a fellow Harvard man. It deserved a majestic reply, thought Alexander. He believed that the flags and the ranks of citizen soldiers and the solemn, steady presence of the police would surely do the job.

The law would be read out loud, and all would hear it, and all would go home. Peace should not be broken for any cause.

Alexander meant to say in his prayer that afternoon that God should protect the working people from leaders like Colin Jarvis, who had encouraged them to bring such misery and heartbreak on themselves.

'Amen,' he said to himself.

And the people came as promised. They came on foot. In order to discourage them, the city fathers had cancelled all streetcar service in that part of the city that day.

There were many children among them, and even infants in arms. One infant would be shot to death and inspire the poem by Henry Niles Whistler, later put to music and still sung today, 'Bonnie Failey'.

Where were the soldiers? They had been standing in front of the factory fence since eight o'clock, with bayonets already fixed, with full packs on their backs. Those packs weighed fifty

25

pounds or more. They were Colonel Redfield's idea of how to make his men more fearsome. They were in a single rank, which stretched the width of the plaza. The battle plan was this: If the crowd would not disperse when told to, the soldiers were to level their bayonets and to clear the plaza slowly but irresistibly, glacially – maintaining a perfectly straight rank that bristled with cold steel, and advancing, always on command, one step, then two, then three, then four ...

Only the soldiers had been outside the fence since eight. The snow had kept on falling. So when the first members of the crowd appeared at the far end of the plaza, they gazed at the factory over an expanse of virgin snow. The only footprints were those they themselves had just made.

And many more people came than had spiritual business to conduct specifically with Cuyahoga Bridge and Iron. The strikers themselves were mystified as to who all these other ragged strangers might be – who also, often, had brought their families along. These outsiders, too, wished to demonstrate to simply anybody their misery and heartbreak at Christmastide. Young Alexander, peering through his binoculars, read a sign a man was carrying that said, 'Erie Coal and Iron unfair to workers.' Erie Coal and Iron wasn't even an Ohio firm. It was in Buffalo, New York.

So it was against considerable odds that Bonnie Failey, the infant killed in the Massacre, was actually the child of a striker against Cuyahoga Bridge and Iron, that Henry Niles Whistler was able to say in the refrain of his poem about her:

> Damn you, damn you, Dan McCone,
> With a soul of pig iron and a heart of stone ...

Young Alexander read the sign about Erie Coal and Iron while standing at the second-storey window in an office wing abutting the north wall of the bell tower. He was in a long gallery, also of Venetian inspiration, which had a window every ten feet and a mirror at its far end. The mirror made its length appear to be infinite. The windows looked out over the plaza. It was in this gallery that the four sharpshooters supplied by Pinkerton set up their places of business. Each installed a table at his chosen window and set a comfortable chair behind that. There was a rifle rest on each table.

The sharpshooter nearest Alexander had put a sandbag on his table and had hammered a groove into it with the edge of his hairy hand. There his rifle would rest, with its butt tucked into his shoulder, as he squinted down his sights at this face or that face in the crowd from his easy chair. The sharpshooter farther down the corridor was a machinist by trade, and had built a squat tripod with a swivelling oarlock on top. This squatted on his table. It was into this oarlock that he would slip his rifle if trouble came.

'Patent applied for,' he had told Alexander of his tripod, and he had patted the thing.

Each man had his ammunition and his cleaning rod and his cleaning patches and his oil laid out on the table, as though they might be for sale.

All the windows were still closed now. At some of the others were far angrier and less orderly men. These were regular company guards, who had been up most of the night. Several had been drinking, so they said, '... to stay awake.' They had been stationed at the windows with their rifles or shotguns – in case the mob should attack the factory at all costs, and nothing but withering fire would turn them away.

They had persuaded themselves by now that this attack would surely come. Their alarm and bravado were the first strong hints young Alexander received, as he would tell young Walter F. Starbuck decades afterward, again stammering, that there were 'certain instabilities inherent in the pageant.'

He himself, of course, was carrying a loaded revolver in his overcoat pocket – and so were his father and brother, who now came into the corridor to approve of the arrangements one last time. It was ten o'clock in the morning. It was time to open the windows, they said. The plaza was full.

*

It was time to go up to the top of the tower, they told Alexander, for the best view of all.

So the windows were opened and the sharpshooters laid their rifles in their cradles of different kinds.

Who were the four sharpshooters, really – and was there really such a trade? There was less work for sharpshooters than there was for hangmen at the time. Not one of the four had ever been hired in this capacity before, nor was he likely, unless war came, to be paid for such work ever again. One was a part-time Pinkerton agent, and the other three were his friends. The four of them hunted together regularly, and had for years praised one another for what unbelievably good shots they were. So when the Pinkerton Agency let it be known that it could use four sharpshooters, they materialized almost instantly, like the company of citizen soldiers.

The man with the tripod had invented the device for the occasion. Nor had the man with the sandbag ever couched his rifle on a sandbag before. So it was, too, with the chairs and tables and the tidy displays of ammunition and all that: They had agreed among themselves as to how truly professional sharpshooters should comport themselves.

Years later Alexander McCone, when asked by Starbuck what he thought the principal cause of the Cuyahoga Massacre had been, would reply: 'American am-am-am-amateurism in muh-muh-matters of luh-life and duh-duh-duh-death.'

When the windows were opened, the oceanic murmurs of the crowd came in with the cold air. The crowd wished to be silent, and imagined itself to be silent – but this person had to whisper a little something, and that one had to reply, and so on. Hence, sounds like a sea.

It was mainly this seeming surf that Alexander heard as he stood with his father and brother in the belfry. The defenders of the factory were quiet. Except for the rattles and bumps of the opening of the windows on the second floor, they had made no reply.

28

Alexander's father said this as they waited: 'It is no dainty thing to shape iron and steel to human needs, my boys. No man in his right mind would do such work, if it were not for fear of cold and hunger. The question is, my boys – how much does the world need iron and steel products? In case anybody wants some, Dan McCone knows how they're made.'

Now there was a tiny quickening of life inside the fence. The chief of police of Cleveland, carrying a piece of paper on which the Riot Act was written, climbed the steps to the top of the scaffold. This was to be the climax of the pageant, young Alexander supposed, a moment of terrible beauty.

But then he sneezed up there in the belfry. Not only were his lungs emptied of air, but his romantic vision was destroyed. What was about to happen below, he realized, was not majestic. It would be insane. There was no such thing as magic, and yet his father and his brother and the governor, and probably even President Grover Cleveland, expected this police chief to become a wizard, a Merlin – to make a crowd vanish with a magic spell.

'It will not work,' he thought. 'It cannot work.'

It did not work.

The chief cast his spell. His shouted words bounced off the buildings, warred with their own echoes, and sounded like Babylonian by the time they reached Alexander's ears.

Absolutely nothing happened.

The chief climbed down from the scaffold. His manner indicated that he had not expected much of anything to happen, that there were simply too many people out there. It was with great modesty that he rejoined his own shock troops, who were armed with shields and lances, but safe inside the fence. He was not about to ask them to arrest anyone, or to do anything provocative against a crowd so large.

But Colonel Redfield was enraged. He had the gate opened a crack, to let him out so he could join his half-frozen troops. He took his place between two farm boys at the centre of the long line. He ordered his men to level their bayonets at those in front of them. Next, he ordered them to take one step forward. This they did.

Looking down on the plaza, young Alexander could see the people at the front of the crowd backing into those behind them as they shrank from the naked steel. People at the back of the crowd, meanwhile, had no idea what was going on, and were not about to depart, to relieve the pressure some.

The soldiers advanced yet another pace and the people retreating put pressure not only on those behind them, but on those beside them, too. Those at either end found themselves squashed against the buildings. The soldiers facing them had no heart for skewering someone so hopelessly immobilized, so they averted their bayonets, opening a space between the blade tips and the unyielding walls.

When the soldiers took yet another step forward, according to Alexander when old, people began '... to squh-squh-squirt around the ends of the luh-luh-line like wuh-wuh-water.' The squirts became torrents, crumpling the flanks of the line and delivering hundreds of people to the space between the factory fence and the undefended rears of the soldiers.

Colonel Redfield, his eyes blazing straight ahead, had no idea what was happening on either side. He ordered yet another advance.

Now the crowd behind the soldiers began to behave quite badly. A youth jumped onto a soldier's pack like a monkey. The soldier sat down hard and struggled most comically, trying to rise again. Soldier after soldier was brought down in this way. If one got back to his feet, he was pulled down again. And the soldiers began to crawl toward each other for mutual protection. They refused to shoot. They formed a defensive heap, instead, a paralysed porcupine.

Colonel Redfield was not among them. He was nowhere to be seen.

*

No one was ever found who would admit to ordering the sharpshooters and the guards to open fire from the windows of the factory, but the firing began.

Fourteen people were killed outright by bullets – one of them a soldier. Twenty-three were seriously wounded.

Alexander would say when an old man that the shooting sounded no more serious than 'puh-puh-popcorn', and that he thought a freakish wind had blown across the plaza below, since the people seemed to be blowing away like 'luh-luh-leaves.'

When it was all over, there was general satisfaction that honour had been served and that justice had been done. Law and order had been restored.

Old Daniel McCone would say to his sons as he looked out over the battlefield, vacant now except for bodies, 'Like it or not, boys, that's the sort of business you're in.'

Colonel Redfield would be found in a side street, naked and out of his head, but otherwise unharmed.

Young Alexander did not try to speak afterward until he had to speak, which was at Christmas dinner that afternoon. He was asked to say grace. He discovered then that he had become a bubbling booby, that his stammer was so bad now that he could not speak at all.

He would never go to the factory again. He would become Cleveland's leading art collector and the chief donor to the Cleveland Museum of Fine Arts, demonstrating that the McCone family was interested in more than money and power for money's and power's sakes.

His stammer was so bad for the rest of his life that he seldom ventured outside his mansion on Euclid Avenue. He had married a Rockefeller one month before his stammer became so bad. Otherwise, as he would later say, he would probably never have married at all.

He had one daughter, who was embarrassed by him, as was his wife. He would make only one friendship after the

Massacre. It would be with a child. It would be with the son of his cook and his chauffeur.

The multimillionaire wanted someone who would play chess with him many hours a day. So he seduced the boy, so to speak, with simpler games first – hearts and old maid, checkers and dominoes. But he also taught him chess. Soon they were playing only chess. Their conversations were limited to conventional chess taunts and teasings, which had not changed in a thousand years.

Samples: 'Have you played this game before?' 'Really?' 'Spot me a queen.' 'Is this a trap?'

The boy was Walter F. Starbuck. He was willing to spend his childhood and youth so unnaturally for this reason: Alexander Hamilton McCone promised to send him to Harvard someday.

– K.V.

Help the weak ones that cry for help, help the prosecuted and the victim, because they are your better friends; they are the comrades that fight and fall as your father and Bartolo fought and fell yesterday for the conquest of the joy of freedom for all the poor workers. In this struggle of life you will find more love and you will be loved.

— NICOLA SACCO (*1891–1927*)
*in his last letter to his thirteen-year-old son,
Dante, August 18, 1927, three days before his
execution in Charlestown Prison, Boston,
Massachusetts. 'Bartolo' was Bartolomeo
Vanzetti (1888–1927), who died the same
night in the same electric chair, the invention
of a dentist. So did an even more forgotten
man, Celestino Madeiros (1894–1927), who
confessed to the crime of which Sacco and
Vanzetti had been convicted, even while his
own conviction for another murder was being
appealed. Madeiros was a notorious criminal,
who behaved unselfishly at the end.*

Jailbird

I

Life goes on, yes – and a fool and his self-respect are soon parted, perhaps never to be reunited even on Judgement Day.

Pay attention, please, for years as well as people are characters in this book, which is the story of my life so far. Nineteen-hundred and Thirteen gave me the gift of life. Nineteen-hundred and Twenty-nine wrecked the American economy. Nineteen-hundred and Thirty-one sent me to Harvard. Nineteen hundred and Thirty-eight got me my first job in the federal government. Nineteen-hundred and Forty-six gave me a wife. Nineteen-hundred and Forty-six gave me an ungrateful son. Nineteen-hundred and Fifty-three fired me from the federal government.

Thus do I capitalize years as though they were proper names.

Nineteen-hundred and Seventy gave me a job in the Nixon White House. Nineteen-hundred and Seventy-five sent me to prison for my own preposterous contributions to the American political scandals known collectively as 'Watergate.'

Three years ago, as I write, Nineteen-hundred and Seventy-seven was about to turn me loose again. I felt like a piece of garbage. I was wearing olive-drab coveralls, the prison uniform. I sat alone in a dormitory – on a cot that I had stripped of its bedding. A blanket, two sheets, and a pillowcase, which were to be returned to my government along with my uniform, were folded neatly on my lap. My speckled old hands were clasped atop these. I stared straight ahead at a wall on the second floor of a barracks at the Federal Minimum Security Adult Correctional Facility on the edge of Finletter Air Force Base – thirty-five miles from Atlanta, Georgia. I was waiting for a guard to conduct me to the Administration Building, where I would be given my release papers and my civilian clothes. There would be no one to greet me at the gate. Nowhere in the world was there anyone who had a forgiving hug for me — or a free meal or a bed for a night or two.

If anyone had been watching me, he would have seen me do something quite mysterious every five minutes or so. Without changing my blank expression, I would lift my hands from the bedding and I would clap three times. I will explain why by and by.

It was nine in the morning on April twenty-first. The guard was one hour late. A fighter plane leaped up from the tip of a nearby runway, destroyed enough energy to heat one hundred homes for a thousand years, tore the sky to shreds. I did not bat an eyelash. The event was merely tedious to old prisoners and guards at Finletter. It happened all the time.

Most of the other prisoners, all of them convicted of nonviolent, white-collar crimes, had been trundled away in purple schoolbuses to work details around the base. Only a small housekeeping crew had been left behind — to wash windows, to mop floors. There were a few others around, writing or reading or napping — too sick, with heart trouble or back trouble, usually, to do manual work of any kind. I myself would have been feeding a mangle in the laundry at the base hospital if it had been a day like any other day. My health was excellent, as they say.

Was I shown no special respect in prison as a Harvard man? It was no distinction, actually. I had met or heard of at least seven others. And no sooner would I leave than my cot would be taken by Virgil Greathouse, former secretary of health, education, and welfare, who was also a Harvard man. I was quite low on the educational ladder at Finletter, with nothing but a poor bachelor's degree. I was not even a Phi Beta Kappa. We must have had twenty or more Phi Beta Kappas, a dozen or more medical doctors, an equal number of dentists, a veterinarian, a Doctor of Divinity, a Doctor of Economics, a Doctor of Philosophy in chemistry, and simply shoals of disbarred lawyers. Lawyers were so common that we had a joke for newcomers that went like this: 'If you find yourself talking to somebody who hasn't been to law school, watch your step. He's either the warden or a guard.'

My own poor degree was in the liberal arts, with some emphasis on history and economics. It was my plan when I entered Harvard to become a public servant, an employee rather than an elected official. I believed that there could be no higher calling in a democracy than to a lifetime in government. Since I did not know what branch of government might take me on, whether the State Department or the Bureau of Indian Affairs or whatever, I would make my wisdom as widely applicable as possible. For this reason did I take a liberal arts degree.

And I speak now of *my* plans and *my* beliefs – but, being so new to the planet in those days, I had been glad to adopt as my own the plans and beliefs of a much older man. He was a Cleveland multimillionaire named Alexander Hamilton McCone, a member of the Harvard class of Eighteen-hundred and Ninety-four. He was the reclusive, stammering son of Daniel McCone. Daniel McCone was a brilliant and brutal Scottish engineer and metallurgist, who founded the Cuyahoga Bridge and Iron Company, the largest single employer in Cleveland when I was born. Imagine being born as long ago as Nineteen-hundred and Thirteen! Will young people of today doubt me if I aver with a straight face that the Ohio skies back then were often darkened by flocks of hooting pterodactyls, and that forty-ton brontosaurs basked and crooned in the Cuyahoga River's ooze? No.

Alexander Hamilton McCone was forty-one years old when I was born into his mansion on Euclid Avenue. He was married to the former Alice Rockefeller, who was even richer than he was, and who spent most of her time in Europe with their one child, a daughter named Clara. Mother and daughter, no doubt embarrassed by Mr McCone's terrible speech impediment, and even more dismayed, perhaps, by his wanting to do nothing with his life but read books all day long, were seldom home. Divorce was unthinkable back then.

Clara — are you still alive? She hated me. Some people did and do.

That's life.

And what was I to Mr McCone, that I should have been born into the unhappy stillness of his mansion? My mother, born Anna Kairys in Russian Lithuania, was his cook. My father, born Stanislaus Stankiewicz in Russian Poland, was his bodyguard and chauffeur. They genuinely loved him.

Mr McCone built a handsome apartment for them, and for me, too, on the second floor of his carriage house. And, as I grew older, I became his playmate, always indoors. He taught me hearts and old maid, checkers and dominoes — and chess. Soon we were playing only chess. He did not play well. I won almost all of the games, and it is possible that he was secretly drunk. He never tried hard to win, I thought. In any event, and very early on, he began to tell me and my parents that I was a genius, which I surely was not, and that he would send me to Harvard. He must have said to my father and mother a thousand times over the years, 'You are going to find yourselves the proud parents of a perfect Harvard gentleman someday.'

To that end, and when I was about ten years old, he had us change our family name from Stankiewicz to Starbuck. I would be better received at Harvard, he said, if I had an Anglo-Saxon name. Thus did Walter F. Starbuck become my name.

He himself had done badly at Harvard, had scarcely squeaked through. He had also been scorned socially, not only for his stammer but for his being the obscenely rich son of an immigrant. There was every reason for him to hate Harvard — but I watched him over the years so sentimentalize and romanticize, and finally so worship the place that, by the time I was in high school, he believed that Harvard professors were the wisest men in the history of the world. America could be paradise, if only all high posts in government were filled by Harvard men.

And, as things turned out: When I went to work for the

government as a bright young man in Franklin Delano Roosevelt's Department of Agriculture, more and more posts were being filled by Harvard men. That seemed only right to me back then. It seems mildly comical to me now. Not even in prison, as I say, is there anything special about Harvard men.

While I was a student, I sometimes caught the whiff of a promise that, after I graduated, I would be better than average at explaining important matters to people who were slow at catching on. Things did not work out that way.

So there I sat in prison in Nineteen-hundred and Seventy-seven, waiting for the guard to come. I wasn't annoyed at his being an hour late so far. I was in no hurry to go anyplace, had no place in particular to go. The guard's name was Clyde Carter. He was one of the few friends I had made in prison. Our chief bond was that we had taken the same correspondence course in bartending from a diploma mill in Chicago, The Illinois Institute of Instruction, a division of The RAMJAC Corporation. On the same day and in the same mail each of us had received his Doctor of Mixology degree. Clyde had then surpassed me by taking the school's course in air conditioning, as well. Clyde was a third cousin to the President of the United States, Jimmy Carter. He was about five years younger than the President, but was otherwise his perfect spit and image. He had the same nice manners, the same bright smile.

A degree in bartending was enough for me. That was all I intended to do with the rest of my life: tend a quiet bar somewhere, ideally in a club for gentlemen.

And I lifted my old hands from the folded bedding and I clapped three times.

Another fighter plane leaped up from the tip of a nearby runway, tore the sky to shreds. I thought this: 'At least I don't smoke anymore.' It was true. I, who used to smoke four packages of unfiltered Pall Malls a day, was no longer a slave to King Nicotine. I would soon be reminded of how much I used to smoke, for the grey, pinstripe, three-piece Brooks Brothers suit awaiting me over in the supply room would be riddled with cigarette burns. There was a hole the size of a dime in the crotch, I remembered. A newspaper photograph was taken of me as I sat in the back of the federal marshal's green sedan, right after I was sentenced to prison. It was widely interpreted as showing how unashamed I was, haggard, horrified, unable to look anyone in the eye. It was in fact a photograph of a man who had just set his pants on fire.

I thought now about Sacco and Vanzetti. When I was young, I believed that the story of their martyrdom would cause an irresistible mania for justice to the common people to spread throughout the world. Does anybody know or care who they were anymore?

No.

I thought about the Cuyahoga Massacre, which was the bloodiest single encounter between strikers and an employer in the history of American labour. It happened in Cleveland, in front of the main gate of Cuyahoga Bridge and Iron, on Christmas morning in Eighteen-hundred and Ninety-four. That was long before I was born. My parents were still children in the Russian Empire when it happened. But the man who sent me to Harvard, Alexander Hamilton McCone, watched it from the factory clock tower in the company of his father and his older brother John. That was when he ceased to be a slight stammerer and became, when the least bit anxious about anything, a bubbling booby of totally blocked language instead.

Cuyahoga Bridge and Iron, incidentally, lost its identity, save in labour history, long ago. It was absorbed by Youngstown Steel shortly after the Second World War, and Youngstown Steel itself has now become a mere division of The RAMJAC Corporation.

Peace.

Yes, and I lifted my old hands from the folded bedding, and I clapped three times. Here was what that was all about, as silly as it was: Those three claps completed a rowdy song I had never liked, and which I had not thought about for thirty years or more. I was making my mind as blank as possible, you see, since the past was so embarrassing and the future so terrifying. I had made so many enemies over the years that I doubted that I could even get a job as a bartender somewhere. I would simply get dirtier and raggedier, I thought, since I would have no money coming in from anywhere. I would wind up on Skid Row and learn to keep the cold out by drinking wine, I thought, although I had never liked alcohol.

The worst thing, I thought, was that I would be asleep in an alley in the Bowery, say, and juvenile delinquents who loathed dirty old men would come along with a can of gasoline. They would soak me in it, and they would touch me off. And the worst thing about that, I thought, would be having my eyeballs lapped by flames.

No wonder I craved an empty mind!

But I could achieve mental vacancy only intermittently. Most of the time, as I sat there on the cot, I settled for an only slightly less perfect peace, which was filled with thoughts that need not scare me – about Sacco and Vanzetti, as I say, and about the Cuyahoga Massacre, about playing chess with old Alexander Hamilton McCone, and on and on.

Perfect blankness, when I achieved it, lasted only ten seconds or so – and then it would be wrecked by the song, sung loudly and clearly in my head by an alien voice, which required for its completion that I clap three times. The words were highly offensive to me when I first heard them, which was at a drunken stag party at Harvard during my freshman year. It was a song to be kept secret from women. It may be that no woman has ever heard it, even at this late date. The intent of the lyricist, obviously, was to so coarsen the feelings of males who sang the song that the singers could never believe again what most of us believed with all our hearts back then: that women were more spiritual, more sacred than men.

I still believe that about women. Is that, too, comical? I have loved only four women in my life – my mother, my late wife, a woman to whom I was once affianced, and one

43

other. I will describe them all by and by. Let it be said now, though, that all four seemed more virtuous, braver about life, and closer to the secrets of the universe than I could ever be.

Be that as it may, I will now set down the words to the frightful song. And even though I have been technically responsible, because of my high position in a corporate structure in recent years, for the publication of some of the most scurrilous books about women ever written, I still find myself shrinking from setting on paper, where they have perhaps never been before, the words to the song. The tune to which they were sung, incidentally, was an old one, a tune that I call 'Ruben, Ruben.' It no doubt has many other names.

Readers of the words should realize, too, that I heard them sung not by middle-aged roughnecks, but by college boys, by children, really, who, with a Great Depression going on and with a Second World War coming, and with most of them mocked by their own virginity, had reason to be petrified of all the things that women of that time would expect of them.

Women would expect them to earn good money after they graduated, and they did not see how they could do that, with all the businesses shutting down. Women would expect them to be brave soldiers, and there seemed every chance that they would go to pieces when the shrapnel and bullets flew. Who could be absolutely responsible for his own reactions when the shrapnel and bullets flew? There would be flame throwers and poison gas. There would be terrific bangs. The man standing beside you could have his head blown off – and his throat would be a fountain.

And women, when they became their wives, would expect them to be perfect lovers even on the wedding night – subtle, tender, raffish, respectful, titillatingly debauched, and knowing as much about the reproductive organs of both sexes as Harvard Medical School.

I recall a discussion of a daring magazine article that appeared at that time. It told of the frequency of sexual intercourse by American males in various professions and trades. Firemen were the most ardent, making love ten times a week.

44

College professors were the least ardent, making love once a month. And a classmate of mine, who, as it happened, would actually be killed in the Second World War, shook his head mournfully and said, 'Gee – I'd give anything to be a college professor.'

The shocking song, then, may really have been a way of honouring the powers of women, of dealing with the fears they inspired. It might properly be compared with a song making fun of lions, sung by lion hunters on a night before a hunt.

The words were these:

> *Sally in the garden,*
> *Sifting cinders,*
> *Lifted up her leg*
> *And farted like a man.*
> *The bursting of her bloomers*
> *Broke sixteen winders.*
> *The cheeks of her ass went –*

Here the singers, in order to complete the stanza, were required to clap three times.

2

My official title in the Nixon White House, the job I was holding when I was arrested for embezzlement, perjury, and obstruction of justice, was this: the President's special advisor on youth affairs. I was paid thirty-six thousand dollars a year. I had an office, but no secretary, in the subbasement of the Executive Office Building, directly underneath, as it happened, the office where burglaries and other crimes on behalf of President Nixon were planned. I could hear people walking overhead and raising their voices sometimes. On my own level in the subbasement my only companions were heating and air-conditioning equipment and a Coca-Cola machine that only I knew about, I think. I was the only person to patronize that machine.

Yes, and I read college and high-school newspapers and magazines, and *Rolling Stone* and *Crawdaddy*, and anything else that claimed to speak for youth. I catalogued political statements in the words of popular songs. My chief qualification for the job, I thought, was that I myself had been a radical at Harvard, starting in my junior year. Nor had I been a dabbler, a mere parlour pink. I had been cochairman of the Harvard chapter of the Young Communist League. I had been cochairman of a radical weekly paper, *The Bay State Progressive*. I was in fact, openly and proudly, a card-carrying communist until Hitler and Stalin signed a nonaggression pact in Nineteen-hundred and Thirty-nine. Hell and heaven, as I saw it, were making common cause against weakly defended peoples everywhere. After that I became a cautious believer in capitalistic democracy again.

It was once so acceptable in this country to be a communist that my being one did not prevent my winning a Rhodes Scholarship to Oxford after Harvard, and then landing a job in Roosevelt's Department of Agriculture after that. What could be so repulsive after all, during the Great Depression, especially, and with yet another war for natural wealth and markets coming, in a young man's belief that each person could work as well as he or she was able, and should be rewarded, sick or well, young or old, brave or frightened, talented or imbecilic, according to his or her simple needs? How could anyone treat me as a person with a diseased mind if I thought that war need never come again – if only common people everywhere would take control of the planet's wealth, disband their national armies, and forget their national boundaries; if only they would think of themselves ever after as brothers and sisters, yes, and as mothers and fathers, too, and children of all other common people – everywhere. The only person who would be excluded from such friendly and merciful society would be one who took more wealth than he or she needed at any time.

And even now, at the rueful age of sixty-six, I find my knees still turn to water when I encounter anyone who still considers it a possibility that there will one day be one big happy and peaceful family on Earth – the Family of Man. If I were this very day to meet myself as I was in Nineteen-hundred and Thirty-three, I would swoon with pity and respectfulness.

So my idealism did not die even in the Nixon White House, did not die even in prison, did not die even when I became, my most recent employment, a vice-president of the Down Home Records Division of The RAMJAC Corporation.

I still believe that peace and plenty and happiness can be worked out some way. I am a fool.

When I was Richard M. Nixon's special advisor on youth affairs, from Nineteen-hundred and Seventy until my arrest in Nineteen-hundred and Seventy-five, smoking four packs of unfiltered Pall Malls a day, nobody ever asked me for facts or opinions or anything. I need not even have come to work, and I might have spent my time better in helping my poor wife with the little interior-decorating business she ran out of our right little, tight little brick bungalow out in Chevy Chase,

Maryland. The only visitors I ever had to my subterranean office, its walls golden-brown with cigarette tars, were the President's special burglars, whose office was above mine. They suddenly realized one day, when I had a coughing fit, that somebody was right below them, and that I might be able to hear their conversations. They performed experiments, with one of them yelling and stamping upstairs, and another one listening in my office. They satisfied themselves at last that I had heard nothing, and was a harmless old poop, in any event. The yeller and stamper was a former Central Intelligence Agency operative, a writer of spy thrillers, and a graduate of Brown University. The listener below was a former agent of the Federal Bureau of Investigation, a former district attorney, and a graduate of Fordham University. I myself, as I may have said already, was a Harvard man.

And this Harvard man, knowing full well that everything he wrote would be shredded and baled with all the rest of the White House wastepaper, unread, still turned out some two hundred or more weekly reports on the sayings and doings of youth, with footnotes, bibliographies, and appendices and all. But the conclusions implied by my materials changed so little over the years that I might as well have simply sent the same telegram each week to limbo. It would have said this:

YOUNG PEOPLE STILL REFUSE TO SEE THE OBVIOUS IMPOSSIBILITY OF WORLD DISARMAMENT AND ECONOMIC EQUALITY. COULD BE FAULT OF NEW TESTAMENT (QUOD VIDE).

> WALTER F. STARBUCK
> PRESIDENT'S SPECIAL ADVISOR
> ON YOUTH AFFAIRS

At the end of every futile day in the subbasement I would go home to the only wife I have ever had, who was Ruth – waiting for me in our little brick bungalow in Chevy Chase, Maryland. She was Jewish, which I am not. So our only child, a son who is now a book reviewer for *The New York*

Times, is half-Jewish. He has further confused racial and religious matters by marrying a black nightclub singer, who has two children by a former husband. The former husband was a nightclub comedian of Puerto Rican extraction named Jerry Cha-cha Rivera, who was shot as an innocent bystander during the robbery of a RAMJAC carwash in Hollywood. My son has adopted the children, so that they are now legally my grandchildren, my only grandchildren.

Life goes on.

My late wife Ruth, the grandmother of these children, was born in Vienna. Her family owned a rare-book store there – before the Nazis took it away from them. She was six years younger than I. Her father and mother and two siblings were killed in concentration camps. She herself was hidden by a Christian family, but was discovered and arrested, along with the head of that family, in Nineteen-hundred and Forty-two. So she herself was in a concentration camp near Munich, finally liberated by American troops, for the last two years of the war. She herself would die in her sleep in Nineteen-hundred and Seventy-four – of congestive heart failure, two weeks before my own arrest. Whither I went, and no matter how clumsily, there did my Ruth go – as long as she could. If I marvelled at this out loud, she would say, 'Where else could I be? What else could I do?'

She might have been a great translator, for one thing. Languages came so easily to her, as they did not to me. I spent four years in Germany after the Second World War, but never mastered German. But there was no European language that Ruth could not speak at least a little bit. She passed the time in the concentration camp, waiting for death, by getting other prisoners to teach her languages she did not know. Thus did she become fluent in Romany, the tongue of the Gypsies, and even learned the words to some songs in Basque. She might have become a portrait artist. That was another thing she had done in prison: With a finger dipped in lamp-black, she had drawn on the walls likenesses of those passing through. She might have been a famous photographer. When she was only sixteen, three years before Germany annexed Austria, she photographed one hundred beggars in Vienna, all of whom were terribly wounded veterans of World War One. These were sold in portfolios, one of which I have found recently, and to my heartbroken amazement, in the collection of New York's Museum of Modern Art. She could also play the piano, whereas I am tone-deaf. I cannot even sing 'Sally in the Garden' on key.

I was Ruth's inferior, you might say.

When things started to go really badly for me in the fifties and sixties, when I was unable to get a decent job anywhere, despite all the high posts I had held in government, despite all the important people I knew, it was Ruth who rescued our unpopular little family out in Chevy Chase. She began with two failures, which depressed her at first, but which would later make her laugh so hard that tears streamed from her eyes. Her first failure was as a piano player in a cocktail lounge. The proprietor, when he fired her, told her that she was too good, that his particular clientele '... didn't appreciate the finer things in life.' Her second failure was as a wedding photographer. There was always an air of prewar doom about her photographs, which no retoucher could eradicate. It was as though the entire wedding party would wind up in the trenches or the gas chambers by and by.

But then she became an interior decorator, beguiling prospective clients with watercolours of rooms she would like to do for them. And I was her clumsy assistant, hanging draperies, holding wallpaper samples against a wall, taking telephone messages from clients, running errands, picking up swatches of this and that – and on and on. I set fire to eleven hundred dollars' worth of blue velvet draperies one time. No wonder my son never respected me.

When did he ever have a chance to?

My God – there his mother was, trying to support the family, and scrimping and saving to get by. And there his unemployed father was, always in the way and helpless, and finally setting fire to a fortune in draperies with a cigarette!

Hooray for a Harvard education! Oh, to be the proud son of a Harvard man!

Ruth was a tiny woman, incidentally — with coppery skin and straight black hair and high cheekbones and deep-set eyes. The first time I laid eyes on her, which was in Nuremberg, Germany, in late August of Nineteen-hundred and Forty-five, she was wearing voluminous army fatigues, and I mistook her for a Gypsy boy. I was a civilian employee of the Defence Department, thirty-two years old. I had never married. I had been a civilian all through the war, often exercising more real power than generals or admirals. Now I was in Nuremberg, ogling the wreckage of war for the first time. I had been sent over to oversee the feeding and housing of the American, British, French, and Russian delegations to the War Crimes Trials. I had previously set up recuperation centres for American soldiers in various resort areas in the United States, so I knew a little something about the hotel trade.

I was to be a dictator to the Germans as far as food and drink and beds were considered. My official vehicle was a white Mercedes touring car, a four-door convertible with a windshield for the backseat as well as the front. It had a siren. It had little sockets on its front fenders for flags. I of course flew American flags. This dreamboat, as young people might call it, had been an anniversary present from Heinrich Himmler, the creator of concentration camps, to his wife in the good old days. Wherever I went, I had an armed chauffeur. My father, remember, had been a millionaire's armed chauffeur.

And I was being driven down the main street, the König-strasse, one August afternoon. The War Crimes Tribunal was meeting in Berlin but was going to move to Nuremberg as soon as I could get things ready there. The street was still blocked by rubble here and there. It being cleared away by German prisoners of war, who laboured, as it happened, under the smouldering gazes of black American military policemen. The American Army was still segregated in those days.

Every unit was all black or all white, except for the officers, who were usually white in any case. I do not recall having felt that there was anything odd in this scheme. I knew nothing about black people. There had been no black people on the household staff of the McCone mansion in Cleveland, no black people in my schools. Not even when I was a communist had I had a black person for a friend.

Near Saint Martha's Church on the Königstrasse, which had had its roof burned off by a firebomb, my Mercedes was halted at a security checkpoint. It was manned by white American Military Police. They were looking for people who were not where they were supposed to be, now that civilization was being started up again. They were seeking deserters from every imaginable army, including the American one, and war criminals not yet apprehended, and lunatics and common criminals, who had simply sauntered from the approaching front lines, and citizens of the Soviet Union, who had defected to the Germans or been captured by them, who would be imprisoned or killed, if they went back home. Russians were supposed, no matter what, to go back to Russia; Poles were supposed to go back to Poland; Hungarians to Hungary; Estonians to Estonia; and on and on. Everybody, no matter what, was supposed to go home.

I was curious as to what sort of interpreters the M.P.'s were using, since I was having trouble finding good ones for my own operations. I particularly needed people who were tri-lingual, who were fluent in both German and English, and in either French or Russian as well. They also had to be trustworthy, polite, and presentable. So I got out of my car to have a closer look at the interrogations. I discovered that they were being conducted, surprisingly, by a seeming Gypsy boy. It was my Ruth, of course. Her hair had all been cut off at a de-lousing station. She was wearing Army fatigues without any badges of unit or rank. She was beautiful to watch as she tried to elicit a glimmer of understanding from a ragbag of a man, whom the M.P.'s held before her. She must have tried seven or eight languages on him, slipping from one to another as easily as a musician changing tempos and keys. Not only that, but she altered her gestures, too, so that her hands were always doing appropriate dances to each language.

Suddenly, the man's hands were dancing as hers were, and the sounds coming from his mouth were like those she was making. As Ruth would tell me later, he was a Macedonian peasant from southern Yugoslavia. The language they had found in common was Bulgarian. He had been taken prisoner by the Germans, even though he had never been a soldier, and had been sent as a slave labourer to strengthen the forts of the Siegfried Line. He had never learned German. Now he wanted to go to America, he told Ruth, to become a very rich man. He was shipped back to Macedonia, I presume.

Ruth was then twenty-six years old — but she had eaten so badly for seven years, mostly potatoes and turnips, that she was an asexual stick. She herself, it turned out, had come to the roadblock only an hour before I had, and had been pressed into service by the M.P.'s because of all the languages she knew. I asked an M.P. sergeant how old he thought she was, and he guessed, 'Fifteen.' He thought she was a boy whose voice had yet to change.

I coaxed her into the backseat of my Mercedes and I questioned her there. I learned that she had been freed from a concentration camp in springtime, about four months before — and had since eluded every agency that might have liked to help her. She should by now have been in a hospital for displaced persons. She was uninterested in ever trusting anybody with her destiny anymore. Her plan was to roam alone and out-of-doors forever, from nowhere to nowhere in a demented sort of religious ecstasy. 'No one ever touches me,' she said, 'and I never touch anyone. I am like a bird in flight. It is so beautiful. There is only God — and me.'

I thought this of her: that she resembled gentle Ophelia in *Hamlet*, who became fey and lyrical when life was too cruel to bear. I have a copy of *Hamlet* at hand, and refresh my memory as to the nonsense Ophelia sang when she would no

longer respond intelligently to those who asked how she was.
This was the song:

> How should I your true love know
> From another one?
> By his cockle hat and staff,
> And his sandal shoon.
> He is dead and gone, lady,
> He is dead and gone;
> At his head a grass-green turf,
> At his heels a stone –

And on and on.

Ruth, one of millions of Europe's Ophelias after the Second World War, fainted in my motorcar.

I took her to a twenty-bed hospital in the *Kaiserburg*, the imperial castle, which wasn't even officially operating yet. It was being set up exclusively for persons associated with the War Crimes Trials. The head of it was a Harvard classmate of mine, Dr Ben Shapiro, who had also been a communist in student days. He was now a lieutenant colonel in the Army Medical Corps. Jews were not numerous at Harvard in my day. There was a strict quota, and a low one, as to how many Jews were let in each year.

'What have we here, Walter?' he said to me in Nuremberg. I was carrying the unconscious Ruth in my arms. She weighed no more than a handkerchief. 'It's a girl,' I said. 'She's breathing. She speaks many languages. She fainted. That's all I know.'

He had an idle staff of nurses, cooks, technicians, and so on, and the finest food and medicines that the Army could give him, since he was likely to have high-ranking persons for patients by and by. So Ruth received, and for nothing, the finest care available on the planet. Why? Mostly because, I think, Shapiro and I were both Harvard men.

One year later, more or less, on October fifteenth of Nineteen-hundred and Forty-six, Ruth would become my wife. The War Crimes Trials were over. On the day we were married, and probably conceived our only child as well, *Reichs-marschall* Hermann Göring cheated the hangman by swallowing cyanide.

It was vitamins and minerals and protein and, of course, tender, loving care, that made all the difference to Ruth. After only three weeks in the hospital she was a sane and witty Viennese intellectual. I hired her as my personal interpreter and took her everywhere with me. Through another Harvard acquaintance, a shady colonel in the Quartermaster Corps in Wiesbaden – a black marketeer, I'm sure – I was able to get her a suitable wardrobe, for which, mysteriously, I was never asked to pay anyone. The woollens were from Scotland, the cottons from Egypt – the silks from China, I suppose. The shoes were French – and prewar. One pair, I remember, was alligator, and came with a bag to match. The goods were priceless, since no store in Europe, or in North America, for that matter, had offered anything like them for years. The sizes, moreover, were exactly right for Ruth. These black-market treasures were delivered to my office in cartons claiming to contain mimeograph paper belonging to the Royal Canadian Air Force. Two taciturn young male civilians delivered them in what had once been a *Wehrmacht* ambulance. Ruth guessed that one was Belgian and the other, like my mother, Lithuanian.

My accepting those goods was surely my most corrupt act as a public servant, and my *only* corrupt act – until Watergate. I did it for love.

I began to speak to Ruth of love almost as soon as she got out of the hospital and went to work for me. Her replies were kind and funny and perceptive – but above all pessimistic. She believed, and was entitled to believe, I must say, that all human beings were evil by nature, whether tormentors or victims, or idle standers-by. They could only create meaningless tragedies, she said, since they weren't nearly intelligent enough to accomplish all the good they meant to do. We were a disease, she said, which had evolved on one tiny cinder in the universe, but could spread and spread.

'How can you speak of love to a woman,' she asked me early in our courtship, 'who feels that it would be just as well if nobody had babies anymore, if the human race did not go on?'

'Because I know you don't really believe that,' I replied. 'Ruth – look at how full of *life* you are!' It was true. There was no movement or sound she made that was not at least accidentally flirtatious – and what is flirtatiousness but an argument that life must go on and on and on?

What a charmer she was! Oh, I got the credit for how smoothly things ran. My own country gave me a Distinguished Service Medal, and France made me a *chevalier* in the Légion d'honneur, and Great Britain and the Soviet Union sent me letters of commendation and thanks. But it was Ruth who worked all the miracles, who kept each guest in a state of delighted forgivingness, no matter what went wrong.

'How can you dislike life and still be so lively?' I asked her.

'I couldn't have a child, even if I wanted to,' she said. 'That's how lively I am.'

She was wrong about that, of course. She was only guessing. She *would* give birth to a son by and by, a very unpleasant person, who, as I have already said, is now a book reviewer for *The New York Times*.

That conversation with Ruth in Nuremberg went on. We were in Saint Martha's Church, close to where fate had first brought us together. It was not yet operating as a church again. The roof had been put back on – but there was a canvas flap where the rose window used to be. The window and the altar, an old custodian told us, had been demolished by a single cannon shell from a British fighter plane. To him, judging from his solemnity, this was yet another religious miracle. And I must say that I seldom met a male German who was saddened by all the destruction in his own country. It was always the ballistics of whatever had done the wrecking that he wished to talk about.

'There is more to life than having babies, Ruth,' I said.

'If I had one, it would be a monster,' she said. And it came to pass.

'Never mind babies,' I said. 'Think of the new era that is being born. The world has learned its lesson at last, at last. The closing chapter to ten thousand years of madness and greed is being written right here and now — in Nuremberg. Books will be written about it. Movies will be made about it. It's the most important turning point in history.' I believed it.

'Walter,' she said, 'sometimes I think you are only eight years old.'

'It's the only age to be,' I said, 'when a new era is being born.'

Clocks struck six all over town. A new voice joined the chorus of public chimes and bells. It was in fact an old voice in Nuremberg, but Ruth and I had never heard it before. It was the deep *bonging* of the *Männleinlaufen*, the bizarre clock of the distant *Frauenkirche*. That clock was built more than four hundred years ago. My ancestors, both Lithuanian and Polish, would have been fighting Ivan the Terrible back then.

The visible part of the clock consisted of seven robots, which represented seven fourteenth-century electors. They were designed to circle an eighth robot, which represented the Holy Roman Emperor Charles the Fourth, and to celebrate his exclusion, in Thirteen-hundred and Fifty-six, of the Papacy from the selection of German rulers. The clock had been knocked out by bombing. American soldiers who were clever with machinery had begun on their own time to tinker with it as soon as they occupied the city. Most Germans I had talked to were so demoralized that they did not care if the *Männleinlaufen* never ran again. But it was running again, anyway. Thanks to American ingenuity, the electors were circling Charles the Fourth again.

'Well,' said Ruth, when the sounds of the bells had died away, 'when you eight-year-olds kill Evil here in Nuremberg, be sure to bury it at a crossroads and drive a stake through its heart — or you might see it again at the next full moooooooo-ooooooooooooooooon.'

3

But my unflagging optimism prevailed. Ruth consented at last to marry me, to let me try to make her the happiest of women, despite all the ghastly things that had happened to her so far. She was a virgin, and so very nearly was I, although I was thirty-three – although, roughly speaking, half my life was over.

Oh, to be sure, I had, while in Washington, 'made love,' as they say, to this woman or that one from time to time. There was a WAC. There was a Navy nurse. There was a stenographer in the Department of Commerce typing pool. But I was fundamentally a fanatical monk in the service of war, war, war. There were many like me. Nothing else in life is nearly so obsessive as war, war, war.

My wedding gift to Ruth was a wood carving commissioned by me. It depicted hands of an old person pressed together in prayer. It was a three-dimensional rendering of a drawing by Albrecht Dürer, a sixteenth-century artist, whose house Ruth and I had visited many times in Nuremberg, during our courting days. That was my invention, so far as I know, having those famous hands on paper rendered in the round. Such hands have since been manufactured by the millions and are staples of dim-witted piety in gift shops everywhere.

Soon after our marriage I was transferred to Wiesbaden, Germany, outside of Frankfurt am Main, where I was placed in charge of a team of civilian engineers, which was winnowing mountains of captured German technical documents for inventions and manufacturing methods and trade secrets American industry might use. It did not matter that I knew no math or chemistry or physics – any more than it had mattered when I went to work for the Department of Agriculture that I had never been near a farm, that I had not even tended a pot of African violets on a windowsill. There was nothing that a humanist could not supervise – or so it was widely believed at the time.

Our son was born by cesarean section in Wiesbaden. Ben Shapiro, who had been my best man, and who had also been transferred to Wiesbaden, delivered the child. He had just been promoted to full colonel. In a few years Senator Joseph R. McCarthy would find that promotion to have been sinister, since it was well known that Shapiro had been a communist before the war. 'Who promoted Shapiro to Wiesbaden?' he would want to know.

We named our son Walter F. Starbuck, Jr. Little did we dream that the name would become as onerous as Judas Iscariot, Jr., to the boy. He would seek legal remedy when he turned twenty-one, would have his name changed to Walter F. Stankiewicz, the name that appears over his columns in *The New York Times*. Stankiewicz, of course, was our discarded family name. And I must laugh now, remembering something my father once told me about his arrival at Ellis Island as an immigrant. He was advised that Stankiewicz had unpleasant connotations to American ears, that people would think he smelled bad, even if he sat in a bathtub all day long.

I returned to the United States with my little human family, to Washington, D.C., again, in the autumn of Nineteen-hundred and Forty-nine. My optimism became bricks and mortar and wood and nails. We bought the only house we would ever own, which was the little bungalow in Chevy Chase, Maryland. Ruth put on the mantelpiece the wood-carving of the praying hands by Albrecht Dürer. There were two things that had made her want to buy that house and no other, she said. One was that it had a perfect resting place for the hands. The other was a gnarled old tree that shaded the walk to our doorstep. It was a flowering crab apple tree.

Was she religious? No. She was from a family that was sceptical about all formal forms of worship, which was classi-fied as Jewish by the Nazis. Its members would not have so classified themselves. I asked her once if she had ever sought the consolations of religion in the concentration camp.

'No,' she said. 'I knew God would never come near such a place. So did the Nazis. That was what made them so hilarious and unafraid. That was the strength of the Nazis,' she said. 'They understood God better than anyone. They knew how to make Him stay away.'

I still ponder a toast Ruth gave one Christmas Eve, in Nineteen-hundred and Seventy-four or so. I was the only person to hear it – the only other person in the bungalow. Our son had not sent us so much as a Christmas card. The toast was this, and I suppose she might just as logically have given it on the day I met her in Nuremberg: 'Here's to God Almighty, the laziest man in town.'

Strong stuff.

Yes – and my speckled old hands were like the Albrecht Dürer hands atop my folded bedding, as I sat on my prison cot in Georgia, waiting for freedom to begin again.

I was a pauper.

I had emptied my savings account and cashed in my life-insurance policies and sold my Volkswagen and my brick bungalow in Chevy Chase, Maryland, in order to pay for my futile defence.

My lawyers said that I still owed them one hundred and twenty-six thousand dollars. Maybe so. Anything was possible.

Nor did I have glamour to sell. I was the oldest and least celebrated of all the Watergate coconspirators. What made me so uninteresting, I suppose, was that I had had so little power and wealth to lose. Other coconspirators had taken belly-whoppers from the tops of church steeples, so to speak. When I was arrested, I was a man sitting on a three-legged stool in the bottom of a well. All they could do to me was to saw off the legs of my little stool.

Not even I cared. My wife had died two weeks before they took me away, and my son no longer spoke to me. Still – they had to put handcuffs on me. It was the custom.

'Your name?' the police sergeant who booked me had asked.

I was impudent with him. Why not? 'Harry Houdini,' I replied.

A fighter plane leaped up from the tip of a nearby runway, tore the sky to shreds. It happened all the time.

'At least I don't smoke anymore,' I thought.

President Nixon himself commented one time on how much I smoked. It was soon after I came to work for him – in the spring of Nineteen-hundred and Seventy. I was summoned to an emergency meeting about the shooting to death of four antiwar protesters at Kent State University by members of the Ohio National Guard. There were about forty other people at the meeting. President Nixon was at the head of the huge oval table, and I was at the foot. This was the first time I had seen him in person since he was a mere congressman – twenty years before. Until now he had no wish to see his special advisor on youth affairs. As things turned out, he would never want to see me again.

Virgil Greathouse, the secretary of health, education, and welfare, and reputedly one of the President's closest friends, was there. He would begin serving his prison term on the same day I completed mine. Vice-President Spiro T. Agnew was there. He would eventually plead *nolo contendere* to charges of accepting bribes and evading income taxes. Emil Larkin, the President's most vindictive advisor and dreaded hatchet man, was there. He would eventually discover Jesus Christ as his personal Saviour as the prosecutors were about to get him for obstruction of justice and perjury. Henry Kissinger was there. He had yet to recommend the carpet-bombing of Hanoi on Christmas Day. Richard M. Helms, head of the C.I.A., was there. He would later be reprimanded for lying under oath to Congress. H. R. Haldeman and John D. Ehrlichman and Charles W. Colson and John N. Mitchell, the attorney general, were there. They, too, would be jailbirds by and by.

61

I had been up all the previous night, drafting and redrafting my suggestions as to what the President might say about the Kent State tragedy. The guardsmen, I thought, should be pardoned at once, and then reprimanded, and then discharged for the good of the service. The President should then order an investigation of National Guard units everywhere, to discover if such civilians in soldiers' costumes were in fact to be trusted with live ammunition when controlling unarmed crowds. The President should call the tragedy a tragedy, should reveal himself as having had his heart broken. He should declare a day or perhaps a week of national mourning, with flags flown at half-mast everywhere. And the mourning should not be just for those who died at Kent State, but for all Americans who had been killed or crippled in any way, directly or indirectly, by the Vietnam War. He would be more deeply resolved than ever, of course, to press the war to an honourable conclusion.

But I was never asked to speak, nor afterward could I interest anyone in the papers in my hand.

My presence was acknowledged only once, and then only as the butt of a joke by the President. I was so nervous as the meeting wore on that I soon had three cigarettes going all at once, and was in the process of lighting a fourth.

The President himself at last noticed the column of smoke rising from my place, and he stopped all business to stare at me. He had to ask Emil Larkin who I was.

He then gave that unhappy little smile that invariably signalled that he was about to engage in levity. That smile has always looked to me like a rosebud that had just been smashed by a hammer. The joke he made was the only genuinely witty comment I ever heard attributed to him. Perhaps that is my proper place in history – as the butt of the one good joke by Nixon.

'We will pause in our business,' he said, 'while our special advisor on youth affairs gives us a demonstration of how to put out a campfire.'

There was laughter all around.

4

A door in the prison dormitory below me opened and banged shut, and I supposed that Clyde Carter had come for me at last. But then the person began to sing 'Swing Low, Sweet Chariot' as he clumped up the stairway, and I knew he was Emil Larkin, once President Nixon's hatchet man. This was a big man, goggle-eyed and liver-lipped, who had been a middle linebacker for Michigan State at one time. He was a disbarred lawyer now, and he prayed all day long to what he believed to be Jesus Christ. Larkin had not been sent out on a work detail or assigned any housekeeping task, incidentally, because of what all his praying on hard prison floors had done to him. He was crippled in both legs with housemaid's knee.

He paused at the top of the stairs, and there were tears in his eyes. 'Oh, Brother Starbuck,' he said, 'it hurt so bad and it hurt so good to climb those stairs.'

'I'm not surprised,' I said.

'Jesus said to me,' he went on, ' "You have one last chance to ask Brother Starbuck to pray with you, and you've got to forget the pain it will cost you to climb those stairs, because you know what? This time Brother Starbuck is going to bend those proud Harvard knees, and he's going to pray with you." '

'I'd hate to disappoint Him,' I said.

'Have you ever done anything else?' he said. 'That's all *I* used to do: disappoint Jesus every day.'

I do not mean to sketch this blubbering leviathan as a religious hypocrite, nor am I entitled to. He had so opened himself to the consolations of religion that he had become an imbecile. In my time at the White House I had feared him as much as my ancestors must have feared Ivan the Terrible, but now I could be as impudent as I liked with him. He was no more sensitive to slights and jokes at his expense than a village idiot.

May I say, further, that on this very day Emil Larkin puts his money where his mouth is. A wholly-owned subsidiary of my division here at RAMJAC, Heartland House, a publisher of religious books in Cincinnati, Ohio, published Larkin's autobiography, *Brother, Won't You Pray with Me?*, six weeks ago. All of Larkin's royalties, which could well come to half a million dollars or more, excluding motion-picture and paperback rights, are to go to the Salvation Army.

'Who told you where I was?' I asked him. I was sorry he had found me. I had hoped to get out of prison without his asking me to pray with him one last time.

'Clyde Carter,' he said.

This was the guard I had been waiting for, the third cousin to the President of the United States. 'Where the heck is he?' I said.

Larkin said that the whole administration of the prison was in an uproar, because Virgil Greathouse, the former secretary of health, education, and welfare and one of the richest men in the country, had suddenly decided to begin serving his sentence immediately, without any further appeals, without any further delay. He was very probably the highest-ranking person any federal prison had ever been asked to contain.

I knew Greathouse mainly by sight – and of course by reputation. He was a famous tough guy, the founder and still majority stockholder in the public relations firm of Greathouse and Smiley, which specialized in putting the most favourable interpretations on the activities of Caribbean and Latin American dictatorships, of Bahamian gambling casinos, of Liberian and Panamanian tanker fleets, of several Central Intelligence Agency fronts around the world, of gangster-dominated unions such as the International Brotherhood of Abrasives and Adhesives Workers and the Amalgamated Fuel Handlers, of international conglomerates such as RAMJAC and Texas Fruit, and on and on.

He was bald. He was jowly. His forehead was wrinkled like

a washboard. He had a cold pipe clamped in his teeth, even when he sat on a witness stand. I got close enough to him one time to discover that he made music on that pipe. It was like the twittering of birds. He entered Harvard six years after I graduated, so we never met there. We made eye-contact only once at the White House – at the meeting where I made a fool of myself by lighting so many cigarettes. I was just a little mouse from the White House pantry, as far as he was concerned. He spoke to me only once, and that was after we were both arrested. We came together accidentally in a courthouse corridor, where we were facing separate arraignments. He found out who I was and evidently thought I might have something on him, which I did not. So he put his face close to mine, his eyes twinkling, his pipe in his teeth, and he made me this unforgettable promise: 'You say anything about me, Buster, and when you get out of jail you'll be lucky to get a job cleaning toilets in a whorehouse in Port Said.'

It was after he said that, that I heard the birdcalls from his pipe.

Greathouse was a Quaker, by the way – and so was Richard M. Nixon, of course. This was surely a special bond between them, one of the things that made them best of friends for a while.

Emil Larkin was a Presbyterian.

I myself was nothing. My father had been secretly baptized a Roman Catholic in Poland, a religion that was suppressed at the time. He grew up to be an agnostic. My mother was baptized a Greek Orthodox in Lithuania, but became a Roman Catholic in Cleveland. Father would never go to church with her. I myself was baptized a Roman Catholic, but aspired to my father's indifference, and quit going to church when I was twelve. When I applied for admission to Harvard, old Mr McCone, a Baptist, told me to classify myself as a Congregationalist, which I did.

My son is an active Unitarian, I hear. His wife told me that she was a Methodist, but that she sang in an Episcopal Church every Sunday for pay. Why not?

And on and on.

Emil Larkin, the Presbyterian, and Virgil Greathouse, the Quaker, had been thick as thieves back in the good old days. They had not only dominated the burglaries and the illegal wiretaps and the harassment of enemies by the Internal Revenue Service and so on, but the prayer breakfasts, as well. So I asked Larkin now how he felt about the reunion in prospect.

'Virgil Greathouse is no more and no less my brother than you or any other man,' he said. 'I will try to save him from hell, just as I am now trying to save you from hell.' He then quoted the harrowing thing that Jesus, according to Saint Matthew, had promised to say in the Person of God to sinners on Judgment Day.

This is it: 'Depart from me, you cursed, into the eternal fire prepared for the devil and his angels.'

These words appalled me then, and they appall me now. They are surely the inspiration for the notorious cruelty of Christians.

'Jesus may have said that,' I told Larkin, 'but it is so unlike most of what else He said that I have to conclude that He was slightly crazy that day.'

Larkin stepped back and he cocked his head in mock admiration. 'I have seen some rough-tough babies in my time,' he said, 'but you really take the prize. You've turned every friend you ever had against you, with all your flip-flops through the years, and now you insult the last Person who still might be willing to help you, who is Jesus Christ.'

I said nothing. I wished he would go away.

'Name me one friend you've got left,' he said.

I thought to myself that Dr Ben Shapiro, my best man, would have remained my friend, no matter what – might have come for me there at prison in his car and taken me to his home. But that was sentimental speculation on my part. He had gone to Israel long ago and gotten himself killed in the Six Day War. I had heard that there was a primary school named in his honour in Tel Aviv.

'Name one,' Emil Larkin persisted.

'Bob Fender,' I said. This was the only lifer in the prison, the only American to have been convicted of treason during the Korean War. He was *Doctor* Fender, since he held a degree in veterinary science. He was the chief clerk in the supply room where I would soon be given my civilian clothes. There was always music in the supply room, for Fender was allowed to play records of the French *chanteuse*, Edith Piaf, all day long. He was a science-fiction writer of some note, publishing many stories a year under various pseudonyms, including 'Frank X. Barlow' and 'Kilgore Trout.'

'Bob Fender is everybody's friend and nobody's friend,' said Larkin.

'Clyde Carter is my friend,' I said.

'I am talking about people on the outside,' said Larkin. 'Who's waiting outside to help you? Nobody. Not even your own son.'

'We'll see,' I said.

'You're going to New York?' he said.

'Yes,' I said.

'Why New York?' he said.

'It's famous for its hospitality to friendless, penniless immigrants who wish to become millionaires,' I said.

'You're going to ask your son for help, even though he's never even written you the whole time you've been here?' he said. He was the mail clerk for my building, so he knew all about my mail.

'If he ever finds out I'm in the same city with him, it will be purely by accident,' I said. The last words Walter had ever said to me were at his mother's burial in a small Jewish cemetery in Chevy Chase. That she should be buried in such a place and in such company was entirely my idea — the idea of an old man suddenly all alone. Ruth would have said, correctly, that it was a crazy thing to do.

She was buried in a plain pine box that cost one hundred and fifty-six dollars. Atop that box I placed a bough, broken not cut, from our flowering crab apple tree.

A rabbi prayed over her in Hebrew, a language she had

never learned, although she must have had endless opportunities to learn it in the concentration camp.

Our son said this to me, before showing his back to me and the open pit and hastening to a waiting taxicab: 'I pity you, but I can never love you. As far as I am concerned, you killed this poor woman. I can't think of you anymore as a father or as any sort of relative. I never want to see or hear of you again.'

Strong stuff.

My prison daydream of New York City did suppose, however, that there were still old acquaintances, although I could not name them, who might help me to get a job. It is a hard daydream to let go of – that one has friends. Those who would have remained my friends, if life had gone a little bit better for me, would have been mainly in New York. I imagined that, if I were to prowl midtown Manhattan day after day, from the theatre district on the west to the United Nations on the east, and from the Public Library on the south to the Plaza Hotel on the north, and past all the foundations and publishing houses and bookstores and clothiers for gentlemen and clubs for gentlemen and expensive hotels and restaurants in between, I would surely meet somebody who knew me, who remembered what a good man I used to be, who did not especially despise me – who would use his influence to get me a job tending bar somewhere.

I would plead with him shamelessly, and rub his nose in my Doctor of Mixology degree.

If I saw my son coming, so went the daydream, I would show him my back until he was safely by.

'Well,' said Larkin, 'Jesus tells me not to give up on anybody, but I'm close to giving up on you. You're just going to sit there, staring straight ahead, no matter what I say.'

'Afraid so,' I said.

'I never saw anybody more determined to be a geek than you are,' he said.

A geek, of course, is a man who lies in a cage on a bed of filthy straw in a carnival freak-show and bites the heads off live chickens and makes subhuman noises, and is billed as having been raised by wild animals in the jungles of Borneo. He has sunk as low as a human being can sink in the American social order, except for his final resting place in a potter's field.

Now Larkin, frustrated, let some of his old maliciousness show. 'That's what Chuck Colson called you in the White House: "The Geek," ' he said.

'I'm sure,' I said.

'Nixon never respected you,' he said. 'He just felt sorry for you. That's why he gave you the job.'

'I know,' I said.

'You didn't even have to come to work,' he said.

'I know,' I said.

'That's why we gave you the office without any windows and without anybody else around – so you'd catch on that you didn't even have to come to work.'

'I tried to be of use anyway,' I said. 'I hope your Jesus can forgive me for that.'

'If you're just going to make fun of Jesus, maybe you better not talk about Him after all,' he said.

'Fine,' I said. 'You brought Him up.'

'Do you know when you started to be a geek?' he said.

I knew exactly when the downward dive of my life began, when my wings were broken forever, when I realized that I would never soar again. That event was the most painful subject imaginable to me. I could not bear to think about it yet again, so I said to Larkin, looking him in the eye at last, 'In the name of mercy, please leave this poor old man alone.'

He was elated. 'By golly – I finally got through the thick Harvard hide of Walter F. Starbuck,' he said. 'I touched a nerve, didn't I?'

'You touched a nerve,' I said.

'Now we're getting somewhere,' he said.

'I hope not,' I said, and I stared at the wall again.

'I was just a little boy in kneepants in Petoskey, Michigan, when I first heard your voice,' he said.

'I'm sure,' I said.

'It was on the radio. My father made me and my little sister sit by the radio and listen hard. "You listen hard," he said. "You're hearing history made."'

The year would have been Nineteen-hundred and Forty-nine. I had just returned to Washington with my little human family. We had just moved into our brick bungalow in Chevy Chase, Maryland, with its flowering crab apple tree. It was autumn. There were tart little apples on the tree. My wife Ruth was about to make jelly out of them, as she would do every year. Where was my voice coming from, that it should have been heard by little Emil Larkin in Petoskey? From a committee room in the House of Representatives. With a brutal bouquet of radio microphones before me I was being questioned, principally by a young congressman from California named Richard M. Nixon, about my previous associations with communists, and about my present loyalty to the United States.

Nineteen-hundred and Forty-nine: Will young people of today doubt me if I aver with a straight face that congressional committees convened in treetops then, since sabre-toothed tigers still dominated the ground? No. Winston Churchill was still alive. Joseph Stalin was still alive. Think of that. Harry S. Truman was President. And the Defence Department had told me, a former communist, to form and head a task force of scientists and military men. Its mission was to propose tactics for ground forces when, as seemed inevitable, small nuclear weapons became available on the battlefield.

The committee wished to know, and especially Mr Nixon, if a man with my political past was to be trusted with such a sensitive job. Might I hand over our tactical schemes to the Soviet Union? Might I rig the schemes to make them impractical, so that in any battle with the Soviet Union the Soviet Union would surely win?

'You know what I heard on that radio?' said Emil Larkin.

'No,' I said – ever so emptily.

'I heard a man do the one thing nobody can ever forgive

him for – and I don't care what their politics are. I heard him do the one thing he can't ever forgive himself for, and that was to betray his best friend.'

I could not smile then at his description of what he thought he had heard, and I cannot smile at it now – but it was ludicrous all the same. It was an impossibly chowder-headed abridgement of congressional hearings and civil suits and finally a criminal trial, which were spread out over two years. As a little boy listening to the radio, he could only have heard a lot of tedious talk, not much more interesting than static. It was only as a grownup, with a set of ethics based on cowboy movies, that Larkin could have decided that he had heard with utmost clarity the betrayal of a man by his best friend.

'Leland Clewes was never my best friend,' I said. This was the name of the man who was ruined by my testimony, and for a while there our last names would be paired in conversations: 'Starbuck and Clewes' – like 'Gilbert and Sullivan'; like 'Sacco and Vanzetti'; like 'Laurel and Hardy'; like 'Leopold and Loeb.'

I don't hear much about us anymore.

Clewes was a Yale man – my age. We first met at Oxford, where I was the coxswain and he was the bowman of a winning crew at Henley. I was short. He was tall. I am still short. He is still tall. We went to work for the Department of Agriculture at the same time and were assigned adjacent cubicles. We played tennis every Sunday morning, when the weather was clement. Those were our salad days, when we were green in judgment.

For a while there we were joint owners of a second-hand Ford Phaeton and often went out together with our girls. Phaeton was the son of Helios, the sun. He borrowed his father's flaming chariot one day and drove it so irresponsibly that parts of northern Africa were turned into deserts. In order to keep the whole planet from being desolated, Zeus had to kill him with a thunderbolt. 'Good for Zeus,' I say. What choice did he have?

But my friendship with Clewes was never deep and it ended

when he took a girl away from me and married her. She was a member of a fine old New England family, which owned the Wyatt Clock Company in Brockton, Massachusetts, among other things. Her brother was my roommate at Harvard in my freshman year, which was how I got to know her. She was one of the four women I have ever truly loved. Sarah Wyatt was her maiden name.

When I accidentally ruined him, Leland Clewes and I had not exchanged any sort of greeting for ten years or more. He and his Sarah had a child, a daughter, three years older than mine. He had become the brightest meteor in the State Department, and it was widely conceded that he would be secretary of state some day, and maybe even president. No one in Washington was better-looking and more charming than Leland Clewes.

I ruined him in this way: Under oath, and in reply to a question by Congressman Nixon, I named a number of men who were known to have been communists during the Great Depression, but who had proved themselves to be outstanding patriots during World War Two. On that roll of honour I included the name of Leland Clewes. No particular comment was made about this at the time. It was only when I got home late that afternoon that I learned from my wife, who had been listening to me and then to every news programme she could find on the radio, that Leland Clewes had never been connected with communism in any way before.

By the time Ruth put on supper – and we had to eat off a packing case since the bungalow wasn't fully furnished yet – the radio was able to give us Leland Clewes's reply. He wished to appear before Congress at the earliest opportunity, in order to swear under oath that he had never been a communist, had never sympathized with any communist cause. His boss, the secretary of state, another Yale man, was quoted as saying that Leland Clewes was the most patriotic American he had ever known, and that he had proved his loyalty beyond question in negotiations with representatives of the Soviet Union. According to him, Leland Clewes had bested the communists again and again. He suggested that I might still be a communist, and that I might have been given the job of ruining Leland Clewes by my masters.

Two horrible years later Leland Clewes was convicted on six counts of perjury. He became one of the first prisoners to serve his sentence in the then new Federal Minimum Security Adult Correctional Facility on the edge of Finletter Air Force Base – thirty-five miles from Atlanta, Georgia.

Small world.

5

Almost twenty years later Richard M. Nixon, having become President of the United States, would suddenly wonder what had become of me. He would almost certainly never have become President, of course, if he had not become a national figure as the discoverer and hounder of the mendacious Leland Clewes. His emissaries would find me, as I say, helping my wife with her decorating business, which she ran out of our little brick bungalow in Chevy Chase, Maryland.

Through them, he would offer me a job.

How did I feel about it? Proud and useful. Richard M. Nixon wasn't merely Richard M. Nixon, after all. He was also the President of the United States of America, a nation I ached to serve again. Should I have refused – on the grounds that America wasn't really my kind of America just then?

Should I have persisted, as a point of honour, in being to all practical purposes a basket case in Chevy Chase instead?

No.

And now Clyde Carter, the prison guard I had been waiting for so long on my cot, came to get me at last. Emil Larkin had by then given up on me and limped away.

'I'm sure sorry, Walter,' said Clyde.

'Perfectly all right,' I told him. 'I'm in no hurry to go anywhere, and there are buses every thirty minutes.' Since no one was coming to meet me, I would have to ride an Air Force bus to Atlanta. I would have to stand all the way, I thought, since the buses were always jammed long before they reached the prison stop.

Clyde knew about my son's indifference to my sufferings. Everybody in the prison knew. They also knew he was a book reviewer. Half the inmates, it seemed, were writing memoirs or spy novels or romans à clef, or what have you, so there

74

was a lot of talk about book reviewing, and especially in *The New York Times*.

And Clyde said to me, 'Maybe I ain't supposed to say this, but that son of yours ought to be shot for not coming down after his daddy.'

'It's all right,' I said.

'That's what you say about everything,' Clyde complained. 'No matter what it is, you say, "It's all right." '

'It usually is,' I said.

'Them was the last words of Caryl Chessman,' he said. 'I guess they'll be your last words, too.'

Caryl Chessman was a convicted kidnapper and rapist, but not a murderer, who spent twelve years on death row in California. He made all his own appeals for stays of execution, and he learned four languages and wrote two best-selling books before he was put into an airtight tank with windows in it, and made to breathe cyanide gas.

And his last words were indeed, as Clyde said, 'It's all right.'

'Well now, listen,' said Clyde. 'When you get yourself a bartending job up there in New York, I just know you're going to wind up owning that bar inside of two years' time.' This was kindness on his part, and not genuine optimism. Clyde was trying to help me be brave. 'And after you've got the most popular bar in New York,' he went on, 'I just hope you'll remember Clyde and maybe send for him. I can not only tend bar – I can also fix your air conditioning. By that time I'll be able to fix your locks, too.'

I knew he had been considering enrolling in The Illinois Institute of Instruction course in locksmithing. Now, apparently, he had taken the plunge. 'So you took the plunge,' I said.

'I took the plunge,' he said. 'Got my first lesson today.'

The prison was a hollow square of conventional, two-storey military barracks. Clyde and I were crossing the vast parade ground at its centre, I with my bedding in my arms. This was where young infantrymen, the glory of their nation, had performed at one time, demonstrating their eagerness to do or die. Now I, too, I thought, had served my country in uniform, had at every moment for two years done precisely what my country asked me to do. It had asked me to suffer. It had not asked me to die.

There were faces at some of the windows – feeble old felons with bad hearts, bad lungs, bad livers, what have you. But there was only one other figure on the parade ground itself. He was dragging a large canvas trash bag after himself as he picked up papers with a spike at the end of a long stick. He was small and old, like me. When he saw us coming, he positioned himself between us and the Administration Building, and he pointed his spike at me, indicating that he had something very important to say to me. He was Dr Carlo di Sanza, who held a Doctorate in law from the University of Naples. He was a naturalized American citizen and was serving his second term for using the mails to promote a Ponzi scheme. He was ferociously patriotic.

'You are going home?' he said.

'Yes,' I said.

'Don't ever forget one thing,' he said. 'No matter what this country does to you, it is still the greatest country in the world. Can you remember that?'

'Yes, sir – I think I can,' I said.

'You were a fool to have been a communist,' he said.

'That was a long time ago,' I said.

'There are no opportunities in a communist country,' he said. 'Why would you want to live in a country with no opportunities?'

'It was a youthful mistake, sir,' I said.

'In America I have been a millionaire two times,' he said, 'and I will be a millionaire again.'

'I'm sure of it,' I said, and I was. He would simply start up his third Ponzi scheme – consisting, as before, of offering fools enormous rates of interest for the use of their money. As before, he would use most of the money to buy himself mansions and Rolls-Royces and speedboats and so on, but returning part of it as the high interest he had promised. More and more people would come to him, having heard of him from gloatingly satisfied recipients of his interest checks, and he would use their money to write more interest checks – and on and on.

I am now convinced that Dr di Sanza's greatest strength was his utter stupidity. He was such a successful swindler because he himself could not, even after two convictions, understand what was inevitably catastrophic about a Ponzi scheme.

'I have made many people happy and rich,' he said. 'Have you done that?'

'No, sir – not yet,' I said. 'But it's never too late to try.'

I am now moved to suppose, with my primitive understanding of economics, that every successful government is of necessity a Ponzi scheme. It accepts enormous loans that can never be repaid. How else am I to explain to my polyglot grandchildren what the United States was like in the nineteen-thirties, when its owners and politicians could not find ways for so many of its people to earn even the most basic necessities, like food and clothes and fuel. It was pure hell to get shoes!

And then, suddenly, there were formerly poor people in officers' clubs, beautifully costumed and ordering filets mignon and champagne. There were formerly poor people in enlisted men's clubs, serviceably costumed and clad and ordering hamburgers and beer. A man who two years before had patched the holes in his shoes with cardboard suddenly had a Jeep or a truck or an airplane or a boat, and unlimited supplies of fuel and ammunition. He was given glasses and bridge-work, if he needed them, and he was immunized against every imaginable disease. No matter where he was on the planet, a way was found to get hot turkey and cranberry sauce to him on Thanksgiving and Christmas.

What had happened?

What could have happened but a Ponzi scheme?

When Dr Carlo di Sanza stepped aside and let Clyde and

me go on, Clyde began to curse himself for his own lack of large-scale vision. 'Bartender, air-conditioner repairman, locksmith – prison guard,' he said. 'What's the matter with me that I think so small?'

He spoke of his long association with white-collar criminals, and he told me one conclusion he had drawn: 'Successful folks in this country never think about little things.'

'Successful?' I said incredulously. 'You're talking about convicted felons, for heaven's sake!'

'Oh, sure,' he said, 'but most of them have plenty of money still stashed away somewheres. Even if they don't, they know how to get plenty more. Everbody does just fine when they get out of here.'

'Remember me as a striking exception,' I said. 'My wife had to support me for most of my married life.'

'You had a million dollars one time,' he said. 'I'll never see a million dollars, if I live a million years.' He was speaking of the *corpus delecti* of my Watergate crime, which was an old-fashioned steamer trunk containing one million dollars unmarked and circulated twenty-dollar bills. It was an illegal campaign contribution. It became necessary to hide it when the contents of all White House safes were to be examined by the Federal Bureau of Investigation and men from the Office of the Special Prosecutor. My obscure office in the subbasement was selected as the most promising hiding place. I acquiesced.

Somewhere in there my wife died.

And then the trunk was found. The police came for me. I knew the people who brought the trunk to my office, and under whose orders they were operating. They were all high-ranking people, some of them labouring like common stevedores. I would not tell the court or my own lawyers or anyone who they were. Thus did I go to prison for a while.

I had learned this much from my mutual disaster with Leland Clewes: It was sickening to send another poor fool to prison. There was nothing quite like sworn testimony to make life look trivial and mean ever after.

Also: My wife had just died. I could not care what happened next. I was a zombie.

Even now I will not name the malefactors with the trunk. It does not matter.

I cannot, however, withhold from American history what one of the malefactors said after the trunk was set down in my office. This was it: 'Whose dumb fucking idea was it to bring this shit to the White House?'

'People like you,' said Clyde Carter, 'find yourselves around millions of dollars all the time. If I'd of went to Harvard, maybe I would, too.'

We were hearing music now. We were nearing the supply room, and it was coming from a phonograph in there. Edith Piaf was singing 'Non, Je ne Regrette Rien.' This means, of course, 'No, I am not sorry about anything.'

The song ended just as Clyde and I entered the supply room, so that Dr Robert Fender, the supply clerk and lifer, could tell us passionately how much he agreed with the song. 'Non!' he said, his teeth gnashing, his eyes blazing, 'je ne regrette rien! Rien!'

This was, as I have already said, a veterinarian and the only American to have been convicted of treason during the Korean War. He could have been shot for what he did, since he was then a first lieutenant in the United States Army, serving in Japan and inspecting meat on its way to the troops in Korea. As a gesture of mercy, his court-martial sentenced him to life imprisonment with no chance of parole.

This American traitor bore a strong resemblance to a great American hero, Charles Augustus Lindbergh. He was tall and big-boned. He had Scandinavian blood. He was a farm boy. He was fairly fluent in a weepy sort of French from having listened to Edith Piaf for so long. He had actually been almost nowhere outside of prison but Ames, Iowa, and Osaka, Japan. He was so shy with women, he told me one time, that he was still a virgin when he reached Osaka. And then he fell crashingly in love with a female nightclub singer who passed herself off as Japanese and sang word-for-word imitations of

Edith Piaf records. She was also a spy for North Korea.

'My dear friend, my dear Walter Starbuck,' he said, 'and how has this day gone for you so far?'

So I told him about sitting on the cot and having the same song run through my head again and again, about Sally in the garden, sifting cinders.

He laughed. He has since put me and the incident into a science fiction story of his, which I am proud to say is appearing this very month in *Playboy*, a RAMJAC magazine. The author is ostensibly Frank X. Barlow. The story is about a former judge on the planet Vicuna, two and a half galaxies away from Earth, who has had to leave his body behind and whose soul goes flying through space, looking for a habitable planet and a new body to occupy. He finds that the universe is virtually lifeless, but he comes at last to Earth and makes his first landing in the enlisted men's parking lot of Finletter Air Force Base – thirty-five miles from Atlanta, Georgia. He can enter any body he likes through its ear, and ride around inside. He wants a body so he can have some sort of social life. A soul without a body, according to the story, can't have any social life – because nobody can see it, and it can't touch anybody or make any noise.

The judge thinks he can leave a body again, any time he finds it or its destiny uncongenial. Little does he dream that the chemistries of Earthlings and Vicunians are such that, once he enters a body, he is going to be stuck inside forever. The story includes a little essay on glues previously known on Earth, and says that the strongest of these was the one that sticks mature barnacles to boulders or boats or pilings, or whatever.

'When they are very young,' Dr Fender writes in the persona of Frank X. Barlow, 'barnacles can drift or creep whence-so-ever they hanker, anywhere in the seven seas and the brackish estuaries thereof. Their upper bodies are encased in cone-shaped armour. Their little tootsies dangle from the cones like clappers from dinnerbells.

'But there comes a time for every barnacle, at childhood's

end, when the rim of its cone secretes a glue that will stick forever to whatever it happens to touch next. So it is no casual thing on Earth to say to a pubescent barnacle or to a homeless soul from Vicuna, "Sit thee doon, sit thee doon." '

The judge from Vicuna in the story tells us that the way the people on his native planet said 'hello' and 'good-bye,' and 'please' and 'thank you,' too. It was this: 'ting-a-ling.' He says that back on Vicuna the people could don and doff their bodies as easily as Earthlings could change their clothing. When they were outside their bodies, they were weightless, transparent, silent awarenesses and sensibilities. They had no musical instruments on Vicuna, he said, since the people themselves were music when they floated around without their bodies. Clarinets and harps and pianos and so on would have been redundant, would have been machinery for making clumsy counterfeits of airborne souls.

But they ran out of time on Vicuna, he says. The tragedy of the planet was that its scientists found ways to extract time from topsoil and the oceans and the atmosphere – to heat their homes and power their speedboats and fertilize their crops with it; to eat it; to make clothes out of it; and so on. They served time at every meal, fed it to household pets, just to demonstrate how rich and clever they were. They allowed great gobbets of it to putrefy to oblivion in their overflowing garbage cans.

'On Vicuna,' says the judge, 'we lived as through there were no tomorrow.'

The patriotic bonfires of time were the worst, he says. When he was an infant, his parents held him up to coo and gurgle with delight as a million years of future were put to the torch in honour of the birthday of the queen. But by the time he was fifty, only a few weeks of future remained. Great rips in reality were appearing everywhere. People could walk through walls. His own speedboat became nothing more than a steering wheel. Holes appeared in vacant lots where children were playing, and the children fell in.

So all the Vicunians had to get out of their bodies and sail out into space without further ado. 'Ting-a-ling,' they said to Vicuna.

'Chronological anomalies and gravitational thunderstorms and magnetic whirlpools tore the Vicunian families apart in space', the story goes on, 'scattered them far and wide.' The judge manages to stay with his formerly beautiful daughter for a while. She isn't beautiful anymore, of course, because she no longer has a body. She finally loses heart, because every planet or moon they come to is so lifeless. Her father, having no way to restrain her, watches helplessly as she enters a crack in a rock and becomes its soul. Ironically, she does this on the moon of Earth, with that most teeming of all planets only two hundred and thirty-nine thousand miles away!

Before he actually lands at the Air Force base, though, he falls in with a flock of turkey buzzards. He wheels and soars with them and almost enters the ear of one. For all he knows about the social situation on Earth, these carrion eaters may be members of the ruling class.

He decides that lives led at the centre of the Air Force base are too busy, too unreflective for him, so he goes up in the air again and spots a much more quiet cluster of buildings, which he thinks may be a meditation centre for philosophers. He has no way of recognizing the place as a minimum security prison for white-collar criminals, since there were no such institutions back on Vicuna.

Back on Vicuna, he says, convicted white-collar criminals, defilers of trustingness, had their ears plugged up, so their souls couldn't get out. Then their bodies were put into artificial ponds filled with excrement – up to their necks. Then deputy sheriffs drove high-powered speedboats at their heads.

The judge says he himself sentenced hundreds of people to this particular punishment and that the felons invariably argued that they had not broken the law, but merely violated its spirit, perhaps, just the least little bit. Before he condemned them, he would put a sort of chamberpot over his head, to make his words more resonant and awesome, and he would pronounce this formula: 'Boys, you didn't just get the spirit of the law. You got its body and soul this time.'

And, according to the judge, you could hear the deputies warming up their speedboats on the pond outside the courthouse: *'vrooom-ah, vrooom-a, va-va-va-rooooooooooooooooo-oooooooooooooooooooom!'*

6

The judge in Dr Bob Fender's story tries to guess which of the philosophers in the meditation centre is the wisest and most contented. He decides that it is a little old man sitting on a cot in a second-storey dormitory. Every so often that little old man is so delighted with his thoughts, evidently, that he claps three times.

So the judge flies into the ear of that little old man and immediately sticks to him forever, sticks to him, according to the story '... as tightly as Formica to an epoxy-coated countertop.' And what does he hear in that little old man's head but this:

> *Sally in the garden,*
> *Sifting cinders,*
> *Lifted up her leg*
> *And farted like a man ...*

And so on.

It is quite an interesting story. There is a rescue of the daughter who has become the soul of a moon rock, and so on. But the true story of how its author came to commit treason in Osaka is a match for it, in my opinion, any day. Bob Fender fell in love with the North Korean agent, the Edith Piaf imitator, from a distance of about twenty feet, in a nightclub frequented by American officers. He never dared close the distance or to send her flowers or a note, but night after night he mooned at her from the same table. He was always alone and usually the biggest man by far in the club, so the singer, whose stage name was simply 'Izumi,' asked some of the other Americans who and what Fender was.

He was a virgin meat inspector, but his fellow officers had fun telling Izumi that he was so solitary and gloomy all the time because his work was so secret and important. They said he was in command of an elite unit that guarded atomic bombs. If she asked him about it, they said, he would claim to be a meat inspector.

So Izumi went to work on him. She sat down at his table without being asked. She reached inside his shirt and tickled his nipples and all that. She told him that she liked big, silent men, and that all other Americans talked too much. She begged him to take her home with him after the club closed at two o'clock that morning. She wanted to find out where the atomic bombs were, of course. Actually, there weren't any atomic bombs in Japan. They were on aircraft carriers and on Okinawa, and so on. For the rest of the evening she sang all her songs directly to him and to nobody else. He nearly fainted from joy and embarrassment. He had a Jeep outside.

When she got into his Jeep at two o'clock in the morning, she said she not only wanted to see where her big American lived, but where he worked. He told her that would be easy, since he lived and worked at the same place. He took her down to a new United States Army Quartermaster Corps dock in Osaka, which had a big shed running down the middle of it. At one end were some offices. At the other end was a two-room apartment for whoever the resident veterinarian happened to be. In between were great, refrigerated meat lockers, filled with carcasses. Fender had inspected or would inspect. There was a fence on the land side and a guard at the gate; but as came out at the court-martial, discipline was lax. All the guard thought he had to watch out for was people trying to sneak out with sides of beef.

So the guard, who would later be acquitted by a court-martial, simply waved Dr Fender's Jeep inside. He did not notice that there was an unauthorized woman lying on the floor.

Izumi asked to look inside some of the meat lockers, which Bob was more than glad to show her. By the time they reached his apartment, which was at the outer end of the dock, she realized that he really was nothing but a meat inspector.

'But she was so nice,' Fender told me one time, 'and I was so nice, if I may say so, that she stayed for the night, anyway. I was scared to death, naturally, since I had never made love before. But then I said to myself, "Just wait a minute. Just calm down. You have always been good with every kind of animal, practically from the minute you were born. Just keep one thing in mind: You've got another nice little animal here."'

As came out at Fender's court-martial: He and other members of the Army Veterinary Corps looked like soldiers, but they had not been trained to think like soldiers. It seemed unnecessary, since all they did anymore was inspect meat. The last veterinarian to be involved in any sort of fighting, it turned out, died at the Little Bighorn, at Custer's Last Stand. Also: There was a tendency on the part of the Army to coddle veterinarians, since they were so hard to recruit. They could make fortunes on the outside – especially in cities, looking after people's pets. This was why they gave Fender such a pleasant, private apartment on the end of a dock. He inspected meat. As long as he did that, nobody was going to think of inspecting *him*.

'If they had inspected my apartment,' he told me, 'they would not have found a speck of dust anywhere.' They would also have found, according to him, 'one of the best private collections of Japanese pottery and fabrics in Osaka.' He had gone berserk for the subtlety and delicacy of all things Japanese. This art mania was surely an apology, among other things, for his own huge and – to him – ugly and useless hands and feet and all.

'Izumi kept looking back and forth between me and the beautiful things on my shelves and walls – in my cupboards, in my drawers,' he told me one time. 'If you could have seen her expressions change when she did that,' he said, 'you would have to agree with me when I say, even though it's a very conceited thing for me to say: She fell in love with me.'

He made breakfast the next morning, all with Japanese utensils, although it was an American breakfast – bacon and eggs. She stayed curled up in bed while he cooked. She reminded him of the young deer, a doe he had raised when a boy. It was not a new thought. He had been taking care of that doe all night. He turned on his radio, which was tuned to the Armed Forces Network. He hoped for music. He got news instead. The biggest news was that a North Korean spy ring had been rounded up in Osaka in the wee hours of the morning. Their radio transmitter had been found. Only one member of the ring was still being hunted, and that was the woman who called herself 'Izumi.'

Fender, by his own account, had '... entered an alternate universe by then.' He felt so much more at home in the new one than in the old one, simply because he was paired now with a woman, that he wasn't going to return to the old one ever again. What Izumi told him about her loyalty to the communist cause did not sound like enemy talk to him. 'It was just common sense on the part of a good person from an alternate universe,' he said.

So he hid her and fed her for eleven days, being careful not to neglect his duties. On the twelfth day he was so disorientated and innocent as to ask a sailor from a ship from New Zealand, which was unloading beef, if for a thousand dollars he would take a young woman on board and away from Japan. The sailor reported this to his captain, who passed it on to American authorities. Fender and Izumi were promptly arrested, separated, and would never see each other again.

Fender was never able to find out what became of her. She vanished. The most believable rumour was that she had been turned over illegally to South Korean agents, who took her to Seoul – where she was shot without trial.

Fender regretted nothing he had done.

Now he was holding up the pants of my civilian suit, a grey, pinstripe Brooks Brothers suit, for me to see. He asked me if I remembered the large cigarette hole there had been in the crotch.

'Yes,' I said.

'Find it,' he said.

I could not. Nor could I find any other holes in the suit. At his own expense he had sent the suit to an invisible mender in Atlanta. 'That, dear Walter,' he said, 'is my going-away present to you.'

Almost everybody, I knew, got a going-away present from Fender. He had little else to do with all the money he made from his science-fiction tales. But the mending of my suit was by far the most personal and thoughtful one I had ever heard of. I choked up. I could have cried. I told him so.

Before he could make a reply, there were shouts and the thunder of scampering feet in offices in the front of the building – offices whose windows faced the four-lane divided highway outside. It was believed that Virgil Greathouse, the former secretary of health, education, and welfare, had arrived out front. It was a false alarm.

Clyde Carter and Dr Fender ran out into the reception area, so that they could see, too. There were no locked doors anywhere in the prison. Fender could have kept right on running outside, if he wanted to. Clyde didn't have a gun, and neither did any of the other guards. If Fender had made a break for it, maybe somebody would have tried to tackle him; but I doubt it. It would have been the first attempted escape from the prison in its twenty-six-year history, and nobody would have had any clear idea as to what to do.

I was incurious about the arrival of Virgil Greathouse. His arrival, like the arrival of any new prisoner, would be a public execution of sorts. I did not want to watch him or anybody become less than a man. So I was all alone in the supply room. I was grateful for the accident of privacy. I took advantage of it. I performed what was perhaps the most obscenely intimate physical act of my life. I gave birth to a broken, querulous little old man by doing this: by putting on my civilian clothes.

There were white broadcloth underpants and calf-length, ribbed black socks from the Tally-ho Gentleman's Shop in Chevy Chase. There was a white Arrow shirt from Garfinckel's Department Store in Washington. There was the Brooks Brothers suit from New York City, and a regimental-stripe tie and black shoes from there, too. The laces on both shoes were broken and mended with square knots. Fender obviously had not taken a close look at them, or there would have been new laces in those shoes.

The necktie was the most antique item. I had actually worn it during the Second World War. Imagine that. An Englishman I was working with on medical supply schemes for the D-Day landings told me that the tie identified me as an officer in the Royal Welsh Fusiliers.

'You were wiped out in the Second Battle of the Somme in the First World War,' he said, 'and now, in this show, you've been wiped out again at El Alamein. You might say, "Not the luckiest regiment in the world." '

The stripe scheme is this: A broad band of pale blue is bordered by a narrow band of forest-green above and orange below. I am wearing that tie on this very day, as I sit here in my office in the Down Home Records Division of the RAM-JAC Corporation.

When Clyde Carter and Dr Fender returned to the supply room, I was a civilian again. I felt as dazed and shy and tremble-legged as any other newborn creature. I did not yet know what I looked like. There was one full-length mirror in the supply room, but its face was turned to the wall. Fender always turned it to the wall when a new arrival was expected. This was another example of Fender's delicacy. The new arrival, if he did not wish to, did not have to see at once how he had been transformed by a prison uniform.

Clyde's and Fender's faces, however, were mirrors enough to tell me that I was something less than a gay *boulevardier* on the order of, say, the late Maurice Chevalier. They were quick to cover their pity with horseplay; but not quick enough.

Fender pretended to be my valet in an embassy somewhere. 'Good morning, Mr Ambassador. Another crisp and bright day,' he said. 'The queen is expecting you for lunch at one.'

Clyde said that it sure was easy to spot a Harvard man, that they all had that certain something. But neither friend made a move to turn the mirror around, so I did it myself.

Here is who I saw reflected: a scrawny old janitor of Slavic extraction. He was unused to wearing a suit and a tie. His shirt collar was much too large for him, and so was his suit, which fit him like a circus tent. He looked unhappy – on his way to a relative's funeral, perhaps. At no point was there any harmony between himself and the suit. He may have found his clothes in a rich man's ash can.

Peace.

7

I sat now on an unsheltered park bench by the highway in front of the prison. I was waiting for the bus. I had beside me a tan canvas-and-leather suitcase designed for Army officers. It had been my constant companion in Europe during my glory days. Draped over it was an old trenchcoat, also from my glory days. I was all alone. The bus was late. Every so often I would pat the pockets of my suitcoat, making sure that I had my release papers, my government voucher for a one-way, tourist-class flight from Atlanta to New York City, my money, and my Doctor of Mixology degree. The sun beat down on me.

I had three hundred and twelve dollars and eleven cents. Two hundred and fifty of that was in the form of a government cheque, which could not easily be stolen from me. It was all my own money. After all the meticulous adding and subtracting that had gone on relative to my assets since my arrest, that much, to the penny, was incontravertibly mine: three hundred and twelve dollars and eleven cents.

So here I was going out into the Free Enterprise System again. Here I was cut loose from the protection and nurture of the federal government again.

The last time this had happened to me was in Nineteen-hundred and Fifty-three, two years after Leland Clewes went to prison for perjury. Dozens of other witnesses had been found to testify against him by then – and more damagingly, too. All I had ever accused him of was membership in the Communist Party before the war, which I would have thought was about as damning for a member of the Depression generation as having stood in a breadline. But others were willing to swear that Clewes had continued to be a communist throughout the war, and had passed secret information to agents of

91

the Soviet Union. I was flabbergasted.

That was certainly news to me, and may not even have been true. The most I had wanted from Clewes was an admission that I had told the truth about something that really didn't matter much. God knows I did not want to see him ruined and sent to jail. And the most I expected for myself was that I would be sorry for the rest of my life, would never feel quite right about myself ever again, because of what I had accidentally done to him. Otherwise, I thought, life could be expected to go on much as before.

True: I had been transferred to a less-sensitive job in the Defence Department, tabulating the likes and dislikes of soldiers of various major American races and religions, and from various educational and economic backgrounds, for various sorts of field rations, some of them new and experimental. Work of that sort, now done brainlessly and eyelessly and handlessly and at the speed of light by computers, was still being done largely by hand in those days. I and my staff now seem as archaic to me as Christian monks illuminating manuscripts with paintbrushes and golf leaf and quills.

And true: People who dealt with me at work, both inferiors and superiors, became more formal, more coldly correct, when dealing with me. They had no time anymore, seemingly, for jokes, for stories about the war. Every conversation was *schnip-schnap*! Then it was time to get back to work. I ascribed this at the time, and even told my poor wife that I admired it, to the spirit of the new, lean, keen, highly mobile and thoroughly professional Armed Forces we were shaping. They were to be a thunderbolt with which we could vaporize any new, would-be Hitler, anywhere in the world. No sooner had the people of a country lost their freedom, than the United States of America would arrive to give it back again.

And true: Ruth's and my social life was somewhat less vivid than the one I had promised her in Nuremberg. I had projected for her a telephone in our home that would never stop ringing, with old comrades of mine on the other end. They would want to eat and drink and talk all night. They would be in the primes of their lives in government service, in their late thirties or early forties, like me – so able and experienced and diplomatic and clever, and at bottom as hard as nails, that they would be the real heads and the guts of their organizations, no matter where in the hierarchy they were supposed to be. I promised Ruth that they would be blowing in from big jobs in Moscow, in Tokyo, in her home town in Vienna, in Jakarta and Timbuktu, and God knows where: What tales they would have to tell us about the world, about what was *really* going on! We would laugh and have another drink, and so on. And local people, of course, would importune us for our colourful, cosmopolitan company and for our inside information as well.

Ruth said that it was perfectly all right that our telephone did not ring – that, if it weren't for the fact that my job required me to be available at all hours of the night or day, she would rather not have a telephone in the house. As for conversations with supposedly well-informed people long into the night, she said she hated to stay up past ten o'clock, and that in the concentration camp she had heard enough supposedly inside information to last her for the rest of her days, and then some. 'I am not one of those people, Walter,' she said, 'who finds it necessary to always know, supposedly, what is really going on.'

It may be that Ruth protected herself from dread of the gathering storm, or, more accurately, from dread of the gathering silence, by reverting during the daytime, when I was at work, to the Ophelia-like elation she had felt after her liberation – when she had thought of herself as a bird all alone with God. She did not neglect the boy, who was five when Leland Clewes went to prison. He was always clean and well-fed. She did not take to secret drinking. She did, however, start to eat a lot.

And this brings me to the subject of body sizes again, something I am very reluctant to discuss – because I don't want to give them more importance than they deserve. Body sizes can be remarkable for their variations from accepted norms, but still explain almost nothing about the lives led inside those bodies. I am small enough to have been a coxswain, as I have already confessed. That explains nothing. And, by the time Leland Clewes came to trial for perjury, my wife, although only five feet tall, weighed one hundred and sixty pounds or so.

So be it.

Except for this: Our son very early on concluded that his notorious little father and his fat, foreign mother were such social handicaps to him that he actually told several playmates in the neighbourhood that he was an adopted child. A neighbour woman invited my wife over for coffee during the daytime exactly once, and with this purpose: to discover if we knew who the boy's real parents were.

Peace.

So a decent interval went by after Leland Clewes was sent to prison, two years, as I say – and then I was called into the office of Assistant Secretary of the Army Shelton Walker. We had never met. He had never been in government service before. He was my age. He had been in the war and had risen to the rank of major in the Field Artillery and had made the landings in North Africa and then, on D-Day, in France. But he was essentially an Oklahoma businessman. Someone would tell me later that he owned the largest tyre distributorship in the state. More startlingly to me: He was a Republican, for General of the Armies Dwight David Eisenhower had now become President – the first Republican to hold that office in twenty years.

Mr Walker wished to express, he said, the gratitude that the whole country should feel for my years of faithful service in both war and peace. He said that I had executive skills that would surely have been more lavishly rewarded if I had employed them in private industry. An economy drive was underway, he said, and the post I held was to be terminated. Many other posts were being terminated, so that he was unable to move me somewhere else, as much as he might have liked to do so. I was fired, in short. I am unable to say even now whether he was being unkind or not when he said to me, rising and extending his hand, 'You can now sell your considerable skills, Mr Starbuck, for their true value in the open marketplace of the Free Enterprise System. Happy hunting! Good luck!'

What did I know about Free Enterprise? I know a great deal about it now, but I knew nothing about it then. I knew so little about it then that I was able to imagine for several months that private industry really would pay a lot for an all-purpose executive like me. I told my poor wife during those first months of unemployment that, yes, that was certainly an option we held, in case all else failed: that I could at any time raise my arms like a man crucified, so to speak, and fall backward into General Motors or General Electric or some such thing. A measure of the kindness of this woman to me: She never asked me why I didn't do that immediately if it was so easy – never asked me to explain why, exactly, I felt that there was something silly and not quite gentlemanly about private industry.

'We may have to be rich, even though we don't want to be,' I remember telling her somewhere in there. My son was six by then, and listening – and old enough, surely, to ponder such a paradox. Could it have made any sense to him? No.

Meanwhile, I visited and telephoned acquaintances in other departments, making light of being 'temporarily at liberty,' as out-of-work actors say. I might have been a man with a comical injury, like a black eye or a broken big toe. Also: All my old acquaintances were Democrats like myself, allowing me to present myself as a victim of Republican stupidity and vengefulness.

But, alas, whereas life for me had been so long a sort of Virginia reel, as friends handed me on from job to job, no one could now think of a vacant post anywhere. Vacancies had suddenly become as extinct as dodo birds.

Too bad.

But the old comrades behaved so naturally and politely toward me that I could not say even now that I was being punished for what I had done to Leland Clewes – if I had not at last appealed for help to an arrogant old man outside of government, who, to my shock, was perfectly willing to show the disgust he felt for me, and to explain it in detail. He was Timothy Beame. He had been an assistant secretary of agriculture under Roosevelt before the war. He had offered me my first job in government. He, too, was a Harvard man and former Rhodes Scholar. Now he was seventy-four years old and the active head of Beame, Mearns, Weld and Weld, the most prestigious law firm in Washington.

I asked him on the telephone if he would have lunch with me. He declined. Most people declined to have lunch with me. He said he could see me for half an hour late that afternoon, but that he could not imagine what we might have to talk about.

'Frankly, sir,' I said, 'I'm looking for work – possibly with a foundation or a museum. Something like that.'

'Ohhhhhhhhhhhhhh – looking for work, are we?' he said. 'Yes – that we should talk about. Come in, by all means. How many years is it now since we've had a good talk?'

'Thirteen years, sir,' I said.

'A lot of water goes over the old dam in thirteen years.'

'Yes, sir,' I said.

'Ta-ta,' he said.

I was fool enough to keep the appointment.

His reception of me was elaborately hearty and false from the first. He introduced me to his young male secretary, told him what a promising young man I had been, clapping me on the back all the time. This was a man who may never have clapped anyone on the back in his life before.

When we got into his panelled office, Timothy Beame directed me to a leather club chair, saying, 'Sit thee doon, sit thee doon.' I have recently come across that same supposedly humorous expression of course, in Dr Bob Fender's science-fiction story about the judge from Vicuna, who got stuck forever to me and my destiny. Again: I doubt if Timothy Beame had ever addressed such an inane locution to anyone ever before. This was a bunchy, shaggy old man, incidentally – accidentally majestic as I was accidentally small. His great hands suggested that he had swung a mighty broadsword long ago, and that they were fumbling for truth and justice now. His white brows were an unbroken thicket from one side to the other, and after he had seated himself at his desk, he dipped his head forward so as to peer at me and speak to me through that hedge.

'I needn't ask what you've been up to lately,' he said.

'No, sir – I guess not,' I said.

'You and young Clewes have managed to make yourselves as famous as Mutt and Jeff,' he said.

'To our sorrow,' I said.

'I would hope so. I would certainly hope that there was much sorrow there,' he said.

This was a man who, as it turned out, had only about two more months to live. He had had no hint of that, so far as I know. It was said, after he died, that he would surely have been named to the Supreme Court, if only he had managed to live until the election of another Democrat to the presidency.

'If you are truly sorrowful,' he went on, 'I hope you know what it is you are mourning, exactly.'

'Sir – ?' I said.

'You thought only you and Clewes were involved?' he said.

'Yes, sir,' I said. 'And our wives, of course.' I meant it.

He gave a mighty groan. 'That is the one thing you should not have said to me,' he said.

'Sir – ?' I said.

'You ninny, you Harvard abortion, you incomparably third-rate little horse's ass,' he said, and he arose from his chair. 'You and Clewes have destroyed the good reputation of the most unselfish and intelligent generation of public servants this country has ever known! My God – who can care about you now, or about Clewes? Too bad he's in jail! Too bad we can't find another job for you!'

I, too, got up. 'Sir,' I said, 'I broke no law.'

'The most important thing they teach at Harvard,' he said,

'is that a man can obey every law and still be the worst criminal of his time.'

Where or when this was taught at Harvard, he did not say. It was news to me.

'Mr Starbuck,' he said, 'in case you haven't noticed: We have recently come through a global conflict between good and evil, during which we grew quite accustomed to beaches and fields littered with the bodies of our own brave and blameless dead. Now I am expected to feel pity for one unemployed bureaucrat, who, for all the damage he has done to this country, should be hanged and drawn and quartered, as far as I am concerned.'

'I only told the truth,' I bleated. I was nauseated with terror and shame.

'You told a fragmentary truth,' he said, 'which has now been allowed to represent the whole! "Educated and compassionate public servants are almost certainly Russian spies." That's all you are going to hear from the semiliterate old-time crooks and spellbinders who want the government back, who think it's rightly theirs. Without the symbiotic idiocies of you and Leland Clewes they could never have made the connection between treason and pity and brains. Now get out of my sight!'

'Sir,' I said. I would have fled if I could, but I was paralysed.

'You are yet another nincompoop, who, by being at the wrong place at the wrong time,' he said, 'was able to set humanitarianism back a full century! Begone!'

Strong stuff.

8

So there I sat on the bench outside the prison, waiting for the
bus, while the Georgia sun beat down on me. A great Cadillac
limousine, with pale blue curtains drawn across its back windows, simmered by slowly on the other side of the median
divider, on the lanes that would take it to the headquarters of
the Air Force base. I could see only the chauffeur, a black
man, who was looking quizzically at the prison. The place was
not clearly a prison. A quite modest sign at the foot of the
flagpole said only this: 'F.M.S.A.C.F., Authorized Personnel
Only.'

The limousine continued on, until it found a crossover
about a quarter of a mile up. Then it came back down and
stopped with its glossy front fender inches from my nose.
There, reflected in that perfect fender, I saw that old Slavic
janitor again. This was the same limousine, it turned out, that
had set off the false alarm about the arrival of Virgil Greathouse somewhat earlier. It had been cruising in search of the
prison for quite some time.

The chauffeur got out, and he asked me if this was indeed
the prison.

Thus was I required to make my first sound as a free man.
'Yes,' I said.

The chauffeur, who was a big, serenely paternal, middle-
aged man in a tan whipcord uniform and black leather puttees,
opened the back door, spoke into the twilit interior. 'Gentlemen,' he said, with precisely the appropriate mixture of sorrow
and respect, 'we have reached our destination.' Letters embroidered in red silk thread on his breast pocket identified his
employer. 'RAMJAC,' they said.

As I would learn later: Old pals of Greathouse had provided
him and his lawyers with swift and secret transportation from

his home to prison, so that there would be almost no witnesses to his humiliation. A limousine from Pepsi-Cola had picked him up before dawn at the service entrance to the Waldorf Towers in Manhattan, which was his home. It had taken him to the Marine Air Terminal next to La Guardia, and directly out onto a runway. A corporate jet belonging to Resorts International was waiting for him there. It flew him to Atlanta, where he was met, again right out on the runway, by a curtained limousine supplied by the Southeastern District Office of The RAMJAC Corporation.

Out clambered Virgil Greathouse – dressed almost exactly as I was, in a grey, pinstripe suit and a white shirt and a regimental-stripe tie. Our regiments were different. He was a Coldstream Guard. As always, he was sucking on his pipe. He gave me the briefest of glances.

And then two sleek lawyers got out – one young, one old.

While the chauffeur went to the limousine's trunk to get the convict's luggage, Greathouse and the two lawyers looked over the prison as though it were a piece of real estate they were thinking of buying, if the price was right. There was a twinkle in the eyes of Greathouse, and he was imitating bird-calls with his pipe. He may have been thinking how tough he was. He had been taking lessons in boxing and *jujitsu* and *karate*, I would learn later from his lawyers, ever since it had become clear to him that he was really going to go to jail.

'Well,' I thought to myself when I heard that, 'there won't be anybody in that particular prison who will want to fight him, but he will get his back broken anyway. Everybody gets his back broken when he goes to prison for the first time. It mends after a while, but never quite the way it was before. As tough as Virgil Greathouse may be, he will never walk or feel quite the same again.'

Virgil Greathouse had failed to recognize me. Sitting there on the bench, I might as well have been a corpse in the mud on a battlefield, and he might have been a general who had come forward during a lull to see how things were going, by and large.

I was surprised. I did think, though, that he might recognize the voice from inside the prison, which we could all hear so clearly now. It was the voice of his closest Watergate coconspirator, Emil Larkin, singing at the top of his lungs the Negro spiritual 'Sometimes I Feel Like a Motherless Child.'

Greathouse had no time to show his reaction to the voice, for a fighter plane leaped up from the tip of a nearby runway, tore the sky to shreds. This was a gut-ripping sound to anyone who had not heard it and heard it and heard it before. There was never a warning build-up. It was always an end-of-the-world explosion overhead.

Greathouse and the lawyers and the chauffeur flung themselves to the ground. Then they got up again, cursing and laughing and dusting themselves off. Greathouse, supposing correctly that he was being watched and sized up by people he could not see, made some boxing feints and looked up into the sky as though to say, clowningly, 'Send me another one. I'm ready this time.' The party did not advance on the prison, however. It waited by the limousine, expecting some sort of welcoming party. Greathouse wanted, I imagine, one last acknowledgment of his rank in society on neutral ground, a sort of surrender at Appomattox, with the warden as Ulysses S. Grant and himself as Robert E. Lee.

But the warden wasn't even in Georgia. He would have been there if he had had any advance notice that Greathouse was going to surrender on this particular day. But he was in Atlantic City, addressing a convention of the American Association of Parole Officers up there. So it was finally Clyde Carter, the spit and image of President Carter, who came out of the front door a few steps and motioned to them.

Clyde smiled. 'You all come on in,' he said.

So in they went, with the chauffeur bringing up the rear, carrying two valises made of buttery leather and a matching case for toiletries. Clyde relieved him of the bags at the threshold, told him politely to return to the limousine.

'You won't be needed in there,' said Clyde.

So the chauffeur got back into the limousine. His name was

Cleveland Lawes, a garbling of the name of the man I had ruined, Leland Clewes. He had only a grammar-school education, but he read five books a week while waiting for people, mostly RAMJAC executives and customers and suppliers. Because he had been captured by the Chinese during the Korean War, and had actually gone to China for a while and worked as a deckhand on a coastwise steamer in the Yellow Sea, he was reasonably fluent in Chinese.

Cleveland Lawes was reading *The Gulag Archipelago* now, an account of the prison system in the Soviet Union by another former prisoner, Aleksandr Solzhenitsyn.

So there I was all alone on a bench in the middle of nowhere again. I entered a period of catatonia again – staring straight ahead at nothing, and every so often clapping my old hands three times.

If it had not been for that clapping, Cleveland Lawes tells me now, he would never have become curious about me.

But I became his business by clapping my hands. He had to find out why I did it.

Did I tell him the truth about the clapping? No. It was too complicated and silly. I told him that I had been daydreaming about the past, and that whenever I remembered an especially happy moment, I would lift my hands from my lap, and I would clap three times.

He offered me a ride into Atlanta.

And there I was now, after only half an hour of freedom, sitting in the front seat of a parked limousine. So far so good.

And if Cleveland Lawes had not offered me a ride into Atlanta, he would never have become what he is today, personnel director of the Transico Division of The RAMJAC Corporation. Transico has limousine services and taxicab fleets and car-rental agencies and parking lots and garages all over the Free World. You can even rent furniture from Transico. Many people do.

I asked him if he thought his passengers would mind my coming along to Atlanta.

He said that he had never seen them before, and that he

never expected to see them again – that they did not work for RAMJAC. He added the piquant detail that he had not known that his chief passenger had been Virgil Greathouse until the arrival at the prison. Until that moment Greathouse had been disguised by a false beard.

I craned my neck for a look into the backseat, and there the beard was, with one of its wire earloops hooked over a door handle.

Cleveland Lawes said as a joke that he wasn't sure Greathouse's lawyers would come back out again. 'When they were looking over the prison,' he said, 'seemed to me they were trying it on for size.'

He asked me if I had ever ridden in a limousine before. For simplicity's sake I told him, 'No.' As a child, of course, I had often ridden beside my father in the front seat of Alexander Hamilton McCone's various limousines. In my youth, as I was preparing for Harvard, I had often ridden in the backseat with Mr McCone, with a glass partition between myself and my father. The partition had not seemed strange or even suggestive to me at the time.

And when in Nuremberg I had been master of that grotesque Fafner of a Mercedes touring car. But it had been an open car, freakish even without the bullet holes in the trunk lid and the rear windshield. The status it gave me among the Bavarians was that of a pirate – in temporary possession of stolen goods that would certainly be restolen, again and again. But, sitting there outside the prison, I realized that I had not sat in a real limousine for perhaps forty-five years! As high as I had risen in public service, I had never been entitled to a limousine, had never been within three promotions of having one of my own or even the occasional use of one. Nor had I ever so beguiled a superior who had one that he had said to me, 'Young man – I want to talk to you more about this. You come in my car with me.'

Leland Clewes, on the other hand, though not entitled to one of his own, was forever riding around in limousines with adoring old men.

No matter.

Calm down.

Cleveland Lawes commented that I sounded like an educated man to him.

I admitted to having gone to Harvard.

This allowed him to tell me about his having been a prisoner of the Chinese communists in North Korea, for the Chinese major in charge of his prison had been a Harvard man. The major would have been about my age, and possibly even a classmate, but I had never befriended any Chinese. According to Lawes, he had studied physics and mathematics, so I would not have known him in any case.

'His daddy was a big landlord,' said Lawes. 'When the communists came, they made his daddy kneel down in front of all his tenants in the village, and then they chopped off his head with a sword.'

'But the son could still be a communist – after that?' I said.

'He said his daddy really had been a very bad landlord,' he said.

'Well,' I said, 'that's Harvard for you, I guess.'

This Harvard Chinese befriended Cleveland Lawes and persuaded him to come to China instead of going back home to Georgia when the war was over. When he was a boy, a cousin of Lawes had been burned alive by a mob, and his father had been dragged out of his house one night and horse-whipped by the Ku Klux Klan, and he himself had been beat up twice for trying to register to vote, right before the Army got him. So he was easy prey for a smooth-talking communist. And he worked for two years, as I say, as a deckhand on the Yellow Sea. He said that he fell in love several times, but that nobody would fall in love with him.

'So that was what brought you back?' I asked.

He said it was the church music more than anything else. 'There wasn't anybody to sing with over there,' he said. 'And the food,' he said.

'The food wasn't any good?' I said.

'Oh, it was good,' he said. 'It just wasn't the kind of food I like to talk about.'

'Um,' I said.

'You can't just eat food,' he said. 'You've got to talk about it, too. And you've got to talk about it to somebody who understands that kind of food.'

I congratulated him on having learned Chinese, and he replied that he could never do such a thing now. 'I know too much now,' he said. 'I was too ignorant then to know how hard it was to learn Chinese. I thought it was like imitating birds. You know: You hear a bird make a sound, then you try to make a sound just like that, and see if you can't fool the bird.'

The Chinese were nice about it when he decided that he wanted to go home. They liked him, and they went to some trouble for him, asking through circuitous diplomatic channels what would be done to him if he went home. America had no representatives in China then, and neither did any of its allies. The messages went through Moscow, which was still friendly with China then.

Yes, and this black, former private first class, whose military specialty had been to carry the base-plate of a heavy mortar, turned out to be worth negotiations at the highest diplomatic levels. The Americans wanted him back in order to punish him. The Chinese said that the punishment had to be brief and almost entirely symbolic, and that he had to be returned nearly at once to ordinary civilian life – or they would not let him go. The Americans said that Lawes would of course be expected to make some sort of public explanation of why he had come home. After that, he would be court-martialled, given a prison sentence of under three years and a dishonourable discharge, with forfeiture of all pay and benefits. The Chinese replied that Lawes had given his promise that he would never speak against the People's Republic of China, which had treated him well. If he was to be forced to break that promise, they would not let him go. They also insisted that he serve no prison time whatsoever, and that he be paid for the time he spent as a prisoner of war. The Americans replied that he would have to be jailed at some point, since no army could allow the crime of desertion to go unpunished. They would like to jail him prior to his trial. They would sentence him to a term equal to the time he had spent as a prisoner of war, and deduct the time he had spent as a prisoner prisoner of war, and send him home. Back pay was out of the question.

And that was the deal.

'They wanted me back, you know,' he told me, 'because they were so embarrassed. They couldn't stand it that even one American, even a black one, would think for even a minute that maybe America wasn't the best country in the world.'

I asked him if he had ever heard of Dr Robert Fender, who was convicted of treason during the Korean War, and was right inside the prison there, measuring Virgil Greathouse for a uniform.

'No,' he said. 'I never kept track of other people in that kind of trouble. I never felt like it was a club or something.'

I asked him if he had ever seen the legendary Mrs Jack Graham, Jr, the majority stockholder in The RAMJAC Corporation.

'That's like asking me if I've seen God,' he said.

The widow Graham had not been seen in public, at that point, for about five years. Her most recent appearance was in a courtroom in New York City, where RAMJAC was being sued by a group of its stockholders for proofs that she was still alive. The accounts in the papers amused my wife so, I remember. 'This is the America I love,' she said. 'Why can't it be like this all the time?'

Mrs Graham came into the courtroom without a lawyer, but with eight uniformed bodyguards from Pinkerton, Inc, a RAMJAC subsidiary. One of them was carrying an amplifier with a loudspeaker and a microphone. Mrs Graham was wearing a voluminous black kaftan with its hood up, and with the hood pinned shut with diaper pins, so that she could peek out, but nobody could see what was inside. Only her hands were visible. Another Pinkerton was carrying an inkpad, some paper, and a copy of her fingerprints from the files of the Federal Bureau of Investigation. Her prints had been forwarded to the F.B.I. after she was convicted of drunken driving in Frankfort, Kentucky, in Nineteen-hundred and Fifty-two, soon after her husband died. She had been put on probation at that time. I myself had just been fired from government service at that time.

The amplifier was turned on, and the microphone was slipped inside her kaftan, so people could hear what she was saying in there. She proved she was who she said she was by fingerprinting herself on the spot and having the prints compared with those possessed by the F.B.I. She said under oath that she was in excellent health, both physically and mentally – and in control of the company's top officers, but never face-to-face. When she instructed them on the telephone, she used a password to identify herself. This password was changed at irregular intervals. At the judge's request, I remember, she gave a sample password, and it seemed so full of magic that it still sticks in my mind. This was it: 'shoemaker.' Every order she gave on the phone was subsequently confirmed by mail, by a letter written entirely by her own hand. At the bottom of each letter was not only her signature, but a full set of prints from her eight little fingers and two little thumbs. She called them that: '... my eight little fingers and my two little thumbs.'

That was that. Mrs Jack Graham was unquestionably alive, and now she was free to disappear again.

'I've seen Mr Leen many times,' said Cleveland Lawes. He was speaking of Arpad Leen, the very public and communicative president and chairman of the board of directors of The RAMJAC Corporation. He would become my boss of bosses, and Cleveland Lawes's boss of bosses, too, when we both became corporate officers of RAMJAC. I say now that Arpad Leen is the most able and informed and brilliant and responsive executive under whom it has ever been my privilege to serve. He is a genius at acquiring companies and keeping them from dying afterward.

He used to say, 'If you can't get along with me, you can't get along with anybody.'

It was true, it was true.

Lawes said that Arpad Leen had come to Atlanta and been Lawes's passenger only two months before. A cluster of new stores and luxury hotels in Atlanta had gone bankrupt, and Leen had tried to snap it all up for RAMJAC. He had been outbid, however, by a South Korean religious cult.

Lawes asked me if I had any children. I said I had a son who worked for *The New York Times*. Lawes laughed and said that he and my son had the same boss now: Arpad Leen. I had missed the news that morning, so he had to explain to me that RAMJAC had just acquired control of *The New York Times* and all of its subsidiaries, which included the second-largest catfood company in the world.

'When he was down here,' said Lawes, 'Mr Leen told me this was going to happen. It was the catfood company he wanted – not *The New York Times*.'

The two lawyers got into the backseat of the limousine. They weren't subdued at all. They were laughing about the guard who looked like the President of the United States. 'I felt like saying to him,' said one, ' "Mr President, why don't you just pardon him right here and now? He's suffered enough, and he could get in some good golf this afternoon." '

One of them tried on the false beard, and the other one said he looked like Karl Marx. And so on. They were incurious about me. Cleveland Lawes told them that I had been visiting my son. They asked me what my son was in for and I said, 'Mail fraud.' That was the end of the conversation.

So off we went to Atlanta. There was a curious object stuck by means of a suction cup to the glove compartment in front of me, I remember. Coming out of the cup and aimed at my breastbone was what looked like about a foot of green garden hose. At the end of the shaft was a white plastic wheel the size of a dinner plate. Once we got going, the wheel began to hypnotize me, bobbing up and down when we went over bumps, swaying this way and then that way as we went around curves.

So I asked about it. It was a toy steering wheel, it turned out. Lawes had a seven-year-old son he sometimes took with him on trips. The little boy could pretend to be steering the limousine with the plastic wheel. There had been no such toy when my own son was little. Then again, he wouldn't have enjoyed it much. Even at seven, young Walter hated to go anywhere with his mother and me.

I said it was a clever toy.

Lawes said it could be an exciting one, too, especially if the person with the real steering wheel was drunk and having close shaves with oncoming trucks and sideswiping parked cars and so on. He said that the President of the United States ought to be given a wheel like that at his inauguration, to remind him and everybody else that all he could do was pretend to steer.

He let me off at the airport.

The planes to New York City were all overbooked, it turned out. I did not get out of Atlanta until five o'clock that afternoon. That was all right with me. I skipped lunch, having no appetite. I found a paperback book in a toilet stall, so I read that for a while. It was about a man who, through ruthlessness, became the head of a big international conglomerate. Women were crazy about him. He treated them like dirt, but they just came back for more. His son was a drug addict and his daughter was a nymphomaniac.

My reading was interrupted once by a Frenchman who spoke to me in French and pointed to my left lapel. I thought at first that I had set myself on fire again, even though I didn't smoke anymore. Then I realized that I was still wearing the narrow red ribbon that identified me as a *chevalier* in the French Légion d'honneur. Pathetically enough, I had worn it all through my trial, and all the way to prison, too.

I told him in English that it had come with the suit, which

I had bought secondhand, and that I had no idea what it was supposed to represent.

He became very icy. '*Permettez-moi, monsieur,*' he said, and he deftly plucked the ribbon from my lapel as though it had been an insect there.

'*Merci,*' I said, and I returned to my book.

When there was at last an airplane seat for me, my name was broadcast over the public-address system several times: 'Mr Walter F. Starbuck, Mr Walter F. Starbuck ...' It had been such a notorious name at one time; but I could not now catch sight of anyone who seemed to recognize it, who raised his or her eyebrows in lewd surmise.

Two and a half hours later I was on the island of Manhattan, wearing my trenchcoat to keep out the evening chill. The sun was down. I was staring at an animated display in the window of a store that sold nothing but toy trains.

It was not as though I had no place to go. I was close to where I was going. I had written ahead. I had reserved a room without bath or television for a week, paying in advance – in the once-fashionable Hotel Arapahoe, now a catch-as-catch-can lazaret and bagnio one minute from Times Square.

9

I had been to the Arapahoe once before – in the autumn of
Nineteen-hundred and Thirty-one. Fire had yet to be domes-
ticated. Albert Einstein had predicted the invention of the
wheel, but was unable to describe its probable shape and uses
in the language of ordinary women and men. Herbert Hoover,
a mining engineer, was President. The sale of alcoholic beverages was against the law, and I was a Harvard freshman.

I was operating under instructions from my mentor, Alexander Hamilton McCone. He told me in a letter that I was to
duplicate a folly he himself had committed when a freshman,
which was to take a pretty girl to the Harvard-Columbia football game in New York, and then to spend a month's allowance
on a lobster dinner for two, with oysters and caviar and all
that, in the famous dining room of the Hotel Arapahoe. We
were to go dancing afterward. 'You must wear your tuxedo,'
he said. 'You must tip like a drunken sailor.' Diamond Jim
Brady, he told me, had once eaten four dozen oysters, four
lobsters, four chickens, four squabs, four T-bone steaks, four
pork chops, and four lamb chops there – on a bet. Lillian
Russell had looked on.

Mr McCone may have been drunk when he wrote that letter
'All work and no play,' he wrote, 'makes Jack a dull boy.'

And the girl I took there, the twin sister of my roommate,
would become one of the four women I would ever truly love.
The first was my mother. The last was my wife.

Sarah Wyatt was the girl's name. She was all of eighteen,
and so was I. She was attending a very easy two-year college
for rich girls in Wellesley, Massachusetts, which was Pine
Manor. Her family lived in Pride's Crossing, north of Boston
– toward Gloucester. While we were in New York City together, she would be staying with her maternal grandmother,

a stockbroker's widow, in a queerly irrelevant enclave of dead-end streets and vest-pocket parks and Elizabethan apartment-hotels called 'Tudor City' – near the East River, and actually bridging Forty-second Street. As luck will have it, my son now lives in Tudor City. So do Mr and Mrs Leland Clewes.

Small world.

Tudor City was quite new, but already bankrupt and nearly empty when I arrived by taxicab – to take my Sarah to the Hotel Arapahoe in Nineteen-hundred and Thirty-one. I was wearing a tuxedo made to my measure by the finest tailor in Cleveland. I had a silver cigarette lighter and a silver cigarette case, both gifts from Mr McCone. I had forty dollars in my billfold. I could have bought the whole state of Arkansas for forty dollars cash in Nineteen-hundred and Thirty-one.

We come to the matter of physical size again: Sarah Wyatt was three inches taller than me. She did not mind. She was so far from minding that, when I fetched her in Tudor City, she was wearing high heels with her evening dress.

A stronger proof that she was indifferent to our disparity in size: In seven years Sarah Wyatt would agree to marry me.

She wasn't quite ready when I arrived, so I had to talk to her grandmother, Mrs Sutton, for a while. Sarah had warned me at the football game that afternoon that I must not mention suicide to Mrs Sutton – because Mr Sutton had jumped out of his office window in Wall Street after the stock market crashed in Nineteen-hundred and Twenty-nine.

'It is a nice place you have here, Mrs Sutton,' I said.

'You're the only person who thinks so,' she said. 'It's crowded. Everything that goes on in the kitchen you can smell out here.'

It was only a two-bedroom apartment. She had certainly come down in the world. Sarah said she used to have a horse farm in Connecticut and a house on Fifth Avenue, and on and on.

The walls of the little entrance hall were covered with blue ribbons from horse shows before the Crash. 'I see you have won a lot of blue ribbons,' I said.

'No,' she said, 'it was the horses that won those.'

We were seated on folding chairs at a card table in the middle of the living room. There were no easy chairs, no couch. But the room was so jammed with breakfronts and escritoires and armoires and highboys and lowboys and Welsh dressers and wardrobes and grandfather clocks and so on, that I could not guess where the windows were. It turned out that she also stockpiled servants, all very old. A uniformed maid had let me in, and then exited sideways into a narrow fissure between two imposing examples of cabinetwork.

Now a uniformed chauffeur emerged from the same fissure to ask Mrs Sutton if she would be going anywhere in 'the electric' that night. Many people, especially old ladies, seemingly, had electric cars in those days. They looked like telephone booths on wheels. Under the floor were terribly heavy storage batteries. They had a top speed of about eleven miles an hour and needed to be recharged every thirty miles or so. They had tillers, like sailboats, instead of steering wheels.

Mrs Sutton said she would not be going anywhere in the electric, so the old chauffeur said that he would be going to the hotel, then. There were two other servants besides, whom I never saw. They were all going to spend the night at a hotel so that Sarah could have the second bedroom, where they ordinarily slept.

'I suppose this all looks very temporary to you,' Mrs Sutton said to me.

'No, ma'am,' I said.

'It's quite permanent,' she said. 'I am utterly helpless to improve my condition without a man. It was the way I was brought up. It was the way I was educated.'

'Yes, ma'am,' I said.

'Men in tuxedos as beautifully made as yours is should never call anyone but the Queen of England "ma'am," ' she said.

'I'll try to remember that,' I said.

'You are only a child, of course,' she said.

'Yes, ma'am,' I said.

'Tell me again how you are related to the McCones,' she said.

I had never told anyone that I was related to the McCones. There was another lie I had told frequently, however – a lie, like everything else about me, devised by Mr McCone. He said it would be perfectly acceptable, even fashionable, to admit that my father was penniless. But it would not do to have a household servant for a father.

The lie went like this, and I told it to Mrs Sutton: 'My father works for Mr McCone as curator of his art collection. He also advises Mr McCone on what to buy.'

'A cultivated man,' she said.

'He studied art in Europe,' I said. 'He is no businessman.'

'A dreamer,' she said.

'Yes,' I said. 'If it weren't for Mr McCone, I could not afford to go to Harvard.'

' "Starbuck –" ' she mused. 'I believe that's an old Nantucket name.'

I was ready for that one, too. 'Yes,' I said, 'but my great-grandfather left Nantucket for the Gold Rush and never returned. I must go to Nantucket sometime and look at the old records, to see where we fit in.'

'A California family,' she said.

'Nomads, really,' I said. 'California, yes – but Oregon, too, and Wyoming, and Canada, and Europe. But they were always bookish people – teachers and so on.'

I was pure phlogiston, an imaginary element of long ago.

'Descended from whaling captains,' she said.

'I imagine,' I said. I was not at all uncomfortable with the lies.

'And from Vikings before that,' she said.

I shrugged.

She had decided to like me a lot – and would continue to do so until the end. As Sarah would tell me, Mrs Sutton often referred to me as her little Viking. She would not live long enough to see Sarah agree to marry me and then to jilt me. She died in Nineteen-hundred and Thirty-seven or so – penniless in an apartment furnished with little more than a card table, two folding chairs, and her bed. She had sold off all her treasures in order to support herself and her old servants, who would have had no place to go and nothing to eat without her. She survived them all. The maid, who was Tillie, was the last of them to die. Two weeks after Tillie died, so did Mrs Sutton depart from this world.

Back there in Nineteen-hundred and Thirty-one, while I was waiting for Sarah to complete her toilette, Mrs Sutton told me that Mr McCone's father, the founder of Cuyahoga Bridge and Iron, built the biggest house where she spent her girlhood summers – in Bar Harbor, Maine. When it was finished, he gave a grand ball with four orchestras, and nobody came.

'It seemed very beautiful and noble to snub him like that,' she said. 'I remember how happy I was the next day. I can't help wondering now if we weren't just a little insane. I don't mean that we were insane to miss a wonderful party or to hurt the feelings of Daniel McCone. Daniel McCone was a perfectly ghastly man. What was insane was the way we all imagined that God was watching, and simply adoring us, guaranteeing us all seats at His right hand for having snubbed Daniel McCone.'

I asked her what had become of the McCone mansion in Bar Harbor. My mentor had never mentioned it to me.

'Mr and Mrs McCone vanished from Bar Harbor the next day,' she said, 'with their two young sons, I believe.'

'Yes,' I said. One son became my mentor. The other son became chairman of the board and president of Cuyahoga Bridge and Iron.

'A month later,' she said, 'around Labor Day, although there was no Labor Day then – when summer was about to end – a special train arrived. There were perhaps eight freight cars and three cars of workmen, who had come all the way from Cleveland. They must have been from Mr McCone's factory. How pale they looked! They were almost all foreigners, I remember – Germans, Poles, Italians, Hungarians. Who could tell? There had never been such people in Bar Harbor before. They slept on the train. They ate on the train. They allowed themselves to be herded like docile cattle between the mansion and the train. They removed only the finest art treasures from the mansion – only paintings and statues and tapestries and rugs that belonged in museums.' Mrs Sutton rolled her eyes. 'Oh, Lord – what they didn't leave behind! And then the workmen took every pane of glass from the windows and doors and skylights. They stripped the slate from the roof. One workman was killed, I remember, by a falling slate. They bored holes in the naked roof. They loaded all the slate and glass on the train, too, so it would not be easy for anyone to make repairs. Then they went away again. No one had spoken to them, and they had not spoken to anyone.

'It was a very special departure, and nobody who saw it ever forgot it,' said Mrs Sutton. 'Trains were great fun in those days, making such hullabaloos at the station with their whistles and bells. But that special train from Cleveland left as quietly as a ghost. I am sure the engineer was under orders from Daniel McCone himself not to blow the whistle or ring the bell.'

Thus was the finest mansion in Bar Harbor and most of its furnishings, with sheets and blankets and quilts still on all the beds, according to Mrs Sutton, with china and crystal still in the cupboards, with thousands of bottles of wine still in the cellar, left to die and die.

Mrs Sutton closed her eyes, remembering the decay of the mansion year by year. 'Served nobody right, Mr Starbuck,' she said.

Young Sarah now came out from between the furniture, ready at last. She wore two orchids, which I had sent to her. They, too, had been the brainstorm of Alexander Hamilton McCone.

'You are so beautiful!' I said, rising raptly from my folding chair. It was true, surely, for she was tall and slender and golden-haired – and blue-eyed. Her skin was like satin. Her teeth were like pearls. But she radiated about as much sexuality as her grandmother's card table.

This would continue to be the case for the next seven years. Sarah Wyatt believed that sex was a sort of pratfall that was easily avoided. To avoid it, she had only to remind a would-be lover of the ridiculousness of what he proposed to do to her. The first time I kissed her, which was in Wellesley the week before, I suddenly found myself being played like a tuba, so to speak. Sarah was convulsed by laughter, with her lips still pressed to mine. She tickled me. She pulled out my shirttails, leaving me in humiliating disarray. It was terrible. Nor was her laughter about sexuality girlish and nervous, something a man might be expected to modulate with tenderness and anatomical skill. It was the unbridled hee-hawing of somebody at a Marx Brothers film.

A phrase keeps asking to be used at this point: 'nobody home.'

It was in fact a phrase used by a Harvard classmate who also took Sarah out, but only twice, as I recall. I asked him what he thought of her, and he replied with some bitterness: 'nobody home!' He was Kyle Denny, a football player from Philadelphia. Somebody told me recently that Kyle died in a fall in his bathtub on the day the Japanese bombed Pearl Harbor. He cracked his head open on a faucet.

So I can fix the date of Kyle Denny's death with pinpoint accuracy: December the seventh, Nineteen-hundred and Forty-one.

'You do look nice, my dear,' said Mrs Sutton to Sarah. She was pitifully ancient – about five years younger than I am now. I thought she might cry about Sarah's beauty, and how that beauty was sure to fade in just a few years, and on and on. She was very wise.

'I feel so silly,' said Sarah.

'You don't believe you're beautiful?' said her grandmother.

'I know I'm beautiful,' said Sarah. 'I look in a mirror, and I think, "I'm beautiful."'

'What's wrong, then?' said her grandmother.

'Beautiful is such a funny thing to be,' said Sarah. 'Somebody else is ugly, but I'm beautiful. Walter says I'm beautiful. You say I'm beautiful. I say I'm beautiful. Everybody says, "Beautiful, beautiful, beautiful," and you start wondering what it is, and what's so wonderful about it.'

'You make people *happy* with your beauty,' said her grand-mother.

'You certainly make *me* happy with it,' I said.

Sarah laughed. 'It's so silly,' she said. 'It's so dumb,' she said.

'Perhaps you shouldn't think about it so much,' said her grandmother.

'That's like telling a midget to stop thinking about being a midget,' said Sarah, and she laughed again.

'You should stop saying everything is silly and dumb,' said her grandmother.

'Everything *is* silly and dumb,' said Sarah.

'You will learn differently as you grow older,' her grand-mother promised.

'I think everybody older just pretends to know what's going on, that it's all so serious and wonderful,' said Sarah. 'Older people haven't really found out anything new that I don't know. Maybe if people didn't get so serious when they got older, we wouldn't have a depression now.'

'There's nothing constructive in laughing all the time,' said her grandmother.

'I can cry, too,' said Sarah. 'You want me to cry?'

'No,' said her grandmother. 'I don't want to hear any more about it. You just go out with this nice young man and have a lovely time.'

'I can't laugh about those poor women who painted the clocks,' said Sarah. 'That's one thing I can't laugh about.'

'Nobody wants you to,' said her grandmother. 'You run along now.'

Sarah was referring to an industrial tragedy that was notori-ous at the time. Sarah's family was in the middle of it, and sick about it. Sarah had already told me that she was sick about it, and so had her brother, my roommate, and so had their father and mother. The tragedy was a slow one that could not be stopped once it had begun, and it began in the family's clock company, the Wyatt Clock Company, one of the oldest companies in the United States, in Brockton, Massachusetts. It was an avoidable tragedy. The Wyatts never tried to justify it, and would not hire lawyers to justify it. It could not be justified.

It went like this: In the nineteen twenties the United States Navy awarded Wyatt Clock a contract to produce several thousand standardized ships' clocks that could be easily read in the dark. The dials were to be black. The hands and the numerals were to be hand-painted with white paint containing the radioactive element radium. About half a hundred Brockton woman, most of them relatives of regular Wyatt Clock Company employees, were hired to paint the hands and numerals. It was a way to make pin money. Several of the women who had young children to look after were allowed to do the work at home.

Now all those women had died or were about to die most horribly with their bones crumbling, with their heads rotting off. The cause was radium poisoning. Every one of them had been told by a foreman, it had since come out in court, that she should keep a fine point on her brush by moistening it and shaping it with her lips from time to time.

And, as luck would have it, the daughter of one of those unfortunate women would become one of the four women I have ever loved in this Vale of Tears – along with my mother, my wife, and Sarah Wyatt. Mary Kathleen O'Looney was her name.

10

I speak only of Ruth as 'my wife.' It would not surprise me, though, if on Judgement Day Sarah Wyatt and Mary Kathleen O'Looney were also certified as having been wives of mine. I surely paired off with both of them – with Mary Kathleen for about eleven months, and with Sarah, off and on, to be sure, for about seven years.

I can hear Saint Peter saying to me: 'It would appear, Mr Starbuck, that you were something of a Don Juan.'

So there I was in Nineteen-hundred and Thirty-one, sashaying into the wedding-cake lobby of the Hotel Arapahoe with beautiful Sarah Wyatt, the Yankee clock heiress, on my arm. Her family was nearly as broke as mine by then. What little they had salvaged from the crashing stock market and the failing banks would soon be dispersed among the survivors of the women who painted all those clocks for the Navy. This dispersal would be compelled in about a year by a landmark decision of the United States Supreme Court as to the personal responsibility of employers for deaths in their places of work caused by criminal negligence.

Eighteen-year-old Sarah now said of the Arapahoe lobby, 'It's so dirty – and there's nobody here.' She laughed. 'I *love* it,' she said.

At that point in time, in the filthy lobby of the Arapahoe, Sarah Wyatt did not know that I was acting with all possible humourlessness on orders from Alexander Hamilton McCone. She would tell me later that she thought I was being witty when I said we should get all dressed up. She thought we were costumed like millionaires in the spirit of Halloween. We would laugh and laugh, she hoped. We would be people in a movie.

Not at all: I was a robot programmed to behave like a genuine aristocrat.

Oh, to be young again!

The dirt in the Arapahoe lobby might not have been so obvious, if somebody had not started to do something about it and then stopped. There was a tall stepladder set against one wall. There was a bucket at the base of it, filled with dirty water and with a brush floating on top. Someone had clearly scaled the ladder with the bucket. He had scrubbed as much of the wall as he could reach from the top. He had created a circle of cleanliness, dribbling filth at its bottom, to be sure, but as bright as a harvest moon.

I do not know who made the harvest moon. There was no one to ask. There had been no doorman to invite us in. There were no bellboys and no guests inside. There wasn't a soul behind the reception desk in the distance. The newsstand and the theatre-ticket kiosk were shuttered. The doors of the un-manned elevators were propped open by chairs.

'I don't think they're in business anymore,' said Sarah.

'Somebody accepted my reservation on the telephone,' I said. 'He called me "*monsieur*." '

'Anybody can call anybody "*monsieur*" on the telephone,' said Sarah.

But then we heard a Gypsy violin crying somewhere – sobbing as though its heart would break. And when I hear that violin's lamenting in my memory now, I am able to add this information: Hitler, not yet in power, would soon cause to be killed every Gypsy his soldiers and policemen could catch.

The music was coming from behind a folding screen in the lobby. Sarah and I dared to move the screen from the wall. We were confronted by a pair of French doors, which were held shut with a padlock and hasp. The panes in the doors were mirrors, showing us yet again how childish and rich we were. But Sarah discovered one pane that had a flaw in its silvering. She peeped through the flaw, then invited me to take a turn.

I was flabbergasted. I might have been peering into the twinkling prisms of a time machine. On the other side of the French doors was the famous dining room of the Hotel Arapahoe in pristine condition, complete with a Gypsy fiddler – almost atom for atom as it must have been in the time of Diamond Jim Brady. A thousand candles in the chandeliers and on the tables became billions of tiny stars because of all the silver and crystal and china and mirrors in there.

The story was this: The hotel and the restaurant, while sharing the same building, one minute from Times Square, were under separate ownerships. The hotel had given up – was no longer taking guests. The restaurant, on the other hand, had just been completely refurbished, its owner believing that the collapse of the economy would be brief, and was caused by nothing more substantial than a temporary loss of nerve by businessmen.

Sarah and I had come in through the wrong door. I told Sarah as much, and she replied, 'That is the story of my life. I always go in the wrong door first.'

So Sarah and I went out into the night again and then in through the door to the place where food and drink awaited us. Mr McCone had told me to order the meal in advance. That I had done. The owner himself received us. He was French. On the lapel of his tuxedo was a decoration that meant nothing to me, but which was familiar to Sarah, since her father had one, too. It meant, she would explain to me, that he was a *chevalier* in the Légion d'honneur.

Sarah had spent many summers in Europe. I had never been there. She was fluent in French, and she and the owner performed a madrigal in that most melodious of all languages. How could I ever have got through life without women to act as my interpreters? Of the four women I ever loved, only Mary Kathleen O'Looney spoke no language but English. But even Mary Kathleen was my interpreter when I was a Harvard communist, trying to communicate with members of the American working class.

The restaurant owner told Sarah in French, and then she

told me, about the Great Depression's being nothing but a loss of nerve. He said that alcoholic beverages would be legal again as soon as a Democrat was elected President, and that life would become fun again.

He led us to our table. The room could seat at least one hundred, I would guess, but there were only a dozen other patrons there. Somehow, they still had cash. And when I try to remember them now, and to guess what they were, I keep seeing the pictures by George Grosz of corrupt plutocrats amidst the misery of Germany after World War One. I had not seen those pictures in Nineteen-hundred and Thirty-one. I had not seen anything.

There was a puffy old woman, I remember, eating alone and wearing a diamond necklace. She had a Pekingese dog in her lap. The dog had a diamond necklace, too.

There was a withered old man, I remember, hunched over his food, hiding it with his arms. Sarah whispered that he ate as though his meal were a royal flush. We would later learn that he was eating caviar.

'This must be a very expensive place,' said Sarah.

'Don't worry about it,' I said.

'Money is so strange,' she said. 'Does it make any sense to you?'

'No,' I said.

'The people who've got it, and the people who don't –' she mused. 'I don't think anybody understands what's really going on.'

'Some people must,' I said. I no longer believe that.

I will say further, as an officer of an enormous international conglomerate, that nobody who is doing well in this economy ever even wonders what is really going on.

We are chimpanzees. We are orangutans.

'Does Mr McCone know how much longer the Depression will last?' she said.

'He doesn't know anything about business,' I said.

'How can he still be so rich, if he doesn't know anything about business?' she said.

'His brother runs everything,' I said.

'I wish my father had somebody to run everything for him,' she said.

I knew that things were going so badly for her father that her brother, my roommate, had decided to drop out of school at the end of the semester. He would never go back to school, either. He would take a job as an orderly in a tuberculosis sanitarium, and himself contract tuberculosis. That would keep him out of the armed forces in the Second World War. He would work as a welder in a Boston shipyard, instead. I would lose touch with him. Sarah, whom I see regularly again, told me that she died of a heart attack in Nineteen-hundred and Sixty-five – in a cluttered little welding shop he ran single-handed in the village of Sandwich, on Cape Cod.

His name was Radford Alden Wyatt. He never married. According to Sarah, he had not bathed in years.

'Shirtsleeves to shirtsleeves in three generations,' as the saying goes.

In the case of the Wyatts, actually, it was more like shirt-sleeves to shirtsleeves in ten generations. They had been richer than most of their neighbours for at least that long. Sarah's father was now selling off at rock-bottom prices all the treasures his ancestors had accumulated – English pewter, silver by Paul Revere, paintings of Wyatts as sea captains and merchants and preachers and lawyers, treasures from the China Trade.

'It's so awful to see my father so low all the time,' said Sarah. 'Is your father low, too?'

She was speaking of my fictitious father, the curator of Mr McCone's art collection. I could see him quite clearly then. I can't see him at all now. 'No,' I said.

'You're so lucky,' she said.

'I guess so,' I said. My real father was in fact in easy circumstances. My mother and he had been able to bank almost every penny they made, and the bank they put their money in had not failed.

'If only people wouldn't care so much about money,' she

said. 'I keep telling father that I don't care about it. I don't care about not going to Europe anymore. I hate school. I don't want to go there anymore. I'm not learning anything. I'm glad we sold our boats. I was bored with them, anyway. I don't need any clothes. I have enough clothes to last me a hundred years. He just won't believe me. "I've let you down. I've let everybody down," he says.'

Her father, incidentally, was an inactive partner in the Wyatt Clock Company. This did not limit his liability in the radium-poisoning case, but his principal activity in the good old days had been as the largest yacht broker in Massachusetts. That business was utterly shot in Nineteen-hundred and Thirty-one, of course. And it, too, in the process of dying, left him with what he once described to me as '. . . a pile of worthless accounts-receivable as high as Mount Washington, and a pile of bills as high as Pike's Peak.'

He, too, was a Harvard man – the captain of the undefeated swimming team of Nineteen-hundred and Eleven. After he lost everything, he would never work again. He would be supported by his wife, who would operate a catering service out of their home. They would die penniless.

So I am not the first Harvard man who had to be supported by his wife.

Peace.

Sarah said to me at the Arapahoe that she was sorry to be so depressing, that she knew we were supposed to have fun. She said she would really try to have fun.

It was then that the waiter, shepherded by the owner, delivered the first course, specified by Mr McCone in Cleveland, so far away. It was a half-dozen Cotuit oysters for each of us. I had never eaten an oyster before.

'*Bon appetit!*' said the owner. I was thrilled. I had never had anybody say that to me before. I was so pleased to understand something in French without the help of an interpreter. I had studied French for four years in a Cleveland public high school, by the way, but I never found anyone who spoke the dialect I learned out there. It may have been French as it was spoken by Iroquois mercenaries in the French and Indian War.

Now the Gypsy violinist came to our table. He played with all possible hypocrisy and brilliance, in the frenzied expectation of a tip. I remembered that Mr McCone had told me to tip lavishly. I had not so far tipped anyone. So I got out my billfold surreptitiously while the music was still going on, and I took from it what I thought was a one-dollar bill. A common labourer in those days would have worked ten hours for a dollar. I was about to make a lavish tip. Fifty cents would have put me quite high up in the spendthrift class. I wadded up the bill in my right hand, so as to tip with the quick grace of a magician when the music stopped.

The trouble was this: It wasn't a one-dollar bill. It was a twenty-dollar bill.

I blame Sarah somewhat for this sensational mistake. While I was taking the money from the billfold, she was satirizing sexual love again, pretending that the music was filling her with lust. She undid my necktie, which I would be unable to retie. It had been tied by the mother of a friend with whom I was staying. Sarah kissed the tips of two of her fingers passionately, and then pressed those fingers to my white collar, leaving a smear of lipstick there.

Now the music stopped. I smiled my thanks. Diamond Jim Brady, reincarnated as the demented son of a Cleveland chauffeur, handed the Gypsy a twenty-dollar bill.

The Gypsy was quite suave at first, imagining that he had received a dollar.

Sarah, believing it to be a dollar, too, thought I had tipped much too much. 'Good God,' she said.

But then, perhaps to taunt Sarah with the bill that she would have liked me to take back, but which was now his, all his, the Gypsy unfolded the wad, so that its astronomical denomination became apparent to all of us for the first time. He was as aghast as we were.

And then, being a Gypsy, and hence one microsecond more cunning about money than we were, he darted out of the restaurant and into the night. I wonder to this day if he ever came back for his fiddlecase.

But imagine the effect on Sarah!

She thought I had done it on purpose, that I was stupid enough to imagine that this would be a highly erotic event for her. Never have I been loathed so much.

'You inconceivable twerp,' she said. Most of the speeches in this book are necessarily fuzzy reconstructions – but when I assert that Sarah Wyatt called me an 'inconceivable twerp,' that is exactly what she said.

To give an extra dimension to the scolding she gave me: The word 'twerp' was freshly coined in those days, and had a specific definition – it was a person, if I may be forgiven, who bit the bubbles of his own farts in a bathtub.

'You unbelievable jerk,' she said. A 'jerk' was a person who masturbated too much. She knew that. She knew all those things.

'Who do you think you are?' she said. 'Or, more to the point, who do you think *I* am? I may be a dumb toot,' she said, 'but how dare you think I am such a dumb toot that I would think what you just did was glamorous?'

This was the lowest point in my life, possibly. I felt worse then than I did when I was put in prison – worse, even, than when I was turned loose again. I may have felt worse then, even, than when I set fire to the drapes my wife was about to deliver to a client in Chevy Chase.

'Kindly take me home,' Sarah Wyatt said to me. We left without eating, but not without paying. I could not help myself: I cried all the way home.

I told her brokenly in the taxicab that nothing about the evening had been my own idea, that I was a robot invented and controlled by Alexander Hamilton McCone. I confessed to being half-Polish and half-Lithuanian and nothing but a chauffeur's son who had been ordered to put on the clothing and airs of a gentleman. I said I wasn't going back to Harvard, and that I wasn't sure I wanted to live anymore.

I was so pitiful, and Sarah was so contrite and interested,

that we became the closest of friends, as I say, off and on for seven years.

She would drop out of Pine Manor. She would become a nurse. While in nurse's training she would become so upset by the sickening and dying of the poor that she would join the Communist Party. She would make me join, too.

So I might never have become a communist, if Alexander Hamilton McCone had not insisted that I take a pretty girl to the Arapahoe. And now, forty-five years later, here I was entering the lobby of the Arapahoe again. Why had I chosen to spend my first nights of freedom there? For the irony of it. No American is so old and poor and friendless that he cannot make a collection of some of the most exquisite little ironies in town.

Here I was again, back where a restaurateur had first said to me, *'Bon appetit!'*

A great chunk of the original lobby was now a travel agency. What remained for overnight guests was a narrow corridor with a reception desk at the far end. It wasn't wide enough to accommodate a couch or chair. The mirrored French doors through which Sarah and I had peered into the famous dining room were gone. The archway that had framed them was still there, but it was clogged now with masonry as brutal and unadorned as the wall that kept communists from becoming capitalists in Berlin, Germany. There was a pay telephone bolted to the barrier. Its coinbox had been pried open. Its handset was gone.

And yet the man at the reception desk in the distance appeared to be wearing a tuxedo, and even a *boutonniere*!

As I advanced on him, it became apparent that my eyes had been tricked on purpose. He was in fact wearing a cotton T-shirt on which were printed a *trompe l'oeil* tuxedo jacket and shirt, with a *boutonniere*, bow tie, shirtstuds, handkerchief in the pocket, and all. I had never seen such a shirt before. I did not find it comical. I was confused. It was not a joke somehow.

The night clerk had a beard that was real, and an even

more aggressively genuine bellybutton, exposed above his low-slung trousers. He no longer dresses that way, may I say, now that he is vice-president in charge of purchasing for Hospitality Associates, Ltd, a division of The RAMJAC Corporation. He is thirty years old now. His name is Israel Edel. Like my son, he is married to a black woman. He holds a Doctor's degree in history from Long Island University, *summa cum laude*, and is a Phi Beta Kappa. When we first met, in fact, Israel had to look up at me from the pages of *The American Scholar*, the Phi Beta Kappa learned monthly. Working as night clerk at the Arapahoe was the best job he could find.

'I have a reservation,' I said.

'You have a what?' he said. He was not being impudent. His surprise was genuine. No one ever made a reservation at the Arapahoe anymore. The only way to arrive there was unexpectedly, in response to some misfortune. As Israel said to me only the other day, when we happened to meet in an elevator, 'Making a reservation at the Arapahoe is like making a reservation in a burn ward.' He now oversees the purchasing at the Arapahoe, incidentally, which, along with about four hundred other hostelries all over the world, including one in Katmandu, is a Hospitality Associates, Ltd, hotel.

He found my letter of reservation in an otherwise vacant bank of pigeonholes behind him. 'A week?' he said incredulously.

'Yes,' I said.

My name meant nothing to him. His area of historical expertise was heresies in thirteenth-century Normandy. But he did glean that I was an ex-jailbird – from the slightly queer return address on my envelope: a box number in the middle of nowhere in Georgia, and some numbers after my name.

'The least we can do,' he said, 'is to give you the Bridal Suite.'

There was in fact no Bridal Suite. Every suite had long ago been partitioned into cells. But there was one cell, and only one, which had been freshly painted and papered – as a result, I would later learn, of a particularly gruesome murder of a teen-age male prostitute in there. Israel Edel was not himself being gruesome now. He was being kind. The room really was quite cheerful.

He gave me the key, which I later discovered would open practically every door in the hotel. I thanked him, and I made a small mistake we irony collectors often make : I tried to share an irony with a stranger. It can't be done. I told him that I had been in the Arapahoe before – in Nineteen-hundred and Thirty-one. He was not interested. I do not blame him.

'I was painting the town red with a girl,' I said.

'Um,' he said.

I persisted, though. I told him how we had peeked through the French doors into the famous restaurant. I asked him what was on the other side of that wall now.

His reply, which he himself considered a bland statement of fact, fell so harshly on my ears that he might as well have slapped me hard in the face. He said this :

'Fist-fucking films.'

I had never heard of such things. I gropingly asked what they were.

It woke him up a little, that I should be so surprised and appalled. He was sorry, as he would tell me later, to have brought a sweet little old man such ghastly news about what was going on right next door. He might have been my father, and I his little child. He even said to me, 'Never mind.'

'Tell me,' I said.

So he explained slowly and patiently, and most reluctantly, that there was a motion-picture theatre where the restaurant used to be. It specialized in films of male homosexual acts of love, and that their climaxes commonly consisted of one actor's thrusting his fist up the fundament of another actor.

I was speechless. Never had I dreamed that the First Amendment of the Constitution of the United States of America and the enchanting technology of a motion-picture camera would be combined to form such an atrocity.

'Sorry,' he said.

'I doubt very much if you're to blame,' I said. 'Good night.'

I went in search of my room.

I passed the brutal wall where the French doors had been – on my way to the elevator. I paused there for a moment. My lips mouthed something that I myself did not understand for a moment. And then I realized what my lips must have said, what they had to say.

It was this, of course : *'Bon appetit.'*

11

What would the next day hold for me?

I would, among other things, meet Leland Clewes, the man I had betrayed in Nineteen-hundred and Forty-nine.

But first I would unpack my few possessions, put them away nicely, read a little while, and then get my beauty sleep. I would be tidy. 'At least I don't smoke anymore,' I thought. The room was so clean to begin with.

Two top drawers in the dresser easily accepted all I owned, but I looked into all the other drawers anyway. Thus I discovered that the bottom drawer contained seven incomplete clarinets – without cases, mouthpieces, or bells.

Life is like that sometimes.

What I should have done, especially since I was an ex-convict, was to march back down to the front desk immediately and to say that I was the involuntary custodian of a drawerful of clarinet parts and that perhaps the police should be called. They were of course stolen. As I would learn the next day, they had been taken from a truck hijacked on the Ohio Turnpike – a robbery in which the driver had been killed. Thus, anyone associated with the incomplete instruments, should they turn up, might also be an accesory to murder. There were notices in every music store in the country, it turned out, saying that the police should be called immediately if a customer started talking about buying or selling sizeable quantities of clarinet parts. What I had in my drawer, I would guess, was about a thousandth of the stolen truckload.

But I simply closed the drawer again. I didn't want to go selling sizeable quantities of clarinet parts. What I had in my room. I would say something in the morning.

I was exhausted, I found. It was not yet curtain time in all the theatres down below. But I could hardly keep my eyes open. So I pulled my windowshade down, and I put myself to bed. Off I went, as my son used to say when he was little, 'to seepy-bye,' which is to say, 'to sleep.'

I dreamed that I was in an easy chair at the Harvard Club of New York, only four blocks away. I was not young again. I was not a jailbird, however, but a very successful man – the head of a medium-sized foundation, perhaps, or assistant secretary of the interior, or executive director of the National Endowment for the Humanities, or some such thing. I really would have been some such thing in my sunset years, I honestly believe, if I had not testified against Leland Clewes in Nineteen-hundred and Forty-nine.

It was a compensatory dream. How I loved it. My clothes were in perfect repair. My wife was still alive. I was sipping brandy and coffee after a fine supper with several other members of the Class of Nineteen-hundred and Thirty-five. One detail from real life carried over into the dream: I was proud that I did not smoke anymore.

But then I absent-mindedly accepted a cigarette. It was simply one more civilized satisfaction to go with the good talk and my warm belly and all. 'Yes, yes –' I said, recalling some youthful shenanigans. I chuckled, eyes twinkling. I put the cigarette to my lips. A friend held a match to it. I inhaled the smoke right down to the soles of my feet.

In the dream I collapsed to the floor in convulsions. In real life I fell out of my bed at the Hotel Arapahoe. In the dream my damp, innocent pink lungs shrivelled into two black raisins. Bitter brown tar seeped from my ears and nostrils.

But worst of all was the *shame*.

Even as I was beginning to perceive that I was not in the Harvard Club, and that old classmates were not sitting forward in their leather chairs and looking down at me, and even after I found I could still gulp down air and it would nourish me – even then I was still strangling on shame.

I had just squandered the very last thing I had to be proud of in life: the fact that I did not smoke anymore.

And as I came awake, I examined my hands in the light that billowed up from Times Square and then bounced down on me from my freshly painted ceiling. I spread my fingers and turned my hands this way and that, as a magician might have done. I was showing an imaginary audience that the cigarette I had held only a moment before had now vanished into thin air.

But I, as magician, was as mystified as the audience as to what had become of the cigarette. I got up off the floor, woozy with disgrace, and I looked around everywhere for a cigarette's tell-tale red eye.

But there was no red eye.

I sat down on the edge of my bed, wide awake at last, and drenched in sweat. I took an inventory of my condition. Yes, I had gotten out of prison only that morning. Yes, I had sat in the smoking section of the airplane, but had felt no wish to smoke. Yes, I was now on the top floor of the Hotel Arapahoe.

No, there was no cigarette anywhere.

As for the pursuit of happiness on this planet: I was as happy as any human being in history.

'Thank God,' I thought, 'that cigarette was only a dream.'

12

At six o'clock on the following morning, which was the prison's time for rising, I walked out into a city stunned by its own innocence. Nobody was doing anything bad to anybody anywhere. It was even hard to *imagine* badness. Why would anybody be bad?

It seemed doubtful that any great number of people lived here anymore. The few of us around might have been tourists in Angkor Wat, wondering sweetly about the religion and commerce that had caused people to erect such a city. And what had made all those people, obviously so excited for a while, decide to go away again?

Commerce would have to be reinvented. I offered a news dealer two dimes, bits of silverfoil as weightless as lint, for a copy of *The New York Times*. If he had refused, I would have understood perfectly. But he gave me a *Times*, and then he watched me closely, clearly wondering what I proposed to do with all that paper spattered with ink.

Eight thousand years before, I might have been a Phoenician sailor who had beached his boat on sand in Normandy, and who was now offering a man painted blue two bronze spearheads for the fur hat he wore. He was thinking: 'Who is this crazy man?' And I was thinking: 'Who is this crazy man?'

I had a whimsical idea: I thought of calling the secretary of the treasury, Kermit Winkler, a man who had graduated from Harvard two years after me, and saying this to him: 'I just tried out two of your dimes on Times Square, and they worked like a dream. It looks like another great day for the coinage!'

I encountered a baby-faced policeman. He was as uncertain about his role in the city as I was. He looked at me sheepishly, as though there were every chance that I was the policeman and he was the old bum. Who could be sure of anything that early in the day?

I looked at my reflection in the black marble façade of a shuttered record store. Little did I dream that I would soon be a mogul of the recording industry, with gold and platinum recordings of moronic cacophony on my office wall.

There was something odd about the position of my arms in my reflection. I pondered it. I appeared to be cradling a baby. And then I understood that this was harmonious with my mood, that I was actually carrying what little future I thought I had as though it were a baby. I showed the baby the tops of the Empire State Building and the Chrysler Building, the lions in front of the Public Library. I carried it into an entrance to Grand Central Station, where, if we tired of the city, we could buy a ticket to simply anywhere.

Little did I dream that I would soon be scuttling through the catacombs beneath the station, and that I would learn the secret purpose of The RAMJAC Corporation down there.

The baby and I headed back west again. If we had kept going east, we would have soon delivered ourselves to Tudor City, where my son lived. We did not want to see him. Yes, and we paused before the window of a store that offered wicker picnic hampers – fitted out with Thermos bottles and tin boxes for sandwiches and so on. There was also a bicycle. I assumed that I could still ride a bicycle. I told the baby in my mind that we might buy a hamper and a bicycle and ride out on an abandoned dock some nice day and eat chicken sandwiches and wash them down with lemonade, while sea-gulls soared and keened overhead. I was beginning to feel hungry. Back in prison I would have been full of coffee and oatmeal by then.

I passed the Century Association on West Forty-third Street, a gentleman's club where, shortly after the Second World War, I had once been the luncheon guest of Peter Gibney, the composer, a Harvard classmate of mine. I was never invited back. I would have given anything now to be a bartender in there, but Gibney was still alive and probably still a member. We had had a falling out, you might say, after I testified against Leland Clewes. Gibney sent me a picture postcard, so that my wife and the postman could read the message, too.

'Dear shithead,' it said, 'why don't you crawl back under a damp rock somewhere?' The picture was of the Mona Lisa, with that strange smile of hers.

Down the block was the Coffee Shop of the Hotel Royalton, and I made for that. The Royalton, incidentally, like the Arapahoe, was a Hospitality Associates, Ltd, hotel; which is to say, a RAMJAC hotel. By the time I reached the coffee-shop door, however, my self-confidence had collapsed. Panic had taken its place. I believed that I was the ugliest, dirtiest little old bum in Manhattan. If I went into the coffee shop, everybody would be nauseated. They would throw me out and tell me to go to the Bowery, where I belonged.

But I somehow found the courage to go in anyway – and imagine my surprise! It was as though I had died and gone to heaven! A waitress said to me, 'Honeybunch, you sit right down, and I'll bring you your coffee right away.' I hadn't said anything to her.

So I did sit down, and everywhere I looked I saw customers of every description being received with love. To the waitresses everybody was 'honeybunch' and 'darling' and 'dear.' It was like an emergency ward after a great catastrophe. It did not matter what race or class the victims belonged to. They were all given the same miracle drug, which was coffee. The catastrophe in this case, of course, was that the sun had come up again.

I thought to myself, 'My goodness – these waitresses and cooks are as unjudgmental as the birds and lizards on the Galapagos Islands, off Ecuador.' I was able to make the comparison because I had read about these peaceful islands in prison, in a *National Geographic* loaned to me by the former lieutenant governor of Wyoming. The creatures there had had

137

no enemies, natural or unnatural, for thousands of years. The idea of anybody's wanting to hurt them was inconceivable to them.

So a person coming ashore there could walk right up to an animal and unscrew its head, if he wanted to. The animal would have no plan for such an occasion. And all the other animals would simply stand around and watch, unable to draw any lessons for themselves from what was going on. A person could unscrew the head of every animal on an island, if that was his idea of business or fun.

I had the feeling that if Frankenstein's monster crashed into the coffee shop through a brick wall, all anybody would say to him was, 'You sit down here, Lambchop, and I'll bring you your coffee right away.'

The profit motive was not operating. The transactions were on the order of sixty-eight cents, a dollar ten, two dollars and sixty-three ... I would find out later that the man who ran the cash register was the owner, but he would not stay at his post to rake the money in. He wanted to cook and wait on people, too, so that the waitresses and cooks kept having to say to him, 'That's my customer, Frank. Get back to the cash register,' or 'I'm the cook here, Frank. What's this mess you've started here? Get back to the cash register,' and so on.

His full name was Frank Ubriaco. He is now executive vice-president of the McDonald's Hamburgers Division of The RAMJAC Corporation.

I could not help noticing that he had a withered right hand. It looked as though it had been mummified, although he could still use his fingers some. I asked my waitress about it. She said he had literally French-fried that hand about a year ago. He accidentally dropped his wristwatch into a vat of boiling cooking oil. Before he realized what he was doing, he had plunged his hand into the oil, trying to rescue the watch, which was a very expensive Bulova Accutron.

So out into the city I went again, feeling much improved.

I sat down to read my newspaper in Bryant Park, behind the Public Library at Forty-second Street. My belly was full and as warm as a stove. It was no novelty for me to read *The New York Times*. About half the inmates back at the prison had mail subscriptions to the *Times*, and to *The Wall Street Journal*, too, and *Time* and *Newsweek* and *Sports Illustrated*, too, and on and on. And *People*. I subscribed to nothing, since the prison trash baskets were forever stuffed with periodicals of every kind.

There was a sign over every trash basket in prison, incidentally, which said, 'Please!' Underneath that word was an arrow that pointed straight down.

In leafing through the *Times*, I saw that my son, Walter Stankiewicz, *né* Starbuck, was reviewing the autobiography of a Swedish motion-picture star. Walter seemed to like it a lot. I gathered that she had had her ups and downs.

What I particularly wanted to read, though, was the *Times*'s account of its having been taken over by The RAMJAC Corporation. The event might as well have been an epidemic of cholera in Bangladesh. It was given three inches of space on the bottom corner of an inside page. The chairman of the board of RAMJAC, Arpad Leen, said in the story that RAMJAC contemplated no changes in personnel or editorial policy. He pointed out that all publications taken over by RAMJAC in the past, including those of Time, Incorporated, had been allowed to go on as they wished, without any interference from RAMJAC.

'Nothing has changed but the ownership,' he said. And I must say, as a former RAMJAC executive myself, that we didn't change companies we take over very much. If one of them started to die, of course – then our curiosity was aroused.

The story said that the publisher of the *Times* had received a handwritten note from Mrs Jack Graham '... welcoming him to the RAMJAC family.' It said she hoped he would stay on in his present capacity. Beneath the signature were the prints of all her fingers and thumbs. There could be no question about the letter's being genuine.

I looked about myself in Bryant Park. Lilies of the valley had raised their little bells above the winter-killed ivy and glassine envelopes that bordered the walks. My wife Ruth and I had had lilies of the valley and ivy growing under the flowering crab apple tree in the front yard of our little brick bungalow in Chevy Chase, Maryland.

I spoke to the lilies of the valley. 'Good morning,' I said.

Yes, and I must have gone into a defensive trance again Three hours passed without my budging from the bench.

I was aroused at last by a portable radio that was turned up loud. The young man carrying it sat down on a bench facing mine. He appeared to be Hispanic. I did not learn his name. If he had done me some kindness, he might now be an executive in The RAMJAC Corporation. The radio was tuned to the news. The newscaster said that the air quality that day was unacceptable.

Imagine that unacceptable air.

The young man did not appear to be listening to his own radio. He may not even have understood English. The newscaster spoke with a barking sort of hilarity, as though life were a comical steeplechase, with unconventional steeds and hazards and vehicles involved. He made me feel that even I was a contestant – in a bathtub drawn by three aardvarks, perhaps. I had as good a chance as anybody to win.

He told about another man in the steeplechase, who had been sentenced to die in an electric chair in Texas. The doomed man had instructed his lawyers to fight anybody, including the governor and the President of the United States, who might want to grant him a stay of execution. The thing he wanted more than anything in life, evidently, was death in the electric chair.

Two joggers came down the path between me and the radio. They were a man and a woman in identical orange-and-gold sweatsuits and matching shoes. I already knew about the jogging craze. We had had many joggers in prison. I found them smug.

About the young man and his radio. I decided that he had bought the thing as a prosthetic device, as an artificial enthusiasm for the planet. He paid as little attention to it as I paid to my false front tooth. I have since seen several young men like that in groups – with their radios tuned to different stations, with their radios engaged in a spirited conversation. The young men themselves, perhaps having been told nothing but 'shut up' all their lives, had nothing to say.

But now the young man's radio said something so horrifying that I got off my bench, left the park, and joined the throng of Free Enterprisers charging along Forty-second Street toward Fifth Avenue.

The story was this: An imbecilic young female drug addict from my home state of Ohio, about nineteen years old, had had a baby whose father was unknown. Social workers put her and the baby into a hotel not unlike the Arapahoe. She bought a full-grown German shepherd police dog for protection, but she forgot to feed it. Then she went out one night on some unspecified errand, and she left the dog to guard the baby. When she got back, she found that the dog had killed the baby and eaten part of it.

What a time to be alive.

So there I was marching as purposefully as anybody toward Fifth Avenue. According to plan, I began to study the faces coming at me, looking for a familiar one that might be of some use to me. I was prepared to be patient. It would be like panning for gold, I thought, like looking for a glint of the precious in a dish of sand.

When I had got no farther than the kerb at Fifth Avenue, though, my warning systems went off earsplittingly: *'Beep, beep, beep! Honk, honk, honk! Rowrr, rowrr, rowrr!'*

Positive identification had been made

Coming right at me was the husk of the man who had stolen Sarah Wyatt from me, the man I had ruined back in Nineteen-hundred and Forty-nine. He had not seen *me* yet. He was Leland Clewes!

He had lost all his hair, and his feet were capsizing in broken shoes, and the cuffs of his trousers were frayed, and his right arm appeared to have died. Dangling at the end of it was a battered sample case. Clewes had become an unsuccessful salesman, as I would find out later, of advertising match-books and calendars.

He is nowadays, incidentally, a vice-president in the Diamond Match Division of The RAMJAC Corporation.

In spite of all that had happened to him, though, his face, as he came toward me, was illuminated as always with an adolescent, goofy good will. He had worn that expression even in a photograph of his entering prison in Georgia, with the warden looking up at him as the secretary of state used to do. When Clewes was young, older men were always looking up at him as though to say, 'That's my boy.'

Now he saw me!

The eye-contact nearly electrocuted me. I might as well have stuck my nose into a lamp socket!

I went right past him and in the opposite direction. I had nothing to say to him, and no wish to stand and listen to all the terrible things he was entitled to say to me.

When I gained the kerb, though, and the lights changed, and we were separated by moving cars, I dared to look back at him.

Clewes was facing me. Plainly, he had not yet come up with a name for me. He pointed at me with his free hand, indicating that he knew I had figured in his life in some way. And then he made that finger twitch like a metronome, ticking off possible names for me. This was fun for him. His feet were apart, his knees were bent, and his expression said that he remembered this much, anyway: We had been involved years ago in some sort of wildness, in a boyish prank of some kind.

I was hypnotized.

As luck would have it, there were religious fanatics behind him, barefoot and chanting and dancing in saffron robes. Thus did he appear to be a leading man in a musical comedy.

Nor was I without my own supporting cast. Willy-nilly, I had placed myself between a man wearing sandwich boards and a top hat, and a little old woman who had no home, who carried all her possessions in shopping bags. She wore enormous purple-and-black basketball shoes. They were so out of scale with the rest of her that she looked like a kangaroo.

My companions were both speaking to passers-by. The man in the sandwich boards was saying such things as 'Put women back in the kitchen,' and 'God never meant women to be the equals of men,' and so on. The shopping-bag lady seemed to be scolding strangers for their obesity, calling them, as I understood her, 'stuck-up fats,' and 'rich fats,' and 'snooty fats,' and 'fats' of a hundred other varieties.

The thing was: I had been away from Cambridge, Massachusetts, so long that I could no longer detect that she was calling people 'farts' in the accent of the Cambridge working class.

And in the toe of one of her capacious basketball shoes, among other things, were hypocritical love letters from me. Small world!

Good God! What a reaper and binder life can be sometimes!

When Leland Clewes, on the other side of Fifth Avenue, realized who I was, he formed his mouth into a perfect 'O.' I could not hear his saying 'Oh,' but I could see his saying 'Oh.' He was making fun of our encounter after all these years, overacting his surprise and dismay like an actor in a silent movie.

Plainly, he was going to come back across the street as soon as the lights changed. Meanwhile, all those fake Hindu imbeciles in saffron robes continued to chant and dance behind him.

There was still time for me to flee. What made me hold my ground, I think, was this: the need to prove myself a gentleman. During the bad old days, when I had testified against him, people who wrote about us, speculating as to who was telling the truth and who was not, concluded for the most part that he was a real gentleman, descended from a long line of gentlemen, and that I was a person of Slavic background only pretending to be a gentleman. Honour and bravery and truthfulness, then, would mean everything to him and very little to me.

Other contrasts were pointed out, certainly. With every new edition of the papers and news magazines, seemingly, I became shorter and he became taller. My poor wife became more gross and foreign, and his wife became more of an American golden girl. His friends became more numerous and respectable, and mine couldn't even be found under damp rocks anymore. But what troubled me most in my very bones was the idea that he was honourable and I was not. Thus, twenty-six years later, did this little Slavic jailbird hold his ground.

Across the avenue he came, the former Anglo-Saxon champion, a happy, ramshackle scarecrow now.

I was bewildered by his happiness. 'What,' I asked myself, 'can this wreck have to be so happy about?'

So there we were reunited, with the shopping-bag lady looking on and listening. He put down his sample case and he extended his right hand. He made a joke, echoing the meeting of Henry Morton Stanley and David Livingstone in Darkest Africa: 'Walter F. Starbuck, I presume.'

And we might as well have been in Darkest Africa, for all anybody knew or cared about us anymore. Most people, if they remembered us at all, believed us dead, I suppose. And we had never been as significant in American history as we had sometimes thought we were. We were, if I may be forgiven, farts in a windstorm – or, as the shopping-bag lady would have called us, 'fats in a windstorm.'

Did I harbour any bitterness against him for having stolen my girl so long ago? No. Sarah and I had loved each other, but we would never have been happy as man and wife. We could never have gotten a sex life going. I had never persuaded her to take sex seriously. Leland Clewes had succeeded where I had failed – much to her grateful amazement, I am sure.

What tender memories did I have of Sarah? Much talk about human suffering and what could be done about it – and then infantile silliness for relief. We collected jokes for each other, to use when it was time for relief. We became addicted to talking to each other on the telephone for hours. Those talks were the most agreeable narcotic I have ever known. We became disembodied – like free-floating souls on the planet Vicuna. If there was a long silence, one or the other of us would end it with the start of a joke.

'What is the difference between an enzyme and a hormone?' she might ask me.

'I don't know,' I would say.

'You can't hear an enzyme,' she would say, and the silly jokes would go on and on – even though she had probably seen something horrible at the hospital that day.

13

I was about to say to him gravely, watchfully but sincerely, 'How are you, Leland? It is good to see you again.'

But I never got to say it. The shopping-bag lady, whose voice was loud and piercing, cried out, 'Oh, my God! Walter F. Starbuck! Is that really you?' I do not intend to reproduce her accent on the printed page.

I thought she was crazy. I thought that she would have parroted any name Clewes chose to hang on me. If he had called me 'Bumptious Q. Bangwhistle,' I thought, she would have cried, 'Oh, my God! Bumptious Q. Bangwhistle! Is that really you?'

Now she began to lean her shopping bags against my legs, as though I were a convenient fireplug. There were six of them, which I would later study at leisure. They were from the most expensive stores in town – Henri Bendel, Tiffany's, Sloane's, Bergdorf Goodman, Bloomingdale's, Abercrombie and Fitch. All but Abercrombie and Fitch, incidentally, which would soon go bankrupt, were subsidiaries of The RAMJAC Corporation. Her bags continued mostly rags, pickings from garbage cans. Her most valuable possessions were in her basketball shoes.

I tried to ignore her. Even as she entrapped me with her bags, I kept my gaze on the face of Leland Clewes. 'You're looking well,' I said.

'I'm feeling well,' he said. 'And so is Sarah, you'll be happy to know.'

'I'm glad to hear it,' I said. 'She's a very good girl.' Sarah was no girl anymore, of course.

Clewes told me now that she was still doing a little nursing, as a part-time thing.

'I'm glad,' I said.

To my horror, I felt as though a sick bat had dropped from the eaves of a building and landed on my wrist. The shopping-bag lady had taken hold of me with her filthy little hand.

'This is your wife?' he said.

'My what?' I said. He thought I had sunk so low that this awful woman and I were a pair! 'I never saw her before in my life!' I said.

'Oh, Walter, Walter, Walter,' she keened, 'how can you say such a thing?'

I pried her hand off me; but the instant I returned my attention to Clewes, she snapped it onto my wrist again.

'Pretend she isn't here,' I said. 'This is crazy. She has nothing to do with me. I will not let her spoil this moment, which means a great deal to me.'

'Oh, Walter, Walter, Walter,' she said, 'what has become of you? You're not the Walter F. Starbuck I knew.'

'That's right,' I said, 'because you never knew any Walter F. Starbuck, but this man did.' And I said to Clewes, 'I suppose you know that I myself have spent time in prison now.'

'Yes,' he said. 'Sarah and I were very sorry.'

'I was let out only yesterday morning,' I said.

'You have some trying days ahead,' he said. 'Is there somebody to look after you?'

'I'll look after you, Walter,' said the shopping-bag lady. She leaned closer to me to say that so fervently, and I was nearly suffocated by her body odour and her awful breath. Her breath was laden not only with the smell of bad teeth but, as I would later realize, with finely-divided droplets of peanut oil. She had been eating nothing but peanut butter for years.

'You can't take care of anybody!' I said to her.

'Oh – you'd be surprised what all I could do for you,' she said.

'Leland,' I said, 'all I want to say to you is that I know what jail is now, and, God damn it, the thing I'm sorriest about in my whole life is that I had anything to do with sending you to jail.'

147

'Well,' he said, 'Sarah and I have often talked about what we would like to say most to you.'

'I'm sure,' I said.

'And it's this,' he said, ' "Thank you very much, Walter. My going to prison was the best thing that ever happened to Sarah and me." I'm not joking. Word of honour: It's true.'

I was amazed. 'How can that be?' I said.

'Because life is supposed to be a test,' he said. 'If my life had kept going the way it was going, I would have arrived in heaven never having faced any problem that wasn't as easy as pie to solve. Saint Peter would have had to say to me, "You never lived, my boy. Who can say what you are?" '

'I see,' I said.

'Sarah and I not only have love,' he said, 'but we have love that has stood up to the hardest tests.'

'It sounds very beautiful,' I said.

'We would be proud to have you see it,' he said. 'Could you come to supper sometime?'

'Yes – I suppose,' I said.

'Where are you staying?' he said.

'The Hotel Arapahoe,' I said.

'I thought they'd torn that down years ago,' he said.

'No,' I said.

'You'll hear from us,' he said.

'I look forward to it,' I said.

'As you'll see,' he said, 'we have nothing in the way of material wealth; but we need nothing in the way of material wealth.'

'That's intelligent,' I said.

'I'll say this though,' he said, 'the food is good. As you may remember, Sarah is a wonderful cook.'

'I remember,' I said.

And now the shopping-bag lady offered the first proof that she really did know a lot about me. 'You're talking about that Sarah Wyatt, aren't you?' she said.

There was a silence among us, although the uproar of the metropolis went on and on. Neither Clewes nor I had mentioned Sarah's maiden name.

I finally managed to ask her, woozy with shapeless misgivings, 'How do you know that name?'

She became foxy and coquettish. 'You think I don't know you were two-timing me with her the whole time?' she said.

Given that much information, I no longer needed to guess who she was. I had slept with her during my senior year at Harvard, while still squiring the virginal Sarah Wyatt to parties and concerts and athletic events.

She was one of the four women I had ever loved. She was the first woman with whom I had had anything like a mature sexual experience.

She was the remains of Mary Kathleen O'Looney!

14

'I was his circulation manager,' said Mary Kathleen to Leland
Clewes very loudly. 'Wasn't I a good circulation manager,
Walter?'

'Yes – you certainly were,' I said. That was how we met:
She presented herself at the tiny office of *The Bay State Progressive* in Cambridge at the start of my senior year, saying
that she would do absolutely anything I told her to do, as long
as it would improve the condition of the working class. I
made her circulation manager, put her in charge of handing
out the paper at factory gates and along breadlines and so on.
She had been a scrawny little thing back then, but tough and
cheerful and highly visible because of her bright red hair. She
was such a hater of capitalism, because her mother was one
of the women who died of radium poisoning after working for
the Wyatt Clock Company. Her father had gone blind after
drinking wood alcohol while a night watchman in a shoe-
polish factory.

Now what was left of Mary Kathleen bowed her head,
responded modestly to my having agreed that she had been a
good circulation manager, and presented her pate to Leland
Clewes and me. She had a bald spot about the size of a silver
dollar. The tonsure that fringed it was sparse and white.

Leland Clewes would tell me later that he almost fainted.
He had never seen a woman's bald spot before.

It was too much for him. He closed his blue eyes and he
turned away. When he manfully faced us again, he avoided
looking directly at Mary Kathleen – just as the mythological
Perseus had avoided looking at the Gorgon's head.

'We must get together soon,' he said.

'Yes,' I said.

'You'll be hearing from me soon,' he said.

'I hope so,' I said.

'Must rush,' he said.

'I understand,' I said.

'Take care,' he said.

'I will,' I said.

He was gone.

Mary Kathleen's shopping bags were still banked around my legs. I was as immobilized and eye-catching as Saint Joan of Arc at the stake. Mary Kathleen still grasped my wrist, and she would not lower her voice.

'Now that I've found you, Walter,' she cried, 'I'll never let you go again!'

Nowhere in the world was this sort of theatre being done anymore. For what it may be worth to modern impresarios: I can testify from personal experience that great crowds can still be gathered by melodrama, provided that the female in the piece speaks loudly and clearly.

'You used to tell me all the time how much you loved me, Walter,' she cried. 'But then you went away, and I never heard from you again. Were you just lying to me?'

I may have made some responsive sound. 'Bluh,' perhaps, or 'fluh.'

'Look at me in the eye, Walter,' she said.

Sociologically, of course, this melodrama was as gripping as *Uncle Tom's Cabin* before the Civil War. Mary Kathleen O'Looney wasn't the only shopping-bag lady in the United States of America. There were tens of thousands of them in major cities throughout the country. Ragged regiments of them had been produced accidentally, and to no imaginable purpose, by the great engine of the economy. Another part of the machine was spitting out unrepentant murderers ten years old, and dope fiends and child batterers and many other bad things. People claimed to be investigating. Unspecified repairs were to be made at some future time.

Good-hearted people were meanwhile as sick about all these tragic by-products of the economy as they would have been about human slavery a little more than a hundred years before. Mary Kathleen and I were a miracle that our audience must have prayed for again and again: the rescue of at least one shopping-bag lady by a man who knew her well.

Some people were crying. I myself was about to cry.

'Hug her,' said a woman in the crowd.

I did so.

I found myself embracing a bundle of dry twigs that was wrapped in rags. That was when I myself began to cry. I was crying for the first time since I had found my wife dead in bed one morning – in my little brick bungalow in Chevy Chase, Maryland.

15

My nose, thank God, had conked out by then. Noses are merciful that way. They will report that something smells awful. If the owner of a nose stays around anyway, the nose concludes that the smell isn't so bad after all. It shuts itself off, deferring to superior wisdom. Thus is it possible to eat Limburger cheese – or to hug the stinking wreckage of an old sweetheart at the corner of Fifth Avenue and Forty-second Street.

It felt for a moment as though Mary Kathleen had died in my arms. To be perfectly frank, that would have been all right with me. Where, after all, could I take her from there? What could be better than her receiving a hug from a man who had known her when she was young and beautiful, and then going to heaven right away?

It would have been wonderful. Then again, I would never have become executive vice-president of the Down Home Records Division of The RAMJAC Corporation. I might at this very moment be sleeping off a wine binge in the Bowery, while a juvenile monster soaked me in gasoline and touched me off with his Cricket lighter.

Mary Kathleen now spoke very softly. 'God must have sent you,' she said.

'There, there,' I said. I went on hugging her.

'There's nobody I can trust anymore,' she said.

'Now, now,' I said.

'Everybody's after me,' she said. 'They want to cut off my hands.'

'There, there,' I said.

'I thought you were dead,' she said.

'No, no,' I said.

'I thought everybody was dead but me,' she said.

'There, there,' I said.

'I still believe in the revolution, Walter,' she said.

'I'm glad,' I said.

'Everybody else lost heart,' she said. 'I never lost heart.'

'Good for you,' I said.

'I've been working for the revolution every day,' she said.

'I'm sure,' I said.

'You'd be surprised,' she said.

'Get her a hot bath,' said somebody in the crowd.

'Get some food in her,' said somebody else.

'The revolution is coming, Walter – sooner than you know,' said Mary Kathleen.

'I have a hotel room where you can rest awhile,' I said. 'I have a little money. Not much, but some.'

'Money,' she said, and she laughed. Her scornful laughter about money had not changed. It was exactly as it had been forty years before.

'Shall we go?' I said. 'My room isn't far from here.'

'I know a better place,' she said.

'Get her some One-a-Day vitamins,' said somebody in the crowd.

'Follow me, Walter,' said Mary Kathleen. She was growing strong again. It was Mary Kathleen who now separated herself from me, and not the other way around. She became raucous again. I picked up three of her bags, and she picked up the other three. Our ultimate destination, it would turn out, was the very top of the Chrysler Building, the quiet showroom of The American Harp Company up there. But first we had to get the crowd to part for us, and she began to call people in our way 'capitalist fats' and 'bloated plutocrats' and 'bloodsuckers' and all that again.

Her means of locomotion in her gargantuan basketball shoes was this: She barely lifted the shoes from the ground, shoving one forward and then the other, like cross-country skis, while her upper body and shopping bags swivelled wildly from side to side. But that oscillating old woman could go like

154

the wind! I panted to keep up with her, once we got clear of the crowd. We were surely the cynosure of all eyes. Nobody had ever seen a shopping-bag lady with an assistant before.

When we got to Grand Central Station, Mary Kathleen said that we had to make sure we weren't being followed. She led me up and down escalators, ramps, and stairways, looking over her shoulders for pursuers all the time. We scampered through the Oyster Bar three times. She brought us at last to an iron door at the end of a dimly lit corridor. We surely were all alone. Our hearts were beating hard.

When we had recovered our breaths, she said to me, 'I am going to show you something you mustn't tell anybody about.'

'I promise,' I said.

'This is our secret,' she said.

'Yes,' I said.

I had assumed that we were as deep in the station as anyone could go. How wrong I was! Mary Kathleen opened the iron door on an iron staircase going down, down, down. There was a secret world as vast as Carlsbad Caverns below. It was used for nothing anymore. It might have been a sanctuary for dinosaurs. It had in fact been a repair shop for another family of extinct monsters – locomotives driven by steam.

Down the steps we went.

My God – what majestic machinery there must have been down there at one time! What admirable craftsmen must have worked there! In conformance with fire laws, I suppose, there were lightbulbs burning here and there. And there were little dishes of rat poison set around. But there were no other signs that anyone had been down there for years.

'This is my home, Walter,' she said.

'Your what?' I said.

'You wouldn't want me sleeping outside, would you?' she said.

'No,' I said.

'Be glad, then,' she said, 'that I have such a nice and private home.'

'I am,' I said.

'You not only talked to me – you hugged me,' she said. 'That's how I knew I could trust you.'

'Um,' I said.

'You're not after my hands,' she said.

'No,' I said.

'You know there are millions of poor souls out on the street, looking for a toilet somebody will let them use?' she said.

'I suppose that's true,' I said.

'Look at this,' she said. She led me into a chamber that contained row on row of toilets.

'It's good to know they're here,' I said.

'You won't tell anybody?' she said.

'No,' I said.

'I'm putting my life in your hands, telling you my secrets like this,' she said.

'I'm honoured,' I said.

And then out of the catacombs we climbed. She led me through a tunnel under Lexington Avenue, and up a staircase into the lobby of the Chrysler Building. She skied across the floor to a waiting elevator, with me trotting behind. A guard shouted at us, but we got into the elevator before he could stop us. The doors shut in his angry face as Mary Kathleen punched the button for the topmost floor.

We had the car all to ourselves, and upward we flew. Within a trice the doors slithered open on a place of unearthly beauty and peace within the building's stainless-steel crown. I had often wondered what was up there. Now I knew. The crown came to a point seventy feet above us. Between us and the point, as I looked upward in awe, there was nothing but a lattice of girders and air, air, air.

'What a glorious waste of space!' I thought. But then I saw that there were tenants after all. Myriads of bright yellow little birds were perched on the girders, or flitting through the prisms of light admitted by the bizarre windows, by the great triangles of glass that pierced the crown.

The vast floor at whose edge we stood was carpeted in grassy green. There was a fountain splashing at its centre. There were garden benches and statues everywhere, and here and there a harp.

As I have already said, this was the showroom of The American Harp Company, which had recently become a subsidiary of The RAMJAC Corporation. The company had occupied this space since the building opened in Nineteen-hundred and Thirty-one. All the birds I saw, which were prothonotary warblers, were descended from a single pair released back then.

There was a Victorian gazebo near the elevator, which contained the desks of the salesman and his secretary. A woman was sobbing in there. What a morning it was for tears! What a book this is for tears!

The oldest man I had ever seen came tottering out of the gazebo. He wore a swallowtail coat and striped trousers and spats. He was the sole salesman, and had been since Nineteen-hundred and Thirty-one. He was the man who had released from the hot cage of his hands and into this enchanted space the first two prothonotary warblers. He was ninety-two years old! He looked like John D. Rockefeller at the end of his life, or like a mummy. The only moisture left in him, seemingly, was faint dew on the surface of his eyes. He was not entirely defenceless, however. He was president of a pistol club that shot at targets shaped like men on weekends, and he had a loaded Luger the size of a Doberman pinscher in his desk. He had been looking forward to a robbery for quite some time.

'Oh – it's you,' he said to Mary Kathleen, and she said that, yes, it was.

She was accustomed to coming here almost every day and sitting for several hours. The understanding was that she was to get out of sight with her shopping bags, in case a customer came in. There was a further understanding, which Mary Kathleen had now violated.

'I thought I told you,' he said to her, 'that you were never to bring anybody else with you, or even to tell anybody else how nice it was up here.'

Since I was carrying three shopping bags, he concluded that I was another derelict, a shopping-bag man.

'He isn't a bum,' said Mary Kathleen. 'He's a Harvard man.'

He did not believe this for a minute. 'I see,' he said, and he looked me up and down. He himself had never even graduated from grammar school, incidentally. There had been no laws against child labour when he was a boy, and he had gone to work in the Chicago factory of The American Harp Company at the age of ten. 'I've heard that you can always tell a Harvard man,' he said, 'but you can't tell him much.'

'I never thought there was anything special about Harvard men,' I said.

'That makes two of us,' he said. He was being most unpleasant, and clearly wanted me out of there. 'This is not the Salvation Army,' he said. This was a man born during the presidency of Grover Cleveland. Imagine that! He said to Mary Kathleen, 'Really – I'm most disappointed in you, bringing somebody else along. Should we expect three tomorrow, and twenty the day after that? Christianity does have its limits, you know.'

I now made a blunder that would land me back in *el calabozo* before noon on what was to have been my first full day of freedom. 'As a matter of fact,' I said, 'I'm here on business.'

'You wish to buy a harp?' he said. 'They're seven thousand dollars and up, you know. How about a kazoo instead?'

'I was hoping you could advise me,' I said, 'as to where I could buy clarinet parts – not whole clarinets, but just clarinet parts.' I was not serious about this. I was extrapolating a business fantasy from the contents of my bottom drawer at the Arapahoe.

The old man was secretly electrified. Thumbtacked to the bulletin board in the gazebo was a circular that advised him to call the police in case anyone expressed interest in buying or selling clarinet parts. As he would tell me later, he had stuck it up there months before – 'like a lottery ticket bought in a moment of folly.' He had never expected to win. His name was Delmar Peale.

Delmar was nice enough later on to make me a present of the circular, which I hung on my office wall at RAMJAC. I became his superior in the RAMJAC family, since American Harp was a subsidiary of my division.

I was certainly no superior of his the first time we met, though. He played cat-and-mouse with me. 'Many clarinet parts, or a few?' he asked cunningly.

'Quite a few, actually,' I said. 'I realize that you yourself don't handle clarinets –'

'You've come to the right place all the same,' he hastened to assure me. 'I know everyone in the business. If you and Madam X would like to make yourselves comfortable, I would be glad to make some telephone calls.'

'You're too kind,' I said.

'Not at all,' he said.

'Madam X,' incidentally, was the only name he had for Mary Kathleen. That was what she had told him her name was. She had simply barged in one day, trying to escape from people she thought were after her. He had worried a lot about shopping-bag ladies, and he was a practising Christian, so he had let her stay.

Meanwhile, the sobbing in the gazebo was abating some.

Delmar conducted us to a bench far from the gazebo, so we could not hear him call the police. He had us sit down. 'Comfy?' he said.

'Yes, thank you,' I said.

He rubbed his hands. 'How about some coffee?' he said.

'It makes me too nervous,' said Mary Kathleen.

'With sugar and cream, if it's not too much trouble,' I said.

'No trouble at all,' he said.

'What's the trouble with Doris?' said Mary Kathleen. That was the name of the secretary who was crying in the gazebo.

Her full name was Doris Kramm. She herself was eighty-seven years old.

At my suggestion, *People* magazine recently did a story on Delmar and Doris as being almost certainly the oldest boss-and-secretary team in the world, and perhaps in all history. It was a cute story. One picture showed Delmar with his Luger, and quoted him to the effect that anybody who tried to rob The American Harp Company '... would be one unhappy robber pretty quick.'

He told Mary Kathleen now that Doris wept because she had had two hard blows in rapid succession. She had been notified on the previous afternoon that she was going to have to retire immediately, now that RAMJAC had taken over. The retirement age for all RAMJAC employees everywhere, except for supervisory personnel, was sixty-five. And then that morning, while she was cleaning out her desk, she got a telegram saying that her great-grandniece had been killed in a head-on collision after a high-school senior prom in Sarasota, Florida. Doris had no descendents of her own, he explained, so her collateral relatives meant a lot to her.

Delmar and Doris, incidentally, did almost no business up there, and continue to do almost no business up there. I was proud, when I became a RAMJAC executive, that American Harp Company harps were the finest harps in the world. You would have thought that the best harps would come from Italy or Japan or West Germany by now, with American craftsmanship having become virtually extinct. But no – musicians even in those countries and even in the Soviet Union agreed: Only an American Harp Company harp can cut the mustard. But the harp business is not and can never be a volume business, except in heaven, perhaps. So the profit picture, the bottom line, was ridiculous. It is so ridiculous that I recently undertook an investigation of why RAMJAC had ever acquired American Harp. I learned that it was in order to capture the incredible lease on the top of the Chrysler Building. The lease ran until the year Two-thousand and Thirty-one, at a rent of two hundred dollars a month! Arpad Leen wanted to turn the place into a restaurant.

That the company also owned a factory in Chicago with sixty-five employees was a mere detail. If it could not be made to show a substantial profit within a year or two, RAMJAC would close it down.

Peace.

16

Mary Kathleen O'Looney was, of course, the legendary Mrs Jack Graham, the majority stockholder in The RAMJAC Corporation. She had her inkpad and pens and writing paper in her basketball shoes. Those shoes were her bank vaults. Nobody could take them off of her without waking her up.

She would claim later that she had told me who she really was on the elevator.

I could only reply, 'If I had heard you say that, Mary Kathleen, I surely would have remembered it.'

If I had known who she really was, all her talk about people who wanted to cut off her hands would have made a lot more sense. Whoever got her hands could pickle them and throw away the rest of her, and control The RAMJAC Corporation with just her fingertips. No wonder she was on the run. No wonder she dared not reveal her true identity anywhere.

No wonder she dared not trust anybody. On this particular planet, where money mattered more than anything, the nicest person imaginable might suddenly get the idea of wringing her neck so that their loved ones might live in comfort. It would be the work of the moment – and easily forgotten as the years went by. Time flies.

She was so tiny and weak. Killing her and cutting off her hands would have been little more horrifying than what went on ten thousand times a day at a mechanized chicken farm. RAMJAC owns Colonel Sanders Kentucky Fried Chicken, of course. I have seen that operation as it looks backstage.

About my not having heard her say she was Mrs Jack Graham on the elevator:

I do remember that I had trouble with my ears toward the top of the elevator ride, because of the sudden change in altitude. We shot up about a thousand feet, with no stops on the way. Also: Temporarily deaf or not, I had my conversational automatic pilot on. I was not thinking about what she was saying, or what I was saying, either. I thought that we were both so far outside the mainstream of human affairs that all we could do was comfort each other with animal sounds. I remember her saying at one point that she owned the Waldorf-Astoria Hotel, and I thought I had not heard her right.

'I'm glad,' I said.

So, as I sat beside her on the bench in the harp showroom, she thought I had a piece of key information about her, which I did not have. And Delmar Peale had meanwhile called the police and had also sent Doris Kramm out, supposedly for coffee, but really to find a policeman out on the street somewhere.

As it happened, there was a small riot going on in the park adjacent to the United Nations, only three blocks away. Every available policeman was over there. Out-of-work white youths armed with baseball bats were braining men they thought were homosexuals. They threw one of them into the East River, who turned out to be the finance minister of Sri Lanka.

I would meet some of those youths later at the police station, and they would assume that I, too, was a homosexual. One of them exposed his private parts to me and said, 'Hey, Pops – you want some of this? Come and get it. Yum, yum, yum,' and so on.

But my point is that the police could not come and get me for nearly an hour. So Mary Kathleen and I had a nice long talk. She felt safe in this place. She felt safe with me. She dared to be sane.

It was most touching. Only her body was decrepit. Her voice and the soul it implied might well have belonged still to what she used to be, an angrily optimistic eighteen-year-old.

'Everything is going to be all right now,' she said to me in the showroom of The American Harp Company. 'Something always told me that it would turn out this way. All's well that ends well,' she said.

What a fine mind she had! What fine minds all of the four women I've loved have had! During the months I more or less lived with Mary Kathleen, she read all the books I had read or pretended to have read as a Harvard student. Those volumes had been chores to me, but they were a cannibal feast to Mary Kathleen. She read my books the way a young cannibal might eat the hearts of brave old enemies. Their magic would become hers. She said of my little library one time: 'the greatest books in the world, taught by the wisest men in the world at the greatest university in the world to the smartest students in the world.'

Peace.

And contrast Mary Kathleen, if you will, with my wife Ruth, the Ophelia of the death camps, who believed that even the most intelligent human beings were so stupid that they could only make things worse by speaking their minds. It was thinkers, after all, who had set up the death camps. Setting up a death camp, with its railroad sidings and its around-the-clock crematoria, was not something a moron could do. Neither could a moron explain why a death camp was ultimately humane.

Again: peace.

So there Mary Kathleen and I were – among all those harps. They are very strange-looking instruments, now that I think about them, and not very far from poor Ruth's idea of civilization even in peacetime – impossible marriages between Greek columns and Leonardo da Vinci's flying machines.

Harps are self-destructive, incidentally. When I found myself in the harp business at RAMJAC, I had hoped that American Harp had among its assets some wonderful old harps that would turn out to be as valuable as Stradivari's and the Amatis' violins. There was zero chance for this dream's coming true. The tensions in a harp are so tremendous and unrelenting that it becomes unplayable after fifty years and

164

belongs on a dump or in a museum.

I discovered something fascinating about prothonotary warblers, too. They are the only birds that are housebroken in captivity. You would think that the harps would have to be protected from bird droppings by canopies – but not at all! The warblers deposit their droppings in teacups that are set around. In a state of nature, evidently, they deposit their droppings in other birds' nests. That is what they think the teacups are.

Live and learn!

But back to Mary Kathleen and me among all those harps – with the prothonotary warblers overhead and the police on their way:

'After my husband died, Walter,' she said, 'I became so unhappy and lost that I turned to alcohol.' That husband would have been Jack Graham, the reclusive engineer who had founded The RAMJAC Corporation. He had not built the company from scratch. He had been born a multimillionaire. So far as I knew, of course, she might have been talking about a plumber or a truck driver or a college professor or anyone.

She told about going to a private sanitorium in Louisville, Kentucky, where she was given shock treatments. These blasted all her memories from Nineteen-hundred and Thirty-five until Nineteen-hundred and Fifty-five. That would explain why she thought she could still trust me now. Her memories of how callously I had left her, and of my later betrayal of Leland Clewes and all that, had been burned away. She was able to believe that I was still the fiery idealist I had been in Nineteen-hundred and Thirty-five. She had missed my part in Watergate. Everybody had missed my part in Watergate.

'I had to make up a lot of memories,' she went on, 'just to fill up all the empty spaces. There had been a war, I knew, and I remembered how much you hated fascism. I saw you on a beach somewhere – on your back, in a uniform, with a rifle, and with the water washing gently around you. Your eyes were wide open, Walter, because you were dead. You were staring straight up at the sun.'

We were silent for a moment. A yellow bird far above us warbled as though its heart would break. The song of a prothonotary warbler is notoriously monotonous, as I am the first to admit. I am not about to risk the credibility of my entire tale by claiming that prothonotary warblers rival the Boston Pops Orchestra with their songs. Still – they are capable of expressing heartbreak – within strict limits, of course.

'I've had the same dream of myself,' I said. 'Many's the time, Mary Kathleen, that I've wished it were true.'

'No! No! No!' she protested. 'Thank God you're still alive! Thank God there's somebody still alive who cares what happens to this country. I thought maybe I was the last one. I've wandered this city for years now, Walter, saying to myself, "They've all died off, the ones who cared." And then there you were.'

'Mary Kathleen,' I said, 'you should know that I just got out of prison.'

'Of course you did!' she said. 'All the good people go to prison all the time. Oh, thank God you're still alive! We will remake this country and then the world. I couldn't do it by myself, Walter.'

'No – I wouldn't think so,' I said.

'I've just been hanging on for dear life,' she said. 'I haven't been able to do anything but survive. That's how alone I've been. I don't need much help, but I do need some.'

'I know the problem,' I said.

'I can still see enough to write, if I write big,' she said, 'but I can't read the stories in newspapers anymore. My eyes –' She said she sneaked into bars and department stores and motel lobbies to listen to the news on television, but that the sets were almost never tuned to the news. Sometimes she would hear a snatch of news on somebody's portable radio, but the person owning it usually switched to music as soon as the news began.

Remembering the news I had heard that morning, about the police dog that ate a baby, I told her that she wasn't really missing much.

'How can I make sensible plans,' she said, 'if I don't know what's going on?'

'You can't,' I said.

'How can you base a revolution on *Lawrence Welk* and *Sesame Street* and *All in the Family*?' she said. All these shows were sponsored by RAMJAC.

'You can't,' I said.

'I need solid information,' she said.

'Of course you do,' I said. 'We all do.'

'It's all such crap,' she said. 'I find this information called *People* in garbage cans,' she said, 'but it isn't about people. It's about crap.'

This all seemed so pathetic to me: that a shopping-bag lady helped to plan her scuttlings about the city and her snoozes among ash cans on the basis of what publications and radio and television could tell her about what was really going on.

It seemed pathetic to her, too. 'Jackie Onassis and Frank Sinatra and the Cookie Monster and Archie Bunker make their moves,' she said, 'and then I study what they have done, and then I decide what Mary Kathleen O'Looney had better do.

'But now I have you,' she said. 'You can be my eyes – and my brains!'

'Your eyes, maybe,' I said. 'I haven't distinguished myself in the brains department recently.'

'Oh – if only Kenneth Whistler were alive, too,' she said.

She might as well have said, 'If only Donald Duck were alive, too.' Kenneth Whistler was a labour organizer who had been my idol in the old days – but I felt nothing about him now, had not thought about him for years.

'What a trio we would make,' she went on. 'You and me and Kenneth Whistler!'

Whistler would have been a bum, too, by now, I supposed

– if he hadn't died in a Kentucky mine disaster in Nineteen-hundred and Forty-one. He had insisted on being a worker as well as a labour organizer, and would have found modern union officials with their soft, pink palms intolerable. I had shaken hands with him. His palm had felt like the back of a crocodile. The lines in his face had had so much coal dust worked into them that they looked like black tattoos. Strangely enough, this was a Harvard man – the class of Nineteen-hundred and Twenty-one.

'Well,' said Mary Kathleen, 'at least there's still us – and now we can start to make our move.'

'I'm always open to suggestions,' I said.

'Or maybe it isn't worth it,' she said.

She was talking about rescuing the people of the United States from their economy, but I thought she was talking about life in general. So I said of life in general that it probably was worth it, but that it did seem to go on a little too long. My life would have been a masterpiece, for example, if I had died on a beach with a fascist bullet between my eyes.

'Maybe people are just no good anymore,' she said. 'They all look so mean to me. They aren't like they were during the Depression. I don't see anybody being kind to anybody anymore. Nobody will even speak to me.'

She asked me if I had seen any acts of kindness anywhere. I reflected on this and I realized that I had encountered almost nothing but kindness since leaving prison. I told her so.

'Then it's the way I look,' she said. This was surely so. There was a limit to how much reproachful ugliness most people could bear to look at, and Mary Kathleen and all her shopping-bag sisters had exceeded that limit.

She was eager to know about individual acts of kindness toward me, to have it confirmed that Americans could still be good-hearted. So I was glad to tell her about my first twenty-four hours as a free man, starting with the kindnesses shown to me by Clyde Carter, the guard, and then by Dr Robert Fender, the supply clerk and science-fiction writer. After that, of course, I was given a ride in a limousine by Cleveland Lawes.

Mary Kathleen exclaimed over these people, repeated their names to make sure she had them right. 'They're saints!' she said. 'So there are still saints around!'

Thus encouraged, I embroidered on the hospitality offered to me by Dr Israel Edel, the night clerk at the Arapahoe, and then by the employees at the Coffee Shop of the Hotel Royalton on the following morning. I was not able to give her the name of the owner of the shop, but only the physical detail that set him apart from the populace. 'He had a French-fried hand,' I said.

'The saint with the French-fried hand,' she said wonderingly.

'Yes,' I said, 'and you yourself saw a man I thought was the worst enemy I had in the world. He was the tall, blue-eyed man with the sample case. You heard him say that he forgave me for everything I had done, and that I should have supper with him soon.'

'Tell me his name again,' she said.

'Leland Clewes,' I said.

'Saint Leland Clewes,' she said reverently. 'See how much you've helped me already? I never could have found out about all these good people for myself.' Then she performed a minor mnemonic miracle, repeating all the names in chronological order. 'Clyde Carter, Dr Robert Fender, Cleveland Lawes, Israel Edel, the man with the French-fried hand, and Leland Clewes.'

Mary Kathleen took off one of her basketball shoes. It wasn't the one containing the inkpad and her pens and paper and her will and all that. The shoe she took off was crammed with memorabilia. There were hypocritical love letters from me, as I've said. But she was particularly eager for me to see a snapshot of what she called '... my two favourite men.'

It was a picture of my one-time idol, Kenneth Whistler, the Harvard-educated labour organizer, shaking hands with a small and goofy-looking college boy. The boy was myself. I had ears like a loving cup.

That was when the police finally came clumping in to get me.

'I'll rescue you, Walter,' said Mary Kathleen. 'Then we'll rescue the world together.'

I was relieved to be getting away from her, frankly. I tried to seem regretful about our parting. 'Take care of yourself, Mary Kathleen,' I said. 'It looks like this is good-bye.'

17

I hung that snapshot of Kenneth Whistler and myself, taken in the autumn of Nineteen-hundred and Thirty-five, dead centre in the Great Depression, on my office wall at RAMJAC – next to the circular about stolen clarinet parts. It was taken by Mary Kathleen, with my bellows camera, on the morning after we first heard Whistler speak. He had come all the way to Cambridge from Harlan County, Kentucky, where he was a miner and a union organizer, to address a rally whose purpose was to raise money and sympathy for the local chapter of the International Brotherhood of Abrasives and Adhesives Workers

The union was run by communists then. It is run by gangsters now. As a matter of fact, the start of my prison sentence overlapped with the end of one being served at Finletter by the lifetime president of the I.B.A.A.W. His twenty-three-year-old daughter was running the union from her villa in the Bahamas while he was away. He was on the telephone to her all the time. He told me that the membership was almost entirely black and Hispanic now. It was lily-white back in the thirties – Scandinavians mostly. I don't think a black or Hispanic would have been allowed to join back in the good old days.

Times change.

Whistler spoke at night. On the afternoon before he spoke, I made love to Mary Kathleen O'Looney for the first time. It was mixed up in our young minds, somehow, with the prospect of hearing and perhaps even touching a genuine saint. How better to present ourselves to him or to any holy person, I suppose, than as Adam and Eve – smelling strongly of apple juice?

Mary Kathleen and I made love in the apartment of an associate professor of anthropology named Arthur von Strelitz. His speciality was the headhunters of the Solomon Islands. He spoke their language and respected their taboos. They trusted him. He was unmarried. His bed was unmade. His apartment was on the third floor of a frame house on Brattle Street.

A footnote to history: Not only that house, but that very apartment would be used later as a set in a very popular motion picture called *Love Story*. It was released during my early days with the Nixon administration. My wife and I went to see it when it came to Chevy Chase. It was a made-up story about a wealthy Anglo-Saxon student who married a poor Italian student, much against his father's wishes. She died of cancer. The aristocratic father was played brilliantly by Ray Milland. He was the best thing in the movie. Ruth cried all through the movie. We sat in the back row of the theatre for two reasons: so I could smoke and so there wouldn't be anybody behind her to marvel at how fat she was. But I could not really concentrate on the story, because I knew the apartment where so much of it was happening so well. I kept waiting for Arthur von Strelitz or Mary Kathleen O'Looney or even me to appear.

Small world.

Mary Kathleen and I had the place for a weekend. Von Strelitz had given me the key. He had then gone to visit some other German émigré friends on Cape Ann. He must have been about thirty then. He seemed old to me. He was born into an aristocratic family in Prussia. He was lecturing at Harvard when Hitler became dictator of Germany in the spring of Nineteen-hundred and Thirty-three. He declined to go home. He applied for American citizenship instead. His father, who never communicated with him in any way again, would command a corps of S.S. and die of pneumonia during the Siege of Leningrad. I know how his father died, since there was testimony about his father at the War Crimes Trials in Nuremberg, where I was in charge of housekeeping.

Again: small world.

His father, acting on written orders from Martin Bormann,

who was tried *in absentia* in Nuremberg, caused to be executed all persons, civilian and military, taken prisoner during the siege. The intent was to demoralize the defenders of Leningrad. Leningrad, incidentally, was younger than New York City. Imagine that! Imagine a famous European city, full of imperial treasures and worth besieging, and yet much younger than New York.

Arthur von Strelitz would never learn how his father died. He himself would be rowed ashore from an American submarine in the Solomon Islands, as a spy, while they were still occupied by the Japanese. He would never be heard of again.

Peace.

He thought it was urgent, I remember, that mankind and womankind be defined. Otherwise, he was sure, they were doomed forever to be defined by the needs of institutions. He had mainly factories and armies in mind.

He was the only man I ever knew who wore a monocle.

Now Mary Kathleen O'Looney, age eighteen, lay in his bed. We had just made love. It would be very pretty to paint her as naked now – a pink little body. But I never saw her naked. She was modest. Never could I induce her to take off all her clothes.

I myself stood stark naked at a window, with my private parts just below the sill. I felt like the great god Thor.

'Do you love me, Walter?' Mary Kathleen asked my bare backside.

What could I reply but this: 'Of course I do.'

There was a knock on the door. I had told my coeditor at *The Bay Suite Progressive* where I could be found in case of emergency. 'Who is it?' I said.

There was a sound like a little gasoline engine on the other side of the door. It was Alexander Hamilton McCone, my mentor, who had decided to come to Cambridge unannounced – to see what sort of life I was leading on his money. He sounded like a motor because of his stammer. He stammered because of the Cuyahoga Massacre in Eighteen-hundred and Ninety-four. He was trying to say his own name.

18

I had somehow neglected to tell him that I had become a communist.

Now he had found out about that. He had come first to my room in Adams House, where he was told that I was most likely at *The Progressive*. He had gone to *The Progressive* and had ascertained what sort of publication it was and that I was its coeditor. Now he was outside the door with a copy folded under his arm.

I remained calm. Such was the magic of having emptied my seminal vesicles so recently.

Mary Kathleen, obeying my silent arm signals, hid herself in the bathroom. I slipped on a robe belonging to von Strelitz. He had brought it home from the Solomon Islands. It appeared to be made of shingles, with wreaths of feathers at its collar and cuffs.

Thus was I clad when I opened the door and said to old Mr McCone, who was in his early sixties then, 'Come in, come in.'

He was so angry with me that he could only continue to make those motor sounds: 'bup-bup-bup-bup-bup ...' But he meanwhile did a grotesque pantomime of how repulsed he was by the paper, whose front-page cartoon showed a bloated capitalist who looked just like him; by my costume; by the unmade bed; by the picture of Karl Marx on von Strelitz's wall.

Out he went again, slamming the door behind him. He was through with me!

Thus did my childhood end at last. I had become a man.

And it was as a man that I went that night, with Mary Kathleen on my arm, to hear Kenneth Whistler speak at the rally for my comrades in the International Brotherhood of

Abrasives and Adhesives Workers.

How could I be so serene, so confident? My tuition for the year had already been paid, so I would graduate. I was about to get a full scholarship to Oxford. I had a superb wardrobe in good repair. I had been saving most of my allowance, so that I had a small fortune in the bank.

If I had to, I could always borrow money from Mother, God rest her soul.

What a daring young man I was!

What a treacherous young man I was! I already knew that I would abandon Mary Kathleen at the end of the academic year. I would write her a few love letters and then fall silent after that. She was too low class.

Whistler had a big bandage over one temple and his right arm was in a plaster cast that night. This was a Harvard graduate, mind you, and from a good family in Cincinnati. He was a Buckeye, like me. Mary Kathleen and I supposed that he had been beat up by the forces of evil yet again – by the police or the National Guard, or by goons or organizers of yellow-dog unions.

I held Mary Kathleen's hand.

Nobody had ever told her he loved her before.

I was wearing a suit and a necktie, and so were most of the men there. We wanted to show that we were as decent and sober citizens as anyone. Kenneth Whistler might have been a businessman. He had even found time to shine his shoes.

Those used to be important symbols of self-respect: shined shoes.

Whistler began his speech by making fun of his bandages. 'The Spirit of Seventy-six,' he said.

Everybody laughed and laughed, although the occasion was surely not a happy one. All the members of the union had been fired about a month before – for joining a union. They were makers of grinding wheels, and there was only one company in the area that could use their skills. That was the Johannsen Grinder Company, and that was the company that had fired them. They were specialized potters, essentially, shaping soft materials and then firing them in kilns. The fathers or grandfathers of most of them had actually been potters in Scandinavia, who were brought to this country to learn this new speciality.

The rally took place in a vacant store in Cambridge. Appropriately enough, the folding chairs had been contributed by a funeral home. Mary Kathleen and I were in the first row.

Whistler, it turned out, had been injured in a routine mining accident. He said he had been working as 'a robber,' taking out supporting pillars of coal from a tunnel where the seam had otherwise been exhausted. Something had fallen on him.

And he went seemlessly from talk of such dangerous work in such a dark place to a recollection of a tea dance at the Ritz fifteen years before, where a Harvard classmate named Nils Johannsen had been caught using loaded dice in a crap game in the men's room. This was the same person who was now the president of Johannsen Grinder, who had fired all these workers. Johannsen's grandfather had started the company. He said that Johannsen had had his head stuck in a toilet bowl at the Ritz, and that the hope was that he would never use loaded dice again.

'But here he is,' said Whistler, 'using loaded dice again.'

He said that Harvard could be held responsible for many atrocities, including the executions of Sacco and Vanzetti, but that it was innocent of having produced Nils Johannsen. 'He never attended a lecture, never wrote a paper, never read a book while he was there,' he said. 'He was asked to leave at the end of his sophomore year.

'Oh, I pity him,' he said. 'I even understand him. How else could he ever amount to anything if he did not use loaded dice? How has he used loaded dice with you? The laws that say he can fire anybody who stands up for the basic rights of workers – those are loaded dice. The policemen who will protect his property rights but not your human rights – those are loaded dice.'

Whistler asked the fired workers how much Johannsen

actually knew or cared about grinding wheels. How shrewd this was! The way to befriend working people in those days, and to get them to criticize their society as brilliantly as any philosopher, was to get them to talk about the one subject on which they were almost arrogantly well-informed: their work.

It was something to hear. Worker after worker testified that Johannsen's father and grandfather had been mean bastards, too, but that they at least knew how to run a factory. Raw materials of the highest quality arrived on time in their day – machinery was properly maintained, the heating plant and the toilets worked, bad workmanship was punished and good workmanship was rewarded, no defective grinding wheel ever reached a customer, and on and on.

Whistler asked them if one of their own number could run the factory better than Nils Johannsen did. One man spoke for them all on that subject. 'God, yes,' he said, 'anyone here.'

Whistler asked him if he thought it was right that a person could inherit a factory.

The man's considered answer was this: 'Not if he's afraid of the factory and everybody in it – no. No, siree.'

This piece of groping wisdom impresses me still. A sensible prayer people could offer up from time to time, it seems to me, might go something like this: 'Dear Lord – never put me in the charge of a frightened human being.'

Kenneth Whistler promised us that the time was at hand for workers to take over their factories and to run them for the benefit of mankind. Profits that now went to drones and corrupt politicians would go to those who worked, and to the old and the sick and the orphaned. All people who could work would work. There would be only one social class – the working class. Everyone would take turns doing the most unpleasant work, so that a doctor, for example, might be expected to spend a week out of each year as a garbage man. The production of luxury goods would stop until the basic needs of every citizen were met. Health care would be free. Food would be cheap and nourishing and plentiful. Mansions and hotels and office buildings would be turned into small apartments, until everyone was decently housed. Dwellings would be assigned by means of a lottery. There would be no more wars and eventually no more national boundaries, since everyone in the world would belong to the same class with identical interests – the interests of the working class.

And on and on.

What a spellbinder he was!

Mary Kathleen whispered in my ear, 'You're going to be just like him, Walter.'

'I'll try,' I said. I had no intention of trying.

The most embarrassing thing to me about this autobiography, surely, is its unbroken chain of proofs that I was never a serious man. I have been in a lot of trouble over the years, but that was all accidental. Never have I risked my life, or even my comfort, in the service of mankind. Shame on me.

People who had heard Kenneth Whistler speak before begged him to tell again about leading the pickets outside Charlestown Prison when Sacco and Vanzetti were executed. And it seems strange to me now that I have to explain who Sacco and Vanzetti were. I recently asked young Israel Edel at RAMJAC, the former night clerk at the Arapahoe, what he knew about Sacco and Vanzetti, and he told me confidently that they were rich, brilliant thrill-killers from Chicago. He had them confused with Leopold and Loeb.

Why should I find this unsettling? When I was a young man, I expected the story of Sacco and Vanzetti to be retold as often and as movingly, to be as irresistible, as the story of Jesus Christ some day. Weren't modern people, if they were to marvel creatively at their own lifetimes, I thought, entitled to a Passion like Sacco and Vanzetti's, which ended in an electric chair?

As for the last days of Sacco and Vanzetti as a modern Passion: As on Golgotha, three lower-class men were executed at the same time by a state. This time, though, not just one of the three was innocent. This time two of the three were innocent.

The guilty man was a notorious thief and killer named Celestino Madeiros, convicted of a separate crime. As the end drew near, he confessed to the murders for which Sacco and Vanzetti had been convicted, too.

Why?

'I seen Sacco's wife come here with the kids, and I felt sorry for the kids,' he said.

Imagine those lines spoken by a good actor in a modern Passion Play.

Madeiros died first. The lights of the prison dimmed three times.

Sacco died next. Of the three, he was the only family man. The actor portraying him would have to project a highly intelligent man who, since English was his second language and since he was not clever with languages, could not trust himself to say anything complicated to the witnesses as he was strapped into the electric chair.

'Long live anarchy,' he said. 'Farewell, my wife, and child, and all my friends,' he said. 'Good evening, gentlemen,' he said. 'Farewell, Mother,' he said. This was a shoemaker. The lights of the prison dimmed three times.

Vanzetti was the last. He sat down in the chair in which Madeiros and Sacco had died before anyone could indicate that this was what he was expected to do. He began to speak to the witnesses before anyone could tell him that he was free to do this. English was his second language, too, but he could make it do whatever he pleased.

Listen to this:

'I wish to tell you,' he said, 'that I am an innocent man. I never committed any crime, but sometimes some sin. I am innocent of all crime – not only this one, but all crime. I am an innocent man.' He had been a fish peddler at the time of his arrest.

'I wish to forgive *some* people for what they are now doing to me,' he said. The lights of the prison dimmed three times.

The story yet again:

Sacco and Vanzetti never killed anybody. They arrived in

America from Italy, not knowing each other, in Nineteen-hundred and Eight. It was the same year in which my parents arrived.

Father was nineteen. Mother was twenty-one.

Sacco was seventeen. Vanzetti was twenty. American employers at that time wanted the country to be flooded with labour that was cheap and easily cowed, so that they could keep wages down.

Vanzetti would say later, 'In the immigration station, I had my first surprise. I saw the steerage passengers handled by the officials like so many animals. Not a word of kindness, of encouragement, to lighten the burden of tears that rest heavily upon the newly arrived on American shores.'

Father and Mother used to tell me much the same thing. They, too, were made to feel like fools who had somehow gone to great pains to deliver themselves to a slaughterhouse.

My parents were recruited at once by an agent of the Cuyahoga Bridge and Iron Company in Cleveland. He was instructed to hire only blond Slavs, Mr McCone once told me, on his father's theory that blonds would have the mechanical ingenuity and robustness of Germans, but tempered with the passivity of Slavs. The agent was to pick up factory workers, and a few presentable domestic servants for the various McCone households, as well. Thus did my parents enter the servant class.

Sacco and Vanzetti were not so lucky. There was no broker in human machinery who had a requisition for shapes like theirs. 'Where was I to go? What was I to do?' wrote Vanzetti. 'Here was the promised land. The elevated rattled by and did not answer. The automobiles and the trolleys sped by heedless of me.' So he and Sacco, still separately and in order not to starve to death, had to begin at once to beg in broken English for any sort of work at any wage – going from door to door.

Time passed.

Sacco, who had been a shoemaker in Italy, found himself welcome in a shoe factory in Milford, Massachusetts, a town where, as chance would have it, Mary Kathleen O'Looney's mother was born. Sacco got himself a wife and a house with a garden. They had a son named Dante and a daughter named Inez. Sacco worked six days a week, ten hours each day. He also found time to speak out and give money and take part in demonstrations for workers on strike for better wages and more humane treatment at work and so on. He was arrested for such activities in Nineteen-hundred and Sixteen.

Vanzetti had no trade and so went from job to job – in restaurants, in a quarry, in a steel mill, in a rope factory. He was an ardent reader. He studied Marx and Darwin and Hugo and Gorki and Tolstoi and Zola and Dante. That much he had in common with Harvard men. In Nineteen-hundred and Sixteen he led a strike against the rope factory, which was The Plymouth Cordage Company in Plymouth, Massachusetts, now a subsidiary of RAMJAC. He was blacklisted by places of work far and wide after that, and became a self-employed peddler of fish to survive.

And it was in Nineteen-hundred and Sixteen that Sacco and Vanzetti came to know each other well. It became evident to both of them, thinking independently, but thinking always of the brutality of business practices, that the battlefields of World War One were simply additional places of hideously dangerous work, where a few men could supervise the wasting of millions of lives in the hopes of making money. It was clear to them, too, that America would soon become involved. They did not wish to be compelled to work in such factories in Europe, so they both joined the same small group of Italian-American anarchists that went to Mexico until the war was over.

Anarchists are persons who believe with all their hearts that governments are enemies of their own people.

I find myself thinking even now that the story of Sacco and Vanzetti may yet enter the bones of future generations. Perhaps it needs to be told only a few more times. If so, then the flight into Mexico will be seen by one and all as yet another expression of a very holy sort of common sense.

Be that as it may: Sacco and Vanzetti returned to Massachusetts after the war, fast friends. Their sort of common sense, holy or not, and based on books Harvard men read routinely and without ill effects, had always seemed contemptible to most of their neighbours. Those same neighbours, and those who liked to guide their destinies without much opposition, now decided to be terrified by that common sense, especially when it was possessed by the foreign-born.

The Department of Justice drew up secret lists of foreigners who made no secret whatsoever about how unjust and self-deceiving and ignorant and greedy they thought so many of the leaders were in the so-called 'Promised Land.' Sacco and Vanzetti were on the list. They were shadowed by government spies.

A printer named Andrea Salsedo, who was a friend of Vanzetti's, was also on the list. He was arrested in New York City by federal agents on unspecified charges, and held incommunicado for eight weeks. On May third of Nineteen-hundred and Twenty, Salsedo fell or jumped or was pushed out of the fourteenth-storey window of an office maintained by the Department of Justice.

Sacco and Vanzetti organized a meeting that was to demand an investigation of the arrest and death of Salsedo. It was scheduled for May ninth in Brockton, Massachusetts, Mary Kathleen O'Looney's home town. Mary Kathleen was then six years old. I was seven.

Sacco and Vanzetti were arrested for dangerous radical activities before the meeting could take place. Their crime was the possession of leaflets calling for the meeting. The penalties could be stiff fines and up to a year in jail.

But then they were suddenly charged with two unsolved murders, too. Two payroll guards had been shot dead during a robbery in South Braintree, Massachusetts, about a month before.

The penalties for that, of course, would be somewhat stiffer, would be two painless deaths in the same electric chair.

19

Vanzetti, for good measure, was also charged with an attempted payroll robbery in Bridgewater, Massachusetts. He was tried and convicted. Thus was he transmogrified from a fish peddler into a known criminal before he and Sacco were tried for murder.

Was Vanzetti guilty of this lesser crime? Possibly so, but it did not matter much. Who said it did not matter much? The judge who tried the case said it did not matter much. He was Webster Thayer, a graduate of Dartmouth College and a descendent of many fine New England families. He told the jury, 'This man, although he may not have actually committed the crime attributed to him, is nevertheless morally culpable, because he is the enemy of our existing institutions.'

Word of honour: This was said by a judge in an American court of law. I take the quotation from a book at hand: *Labor's Untold Story*, by Richard O. Boyer and Herbert M. Morais. (United Front: San Francisco, 1955.)

And then this same Judge Thayer got to try Sacco and the known criminal Vanzetti for murder. They were found guilty about one year after their arrest – in July of Nineteen-hundred and Twenty-one, when I was eight years old.

They were finally electrocuted when I was fifteen. If I heard anybody in Cleveland say anything about it, I have forgotten now.

I talked to a messenger boy in an elevator in the RAMJAC Building the other morning. He was about my age. I asked him if he remembered anything about the execution when he was a boy. He said that, yes, he had heard his father say he was sick and tired of people talking about Sacco and Vanzetti all the time, and that he was glad it was finally over with.

I asked him what line of work his father had been in.

'He was a bank president in Montpelier, Vermont,' he said. This was an old man in a war-surplus United States Army overcoat.

Al Capone, the famous Chicago gangster, thought Sacco and Vanzetti should have been executed. He, too, believed that they were enemies of the American way of thinking about America. He was offended by how ungrateful to America these fellow Italian immigrants were.

According to *Labor's Untold Story*, Capone said, 'Bolshevism is knocking at our gates ... We must keep the worker away from red literature and red ruses.'

Which reminds me of a story written by Dr Robert Fender, my friend back in prison. The story was about a planet where the worst crime was ingratitude. People were executed all the time for being ungrateful. They were executed the way people used to be executed in Czechoslovakia. They were defenestrated. They were thrown out of altitudinous windows.

The hero in Fender's story was finally thrown out of a window for ingratitude. His last words, as he went sailing out of a window thirty floors up, were these: 'Thanks a miiiiiiiiiiiiiiiiiiiillionnnnnnnnnn!'

Before Sacco and Vanzetti could be executed for ingratitude in the Massachusetts style, however, huge crowds turned out in protest all over the world. The fish peddler and the shoe-maker had become planetary celebrities.

'Never in our full life,' said Vanzetti, 'could we hope to do such work for tolerance, for justice, for man's understanding of man, as now we do by accident.'

If this were done as a modern Passion Play, the actors playing the authorities, the Pontius Pilates, would still have to express scorn for the opinions of the mob. But they would be in favour rather than against the death penalty this time.

And they would never wash their hands.

They were in fact so proud of what they were about to do that they asked a committee composed of three of the wisest, most respected, most fair-minded and impartial men within the boundaries of the state to say to the world whether or not justice was about to be done.

It was only this part of the Sacco and Vanzetti story that Kenneth Whistler chose to tell – that night so long ago, when Mary Kathleen and I held hands while he spoke.

He dwelt most scornfully on the resonant credentials of the three wise men.

One was Robert Grant, a retired probate judge, who knew what the laws were and how they were meant to work. The chairman was the president of Harvard, and he would still be president when I became a freshman. Imagine that. He was A. Lawrence Lowell. The other, who according to Whistler '... knew a lot about electricity, if nothing else,' was Samuel W. Stratton, the president of the Massachusetts Institute of Technology.

During their deliberations, they received thousands of telegrams, some in favour of the executions, but most opposed. Among the telegraphers were Romain Rolland, George Bernard Shaw, Albert Einstein, John Galsworthy, Sinclair Lewis, and H. G. Wells.

The triumvirate declared at last that it was clear to them that, if Sacco and Vanzetti were electrocuted, justice would be done.

So much for the wisdom of even the wisest human beings.

And I am now compelled to wonder if wisdom has ever existed or can ever exist. Might wisdom be as impossible in this particular universe as a perpetual-motion machine?

Who was the wisest man in the Bible, supposedly – wiser even, we can suppose, than the president of Harvard? He was King Solomon, of course. Two women claiming the same baby appeared before Solomon, asking him to apply his legendary wisdom to their case. He suggested cutting the baby in two.

And the wisest men in Massachusetts said that Sacco and Vanzetti should die.

When their decision was rendered, my hero Kenneth Whistler was in charge of pickets before the Massachusetts State House in Boston, by his own account. It was raining.

'Nature sympathized,' he said, looking straight at Mary

Kathleen and me in the front row. He laughed.

Mary Kathleen and I did not laugh with him. Neither did anybody else in the audience. His laugh was a chilling laugh about how little Nature ever cares about what human beings think is going on.

And Whistler kept his pickets before the State House for ten more days, until the night of the execution. Then he led them through the winding streets and across the bridge to Charlestown, where the prison was. Among his pickets were Edna St Vincent Millay and John Dos Passos and Haywood Broun.

National Guardsmen and police were waiting for them. There were machine gunners on the walls, with their guns aimed out at the general populace, the people who wanted Pontius Pilate to be merciful.

And Kenneth Whistler had with him a heavy parcel. It was an enormous banner, long and narrow and rolled up tight. He had had it made that morning.

The prison lights began their dimming.

When they had dimmed nine times Whistler and a friend hurried to the funeral parlour where the bodies of Sacco and Vanzetti were to be displayed. The state had no further use for the bodies. They had become the property of relatives and friends again.

Whistler told us that two pairs of sawhorses had been set up in the front room of the funeral parlour, awaiting the coffins. Now Whistler and his friend unfurled their banner, and they nailed it to the wall over the sawhorses.

On the banner were painted the words that the man who had sentenced Sacco and Vanzetti to death, Webster Thayer, had spoken to a friend soon after he passed the sentence:

DID YOU SEE WHAT I DID TO THOSE ANARCHIST BASTARDS THE OTHER DAY?

20

Sacco and Vanzetti never lost their dignity – never cracked up. Walter F. Starbuck finally did.

I seemed to hold up quite well when I was arrested in the showroom of The American Harp Company. When old Delmar Peale showed the two policemen the circular about the stolen clarinet parts, when he explained what I was to be arrested for, I even smiled. I had the perfect alibi, after all: I had been in prison for the past two years.

When I told them that, though, it did not relax them as much as I had hoped. They decided that I was perhaps more of a desperado than they had at first supposed.

The police station was in an uproar when we arrived. Television crews and newspaper reporters were trying to get at the young men who had rioted in the gardens of the United Nations, who had thrown the finance minister of Sri Lanka into the East River. The Sri Lankan had not been found yet, so it was assumed that the rioters would be charged with murder.

Actually, the Sri Lankan would be rescued by a police launch about two hours later. He would be found clinging to a bell buoy off Governor's Island. The papers the next morning would describe him as 'incoherent.' I can believe it.

There was no one to question me at once. I was going to have to be locked up for a while. The police station was so busy that there wasn't even an ordinary cell for me. I was given a chair in the corridor outside the cells. It was there that the rioters insulted me from behind bars, imagining that I would enjoy nothing so much as making love to them.

I was eventually taken to a padded cell in the basement. It was designed to hold a maniac until an ambulance could come for her or him. There wasn't a toilet in there, because a maniac might try to bash his or her brains out on a toilet's rim. There was no cot, no chair. I would have to sit or lie on the padded floor. Oddly enough, the only piece of furniture was a large bowling trophy, which somebody had stored in there. I got to know it well.

So there I was back in a quiet basement again.

And, as had happened to me when I was the President's special advisor on youth affairs, I was forgotten again.

I was accidentally left there from noon until eight o'clock that night, without food or water or a toilet or the slightest sound from the outside – on what was to have been my first full day of freedom. Thus began a test of my character that I failed.

I thought about Mary Kathleen and all she had been through. I still did not know that she was Mrs Jack Graham, but she had told me something else very interesting about herself: After I left Harvard, after I stopped answering her letters or even thinking much about her anymore, she hitch-hiked to Kentucky, where Kenneth Whistler was still working as a miner and an organizer. She arrived at sundown at the shack where he was living alone. The place was unlocked, having nothing inside worth stealing. Whistler was still at work. Mary Kathleen had brought food with her. When Whistler came home, there was smoke coming out of his chimney. There was a hot meal waiting for him inside.

That was how she got down into the coalfields. And that was how she happened, when Kenneth Whistler became violent late at night because of alcohol, to run out into the moon-lit street of a shanty town and into the arms of a young mining engineer. He was, of course, Jack Graham.

And then I regaled myself with a story by my prison friend Dr Robert Fender, which he had published under the name of 'Kilgore Trout.' It was called 'Asleep at the Switch.' It was about a huge reception centre outside the Pearly Gates of heaven – filled with computers and staffed by people who had been certified public accountants or investment counsellors or business managers back on Earth.

188

You could not get into heaven until you had submitted to a full review of how well you handled the business opportunities God, through His angels, had offered to you on Earth.

All day long and in every cubicle you could hear the experts saying with utmost weariness to people who had missed this opportunity and then that one: 'And there you were, asleep at the switch again.'

How much time had I spent in solitary by then? I will make a guess: five minutes.

'Asleep at the Switch' was quite a sacrilegious story. The hero was the ghost of Albert Einstein. He himself was so little interested in the wealth that he scarcely heard what his auditor had to say to him. It was some sort of balderdash about how he could have become a billionaire, if only he had gotten a second mortgage on his house in Berne, Switzerland, in Nineteen-hundred and Five, and invested the money in known uranium deposits before telling the world that $E = Mc^2$.

'But there you were – asleep at the switch again,' said the auditor.

'Yes,' said Einstein politely, 'it does seem rather typical.'

'So you see,' said the auditor, 'life really was quite fair. You did have a remarkable number of opportunities, whether you took them or not.'

'Yes, I see that now,' said Einstein.

'Would you mind saying that in so many words?' said the auditor.

'Saying what?' said Einstein.

'That life was fair.'

'Life was fair,' said Einstein.

'If you don't really mean it,' said the auditor, 'I have many more examples to show you. For instance, just forgetting atomic energy: If you had simply taken the money you put into a savings bank when you were at the Institute for Advanced Studies at Princeton, and you had put it, starting in Nineteen-hundred and Fifty, say, into IBM and Polaroid and Xerox – even though you had only five more years to live –'

The auditor raised his eyes suggestively, inviting Einstein to show how smart he could be.

'I would have been rich?' said Einstein.

'"Comfortable," shall we say?' said the auditor smugly. 'But there you were again –' And again his eyebrows went up.

'Asleep at the switch?' asked Einstein hopefully.

The auditor stood and extended his hand, which Einstein accepted unenthusiastically. 'So you see, Doctor Einstein,' he said, 'we can't blame God for everything, now can we?' He handed Einstein his pass through the Pearly Gates. 'Good to have you aboard,' he said.

So into heaven Einstein went, carrying his beloved fiddle. He thought no more about the audit. He was a veteran of countless border crossings by then. There had always been senseless questions to answer, empty promises to make, meaningless documents to sign.

But once inside heaven Einstein encountered ghost after ghost who was sick about what his or her audit had shown. One husband and wife team, which had committed suicide after losing everything in a chicken farm in New Hampshire, had been told that they had been living the whole time over the largest deposit of nickel in the world.

A fourteen-year-old Harlem child who had been killed in a gang fight was told about a two-carat diamond ring that lay for weeks at the bottom of a catch basin he passed every day. It was flawless and had not been reported as stolen. If he had sold it for only a tenth of its value, four hundred dollars, say, according to his auditor, and speculated in commodities futures, especially in cocoa at that time, he could have moved his mother and sisters and himself into a Park Avenue condominium and sent himself to Andover and then to Harvard after that.

There was Harvard again.

All the auditing stories that Einstein heard were told by Americans. He had chosen to settle in the American part of heaven. Understandably, he had mixed feelings about Europeans, since he was a Jew. But it wasn't only Americans who were being audited. Pakistanis and pygmies from the Philippines and even communists had to go through the very same thing.

It was in character for Einstein to be offended first by the mathematics of the system the auditors wanted everybody to be so grateful for. He calculated that if every person on Earth took full advantage of every opportunity, became a millionaire and then a billionaire and so on, the paper wealth on that one little planet would exceed the worth of all the minerals in the universe in a matter of three months or so. Also: There would be nobody left to do any useful work.

So he sent God a note. It assumed that God had no idea what sorts of rubbish His auditors were talking. It accused the auditors rather than God of cruelly deceiving new arrivals about the opportunities they had had on Earth. He tried to guess the auditors' motives. He wondered if they might not be sadists.

The story ended abruptly. Einstein did not get to see God. But God sent out an archangel who was boiling mad. He told Einstein that if he continued to destroy ghosts' respect for the audits, he was going to take Einstein's fiddle away from him for all eternity. So Einstein never discussed the audits with anybody ever again. His fiddle meant more to him than anything.

The story was certainly a slam at God, suggesting that He was capable of using a cheap subterfuge like the adults to get out of being blamed for how hard economic life was down here.

I made my mind a blank.

But then it started singing about Sally in the garden again.

Mary Kathleen O'Looney, exercising her cosmic powers as Mrs Jack Graham, had meanwhile telephoned Arpad Leen, the top man at RAMJAC. She ordered him to find out what the police had done with me, and to send the toughest lawyer in New York City to rescue me, no matter what the cost.

He was to make me a RAMJAC vice-president after that While she was at it, she said, she had a list of other good people who were to be rounded up and also made vice-presidents. These were the people I had told her about, of course – the strangers who had been so nice to me.

She also ordered him to tell Doris Kramm, the old secretary at The American Harp Company, that she didn't have to retire, no matter how old she was.

Yes, and there in my padded cell I told myself a joke I had read in *The Harvard Lampoon* when a freshman. It had amazed me back then because it seemed so dirty. When I became the President's special adviser on youth affairs, and had to read college humour again, I discovered that the joke was still being published many times a year – unchanged. This was it:

SHE: How dare you kiss me like that?
HE: I was just trying to find out who ate all the macaroons.

So I had a good laugh about that there in solitary. But then I began to crack. I could not stop saying to myself, 'Macaroons, macaroons, macaroons ...'

Things got much worse after that. I sobbed. I bounced myself off the walls. I took a crap in a corner. I dropped the bowling trophy on top of the crap.

I screamed a poem I had learned in grammar school:

Don't care if I do die,
Do die, do die!
Like to make the juice fly,
Juice fly, juice fly!

I may even have masturbated. Why not? We old folks have much richer sex lives than most young people imagine.

I eventually collapsed.

At seven o'clock that night the toughest attorney in New York entered the police station upstairs. He had traced me that far. He was a famous man, known to be extremely ferocious and humourless in prosecuting or defending almost anyone. The police were thunderstruck when such a dreaded celebrity appeared. He demanded to know what had become of me.

Nobody knew. There was no record anywhere of my having been released or transferred elsewhere. My lawyer knew I hadn't gone home, because he had already asked after me there. Mary Kathleen had told Arpad Leen and Leen had told the lawyer that I lived at the Arapahoe.

They could not even find out what I had been arrested for.

So all the cells were checked. I wasn't in any of them, of course. The people who had brought me in and the man who had locked me up had all gone off-duty. None of them could be reached at home.

But the detective who was trying to placate my lawyer remembered the cell downstairs and decided to have a look inside it, just in case.

When the key turned in the lock, I was lying on my stomach like a dog in a kennel, facing the door. My stocking feet extended in the direction of the bowling trophy and the crap. I had removed my shoes for some reason.

When the detective opened the door, he was appalled to see me, realizing how long I must have been in there. The City of New York had accidentally committed a very serious crime against me.

'Mr Starbuck –?' he asked anxiously.

I said nothing. I did sit up. I no longer cared where I was or what might happen next. I was like a hooked fish that had done all the fighting it could. Whatever was on the other end of the line was welcome to reel me in.

When the detective said, 'Your lawyer is here,' I did not protest even inwardly that nobody knew I was in jail, that I had no lawyer, no friends, no anything. So be it: My lawyer was there.

Now the lawyer showed himself. It would not have surprised me if he had been a unicorn. He was, in fact, almost that fantastic – a man who, when only twenty-six years old, had been chief counsel of the Senate Permanent Investigating

Committee, whose chairman was Senator Joseph R. McCarthy, the most spectacular hunter of disloyal Americans since World War Two.

He was in his late forties now – but still unsmiling and nervously shrewd. During the McCarthy Era, which came after Leland Clewes and I had made such fools of ourselves, I had hated and feared this man. He was on my side now.

'Mr Starbuck,' he said, 'I am here to represent you, if you want me to. I have been retained on your behalf by The RAMJAC Corporation. Roy M. Cohn is my name.'

What a miracle-worker he was!

I was out of the police station and into a waiting limousine before you could say, '*Habeas corpus!*'

Cohn, having delivered me to the limousine, did not himself get in. He wished me well without shaking my hand, and was gone. He never touched me, never gave any indication that he knew that I, too, had played a very public part in American history in olden times.

So there I was in a limousine again. Why not? Anything was possible in a dream. Hadn't Roy M. Cohn just gotten me out of jail, and hadn't I left my shoes behind? So why shouldn't the dream go on – and have Leland Clewes and Israel Edel, the night clerk at the Arapahoe, already sitting in the back of the limousine, with a space between them for me? This it did.

They nodded to me uneasily. They, too, felt that life wasn't making good sense just now.

What was going on, of course, was that the limousine was cruising around Manhattan like a schoolbus, picking up people Mary Kathleen O'Looney had told Arpad Leen to hire as RAMJAC vice-presidents. This was Leen's personal limousine. It was what I have since learned is called a 'stretch' limousine. The American Harp Company could have used the backseat for a showroom.

Clewes and Edel and the next person we were going to pick up had all been telephoned personally by Leen – after some of his assistants had found out more about who they were and where they were. Leland Clewes had been found in the phonebook. Edel had been found behind the desk at the Arapahoe. One of the assistants had gone to the Coffee Shop of the Royalton to ask for the name of a person who worked there and had a French-fried hand.

Other calls had gone to Georgia – one to the RAMJAC regional office, asking if they had a chauffeur named Cleveland Lawes working for them, and another one to the Federal Minimum Security Adult Correctional Facility at Finletter Air Force Base, asking if they had a guard named Clyde Carter and a prisoner named Dr Robert Fender there.

Clewes asked me if I understood what was going on.

'No,' I said. 'This is just the dream of a jailbird. It's not supposed to make sense.'

Clewes asked me what had happened to my shoes.

'I left them in the padded cell,' I said.

'You were in a padded cell?' he said.

'It's very nice,' I said. 'You can't possibly hurt yourself.'

A man in the front seat next to the chauffeur now turned his face to us. I knew him, too. He had been one of the lawyers who had escorted Virgil Greathouse into prison on the morning before. He was Arpad Leen's lawyer, too. He was worried about my having lost my shoes. He said we would go back to the police station and get them.

'Not on your life!' I said. 'They've found out by now that I threw the bowling trophy down in the shit, and they'll just arrest me again.'

Edel and Clewes now drew away from me some.

'This has to be a dream,' said Clewes.

'Be my guest,' I said. 'The more the merrier.'

'Gentlemen, gentlemen –' said the lawyer genially. 'Please, you mustn't worry so. You are about to be offered the opportunity of your lives.'

'When the hell did she see me?' said Edel. 'What was the wonderful thing she saw me do?'

'We may never know,' said the lawyer. 'She seldom explains herself, and she's a mistress of disguise. She could be anybody.'

'Maybe she was that big black pimp that came in after you last night,' Edel said to me. 'I was nice to him. He was eight feet tall.'

'I missed him,' I said.

'You're lucky,' said Edel.

'You two know each other?' said Clewes.

'Since childhood!' I said. I was going to blow this dream wide open by absolutely refusing to take it seriously. I was damn well going to get back to my bed at the Arapahoe or my cot in prison. I didn't care which.

Maybe I could even wake up in the bedroom of my little brick bungalow in Chevy Chase, Maryland, and my wife would still be alive.

'I can promise you she wasn't the tall pimp,' said the lawyer. 'That much we can be sure of: Whatever she looks like, she is not tall.'

'Who isn't tall?' I said.

'Mrs Jack Graham,' said the lawyer.

'Sorry I asked,' I said.

'You must have done her some sort of favour, too,' the lawyer said to me, 'or done something she saw and admired.'

'It's my Boy Scout training,' I said.

So we came to a stop in front of a rundown apartment building on the Upper West Side. Out came Frank Ubriaco, the owner of the Coffee Shop. He was dressed for the dream in a pale-blue velvet suit and green-and-white cowboy boots with high, high heels. His French-fried hand was elegantly sheathed in a white kid glove. Clewes pulled down a jumpseat for him.

I said hello to him.

'Who are you?' he said.

'You served me breakfast this morning,' I said.

'I served everybody breakfast this morning,' he said.

'You know him, too?' said Clewes.

'This is my town,' I said. I addressed the lawyer, more convinced than ever that this was a dream, and I told him, 'All right – let's pick up my mother next.'

He echoed me uncertainly. 'Your mother?'

'Sure. Why not? Everybody else is here,' I said.

He wanted to be cooperative. 'Mr Leen didn't say anything specific about your not bringing anybody else along. You'd like to bring your mother?'

'Very much,' I said.

'Where is she?' he said.

'In a cemetery in Cleveland,' I said, 'but that shouldn't slow *you* down.'

He thereafter avoided direct conversations with me.

When we got underway again, Ubriaco asked those of us in the backseat who we were.

Clewes and Edel introduced themselves. I declined to do so.

'They're all people who caught the eye of Mrs Graham, just as you did,' said the lawyer.

'You guys know her?' Ubriaco asked Clewes and Edel and me.

We all shrugged.

'Jesus Christ,' said Ubriaco. 'This better be a pretty good job you got to offer. I like what I do.'

'You'll see,' said the lawyer.

'I broke a date for you monkeys,' said Ubriaco.

'Yes – and Mr Leen broke a date for you,' said the lawyer. 'His daughter is having her debut at the Waldorf tonight, and he won't be there. He'll be talking to you gentlemen instead.'

'Fucking crazy,' said Ubriaco. Nobody else had anything to say. As we crossed Central Park to the East Side, Ubriaco spoke again. 'Fucking debut,' he said.

Clewes said to me, 'You're the only one who knows everybody else here. You're in the middle of this thing somehow.'

'Why wouldn't I be?' I said. 'It's my dream.'

And we were delivered without further conversation to the penthouse dwelling of Arpad Leen. We were told by the lawyer to leave our shoes in the foyer. It was the custom of the house. I, of course, was already in my stocking feet.

Ubriaco asked if Leen was a Japanese, since the Japanese commonly took off their shoes indoors.

The lawyer assured him that Leen was a Caucasian, but that he had grown up in Fiji, where his parents ran a general store. As I would find out later, Leen's father was a Hungarian Jew, and his mother was a Greek Cypriot. His parents met when they were working on a Swedish cruise ship in the late twenties. They jumped ship in Fiji, and started the store.

Leen himself looked like an idealized Plains Indian to me. He could have been a movie star. And he came out into the foyer in a striped silk dressing gown and black socks and garters. He still hoped to make it to his daughter's debut.

Before he introduced himself to us, he had to tell the lawyer an incredible piece of news. 'You know what the son of a bitch is in prison for?' he said. 'Treason! And we're supposed to get him out and give him a job. Treason! How do you get somebody out of jail who's committed treason? How do we give him even a lousy job without every patriot in the country raising hell?'

The lawyer didn't know.

'Well,' said Leen, 'what the hell. Get me Roy Cohn again. I wish I were back in Nashville.'

This last remark alluded to Leen's having been the leading publisher of country music in Nashville, Tennessee, before his little empire was swallowed up by RAMJAC. His old company, in fact, was the nucleus of the Down Home Records Division of RAMJAC.

Now he looked us over and he shook his head in wonderment. We were a freakish crew. 'Gentlemen,' he said, 'you have all been noticed by Mrs Jack Graham. She didn't tell me where or when. She said you were honest and kind.'

'Not me,' said Ubriaco.

'You're free to question her judgement, if you want,' said Leen. 'I'm not. I have to offer you good jobs. I don't mind doing that, though, and I'll tell you why: She never told me to do anything that didn't turn out to be in the best interests

198

of the company. I used to say that I never wanted to work for anybody, but working for Mrs Jack Graham has been the greatest privilege of my life.' He meant it.

He did not mind making us all vice-presidents. The company had seven hundred vice-presidents of this and that on the top level, the corporate level, alone. When you got out into the subsidiaries, of course, the whole business of presidents and vice-presidents started all over again.

'*You* know what she looks like?' Ubriaco wanted to know.

'I haven't seen her recently,' said Leen. This was an urbane lie. He had never seen her, which was a matter of public record. He would confess to me later that he did not even know how he had come to Mrs Graham's attention. He thought she might have seen an article on him in the Diners Club magazine, which had featured him in their 'Man on the Move' department.

In any event, he was abjectly loyal to her. He loved and feared his idea of Mrs Graham the way Emil Larkin loved and feared his idea of Jesus Christ. He was luckier than Larkin in his worship, of course, since the invisible superior being over him called him up and wrote him letters and told him what to do.

He actually said one time, 'Working for Mrs Graham has been a religious experience for me. I was adrift, no matter how much money I was making. My life had no purpose until I became president of RAMJAC and placed myself at her beck and call.'

All happiness is religious, I have to think sometimes.

Leen said he would talk to us one by one in his library. 'Mrs Graham didn't tell me about your backgrounds, what your special interests might be – so you're just going to have to tell me about yourselves.' He said for Ubriaco to come into the library first, and asked the rest of us to wait in the living room. 'Is there anything my butler can bring you to drink?' he said.

Clewes didn't want anything. Edel asked for a beer. I, still hoping to blow the dream wide open, ordered a *pousse-café*, a rainbow-coloured drink that I had never seen, but which I had studied while earning my Doctor of Mixology degree. A heavy liqueur was put into the bottom of a glass, then a lighter one of a different colour was carefully spooned in on top of that, and then a lighter one still on top of that, and on and on, with each bright layer undisturbed by the one above or below.

Leen was impressed with my order. He repeated it, to make sure he had heard it right.

'If it's not too much trouble,' I said. It was no more trouble, surely, than building a full-rigged ship model in a bottle, say.

'No problem!' said Leen. This, I would learn, was a favourite expression of his. He told the butler to give me a *pousse-café* without further ado.

He and Ubriaco went into the library, and the rest of us entered the living room, which had a swimming pool. I had never seen a living room with a swimming pool before. I had heard of such a thing, of course, but hearing of and actually seeing that much water in a living room are two very different things.

I knelt by the pool and swirled my hand in the water, curious about the temperature, which was soupy. When I withdrew my hand and considered its wetness, I had to admit to myself that the wet was undreamlike. My hand was really wet and would remain so for some time, unless I did something about it.

All this was really going on. As I stood, the butler arrived with my *pousse-café*.

Outrageous behaviour was not the answer. I was going to have to start paying attention again. 'Thank you,' I said to the butler.

'You're welcome, sir,' he replied.

Clewes and Edel were seated at one end of a couch about half a block long. I joined them, wanting their appreciation for how sedate I had become.

They were continuing to speculate as to when Mrs Graham might have caught them behaving so virtuously.

Clewes mourned that he had not had many opportunities to be virtuous, selling advertising matchbooks and calendars from door to door. 'About the best I can do is let a building custodian tell me his war stories,' he said. He remembered a custodian in the Flatiron Building who claimed to have been the first American to cross the bridge over the Rhine at Remagan, Germany, during World War Two. The capture of this bridge had been an immense event, allowing the Allied Armies to pour at high speed right into the heart of Germany. Clewes doubted that the custodian could have been Mrs Jack Graham, though.

Israel Edel supposed that Mrs Graham could be disguised as a man, though. 'I sometimes think that about half our customers at the Arapahoe are transvestites,' he said.

The possibility of Mrs Graham's being a transvestite would be brought up again soon, and most startlingly, by Arpad Leen.

Meanwhile, though, Clewes got back on the subject of World War Two. He got personal about it. He said that he and I, when we were wartime bureaucrats, had only imagined that we had something to do with defeats and victories. 'The war was won by fighters, Walter. All the rest was dreams.'

It was his opinion that all the memoirs written about that war by civilians were swindles, pretences that the war had been won by talkers and writers and socialists, when it could only have been won by fighters.

A telephone rang in the foyer. The butler came in to say that the call was for Clewes, who could take it on the telephone on the coffee table in front of us. The telephone was black-and-white plastic and shaped like 'Snoopy,' the famous dog in the comic strip called 'Peanuts.' Peanuts was owned by what was about to become my division of RAMJAC. To converse on that telephone, as I would soon discover, you had to put your mouth over the dog's stomach and stick his nose in your ear. Why not?

It was Clewes's wife Sarah, my old girlfriend, calling from their apartment. She had just come home from a private nursing case, had found his note, which said where he was and what he was doing there and how he could be reached by telephone.

He told her that I was there, too, and she could not believe it. She asked to talk to me. So Clewes handed me the plastic dog.

'Hi,' I said.

'This is crazy,' she said. 'What are you doing there?'

'Drinking a *pousse-café* by the swimming pool,' I said.

'I can't imagine you drinking a *pousse-café*,' she said.

'Well, I am,' I said.

She asked how Clewes and I had met. I told her. 'Such a small world, Walter,' she said, and so on. She asked me if Clewes had told me that I had done them a big favour when I testified against him.

'I would have to say that that opinion is moot,' I told her.

'Is what?' she said.

'Moot,' I said. It was a word she had somehow never heard before. I explained it to her.

'I'm so dumb,' she said. 'There's so much I don't know, Walter.' She sounded just like the same old Sarah on the telephone. It could have been Nineteen-hundred and Thirty-five again, which made what she said next especially poignant: 'Oh, my God, Walter! We're both over sixty years old! How is that possible?'

'You'd be surprised, Sarah,' I said.

She asked me to come home with Clewes for supper, and I said I would if I could; that I didn't know what was going to happen next. I asked her where she lived.

It turned out that she and Clewes lived in the basement of the same building where her grandmother used to live – in Tudor City. She asked me if I remembered her grandmother's apartment, all the old servants and furniture jammed into only four rooms.

I said I did, and we laughed.

I did not tell her that my son also lived somewhere in Tudor City. I would find out later that there was nothing vague about

202

his proximity to her, with his musical wife and his adopted children. Stankiewicz of *The New York Times* was in the same building, and notoriously so, because of the wildness of the children – and only three floors above Leland and Sarah Clewes.

She said that it was good that we could still laugh, despite all we had been through. 'At least we still have our sense of humour,' she said. That was something Julie Nixon had said about her father after he got bounced out of the White House: 'He still has his sense of humour.'

'Yes – at least that,' I agreed.

'Waiter,' she said, 'what's this fly doing in my soup?'

'What?' I said.

'What's this fly doing in my soup?' she persisted.

And then it came back to me: This was the opening line in a daisychain of jokes we used to tell each other on the telephone. I closed my eyes. I gave the answering line, and the telephone became a time machine for me. It allowed me to escape from Nineteen-hundred and Seventy-seven and into the fourth dimension.

'I believe that's the backstroke, madam,' I said.

'Waiter,' she said, 'there's also a needle in my soup.'

'I'm sorry, madam,' I said, 'that's a typographical error. That should have been a noodle.'

'Why do you charge so much for cream?' she said.

'It's because the cows hate to squat on those little bottles,' I said.

'I keep thinking it's Tuesday,' she said.

'It *is* Tuesday,' I said.

'That's what I keep thinking,' she said. 'Tell me, do you serve flannelcakes?'

'Not on the menu today,' I said.

'Last night I dreamed I was eating flannelcakes,' she said.

'That must have been very nice,' I said.

'It was terrible,' she said. 'When I woke up, the blanket was gone.'

She, too, had reason to escape into the fourth dimension. As

I would find out later, her patient had died that night. Sarah had liked her a lot. The patient was only thirty-six, but she had a congenitally defective heart – huge and fatty and weak.

And imagine, if you will, the effect this conversation was having on Leland Clewes, who was sitting right next to me. My eyes were closed, as I say, and I was in such an ecstasy of timelessness and placelessness that I might as well have been having sexual intercourse with his wife before his eyes. He forgave me, of course. He forgives everybody for everything. But he still had to be impressed by how lazily in love Sarah and I could still be on the telephone.

What is more protein than adultery? Nothing in this world.

'I am thinking of going on a diet,' said Sarah.

'I know how you can lose twenty pounds of ugly fat right away,' I said.

'How?' she said.

'Have your head cut off,' I said.

Clewes could hear only my half of the conversation, of course, so he could only hear the premise or the snapper of a joke, but never both. Some of the lines were highly suggestive.

I asked Sarah, I remember, if she smoked after intercourse.

Clewes never heard her reply, which was this: 'I don't know. I never looked.' And then she went on: 'What did you do before you were a waiter?'

'I used to clean birdshit out of cuckoo clocks,' I said.

'I have often wondered what the white stuff in birdshit was,' she said.

'That's birdshit, too,' I told her. 'What kind of work do *you* do?'

'I work in the bloomer factory,' she said.

'Is it a good job in the bloomer factory?' I inquired archly.

21

'Oh,' she said, 'I can't complain. I pull down about ten thousand a year.' Sarah coughed, and that, too, was a cue, which I nearly missed.

'That's quite a cough you have there,' I said in the nick of time.

'It won't stop,' she said.

'Take two of these pills,' I said. 'They're just the thing.'

So she made swallowing sounds: 'gluck, gluck, gluck.' And then she asked what was in the pills.

'The most powerful laxative known to medical science,' I said.

'Laxative!' she said.

'Yes,' I said, 'now you don't dare cough.'

We did the joke, too, about a sick horse I supposedly had. I have never really owned a horse. The veterinarian gave me half a pound of purple powder that I was to give the horse, supposedly. The veterinarian told me to make a tube out of paper, and to put the powder inside the tube, and then to slip the tube into the horse's mouth, and to blow it down its throat.

'How is the horse?' said Sarah.

'Oh, the horse is fine,' I said.

'You don't look so good,' she said.

'No,' I said, 'that is because the horse blew first.'

'Can you still imitate your mother's laugh?' she said.

This was not the premise of yet another joke. Sarah genuinely wanted to hear me imitate my mother's laugh, something I used to do a lot for Sarah on the telephone. I had not tried the trick in years. I not only had to make my voice high: I also had to make it beautiful.

The thing was this: Mother never laughed out loud. She

had been trained to stifle her laughter when a servant girl in Lithuania. The idea was that a master or guest, hearing a servant laughing somewhere in the house, might suspect that the servant was laughing about him.

So when my mother could not help laughing, she made tiny, pure sounds like a music box – or perhaps like bells far away. It was accidental that they were so beautiful.

So – forgetful of where I was, I now filled my lungs and tightened my throat, and to please my old girlfriend, I reincarnated the laughing part of my mother.

It was at that point that Arpad Leen and Frank Ubriaco came back into the living room. They heard the end of my song.

I told Sarah that I had to hang up now, and I did hang up.

Arpad Leen stared at me hard. I had heard women speak of men's undressing them mentally. Now I was finding out what that felt like. As things turned out, that was exactly what Leen was doing to me: imagining what I would look like with no clothes on.

He was beginning to suspect that I was Mrs Jack Graham, checking up on him while disguised as a man.

22

I could not know that, of course – that he thought I might be Mrs Graham. So his subsequent courting of me was as inexplicable as anything that had happened to me all day.

I tried to believe that he was being so attentive in order to soften the bad news he had to give me by and by: that I was simply not RAMJAC material, and that his limousine was waiting down below to take me back, still jobless, to the Arapahoe. But the messages in his eyes were more passionate than that. He was ravenous for my approval of everything he did.

He told me, and not Leland Clewes or Israel Edel, that he had just made Frank Ubriaco a vice-president of the McDonald's Hamburgers Division of RAMJAC.

I nodded that I thought that was nice.

The nod was not enough for Leen. 'I think it's a wonderful example of putting the right man in the right job,' he said. 'Don't you? That's what RAMJAC is all about, don't you think – putting good people where they can use their talents to the fullest?'

The question was for me and nobody else, so I finally said, 'Yes.'

I had to go through the same thing after he had interviewed and hired Clewes and Edel. Clewes was made a vice-president of the Diamond Match Division, presumably because he had been selling advertising matchbooks for so long. Edel was made a vice-president of the Hilton Department of the Hospitality Associates, Ltd, Division, presumably because of his three weeks of experience as a night clerk at the Arapahoe.

It was then my turn to go into the library with him. 'Last but not least,' he said coyly. After he closed the door on the rest of the house, his flirtatiousness became even more out-

207

rageous. 'Come into my parlour,' he murmured, 'said the spider to the fly.' He winked at me broadly.

I hated this. I wondered what had happened to the others in here.

There was a Mussolini-style desk with a swivel chair behind it. 'Perhaps *you* should sit there,' he said. He made his eyebrows go up and down. 'Doesn't that look like your kind of chair? Eh? Eh? Your kind of chair?'

This could only be mockery, I thought. I responded to it humbly. I had had no self-respect for years and years. 'Sir,' I said, 'I don't know what's going on.'

'Ah,' he said, holding up a finger, 'that *does* happen sometimes.'

'I don't know how you found me, or even if I'm who you think I am,' I said.

'I haven't told you yet who I think you are,' he said.

'Walter F. Starbuck,' I said bleakly.

'If you say so,' he said.

'Well,' I said, 'whoever I am, I'm not much anymore. If you're really offering jobs, all I want is a little one.'

'I'm under orders to make you a vice-president,' he said, 'orders from a person I respect very much. I intend to obey.'

'I want to be a bartender,' I said.

'Ah!' he said. 'And mix *pousse-cafés*!'

'I can, if I have to,' I said. 'I have a Doctor of Mixology degree.'

'You also have a lovely high voice when you want to,' he said.

'I think I had better go home now,' I said. 'I can walk. It isn't far from here.' It was only about forty blocks. I had no shoes; but who needed shoes? I would get home somehow without them.

'When it's time to go home,' he said, 'you shall have my limousine.'

'It's time to go home now,' I said. 'I don't care how I get there. It has been a very tiring day for me. I don't feel very clever. I just want to sleep. If you know anybody who needs a bartender, even part-time, I can be found at the Arapahoe.'

'What an actor you are!' he said.

I hung my head. I didn't even want to look at him or at anybody anymore. 'Not at all,' I said. 'Never was.'

'I will tell you something very strange,' he said.

'I won't understand it,' I said.

'Everyone here tonight remembers having seen you, but they've never seen each other before,' he said. 'How would you explain that?'

'I have no job,' I said. 'I just got out of prison. I've been walking around town with nothing to do.'

'Such a complicated story,' he said. 'You were in *prison*, you say?'

'It happens,' I said.

'I won't ask what you were in prison for,' he said. What he meant, of course, was that I, as Mrs Graham disguised as a man, did not have to go on telling taller and taller lies, unless it entertained me to do so.

'Watergate,' I said.

'Watergate!' he exclaimed. 'I thought I knew the names of almost all the Watergate people.' As I would find out later, he not only knew their names: He knew many of them well enough to have bribed them with illegal campaign contributions, and to have chipped in for their defences afterward. 'Why is it that I have never heard the name Starbuck associated with Watergate before?'

'I don't know,' I said, my head still down. 'It was like being in a wonderful musical comedy where the critics mentioned everybody but me. If you can find an old programme, I'll show you my name.'

'The prison was in Georgia, I take it,' he said.

'Yes,' I said. I supposed that he knew that because Roy M. Cohn had looked up my record when he had to get me out of jail.

'That explains Georgia,' he said.

I couldn't imagine why anybody would want Georgia explained.

'So that's how you know Clyde Carter and Cleveland Lawes and Dr Robert Fender,' he said.

'Yes,' I said. Now I started to be afraid. Why would this man, one of the most powerful corporate executives on the planet, bother to find out so much about a pathetic little jailbird like me? Was there a suspicion somewhere that I knew some spectacular secret that could still be revealed about Watergate? Might he be playing cat-and-mouse with me before having me killed some way?

'And Doris Kramm,' he said, 'I'm sure you know her, too.'

I was so relieved not to know her! I was innocent after all! His whole case against me would collapse now. He had the wrong man, and I could prove it! I did not know Doris Kramm! 'No, no, no,' I said. 'I don't know Doris Kramm.'

'The lady you asked me not to retire from The American Harp Company,' he said.

'I never asked you anything,' I said.

'A slip of the tongue,' he said.

And then horror grew in me as I realized that I really did know Doris Kramm. She was the old secretary who had been sobbing and cleaning out her desk at the harp showroom. I wasn't about to tell him that I knew her, though.

But he knew I knew her, anyway! He knew everything! 'You will be happy to learn that I telephoned her personally and assured her that she did not have to retire, after all. She can stay on as long as she likes. Isn't that lovely?'

'No,' I said. It was as good an answer as any. But now I was remembering the harp showroom. I felt as though I had been there a thousand years ago, perhaps, in some other life, before I was born. Mary Kathleen O'Looney had been there. Arpad Leen, in his omniscience, would surely mention her next.

And then the nightmare of the past hour suddenly revealed itself as having been logical all along. I knew something that Leen himself did not know, that probably nobody in the world but me knew. It was impossible, but it had to be true:

Mary Kathleen O'Looney and Mrs Jack Graham were the same.

It was then that Arpad Leen raised my hand to his lips and kissed it. 'Forgive me for penetrating your disguise, madam,' he said, 'but I assume you made it so easy to penetrate on purpose. Your secret is safe with me. I am honoured at last to meet you face to face.'

He kissed my hand again, the same hand Mary Kathleen's dirty little claw had grasped that morning. 'High time, madam,' he said. 'We have worked together so well so long. High time.'

My revulsion at being kissed by a man was so fully automatic that I became a veritable Queen Victoria! My rage was imperial, although my language came straight from the playgrounds of my Cleveland adolescence. 'What the hell do you think you're doing?' I demanded to know. 'I'm no God damn woman!' I said.

I have spoken of losing my self-respect over the years. Arpad Leen had now lost his in a matter of seconds, with this preposterous misapprehension of his.

He was speechless and white.

When he tried to recover, he did not recover much. He was beyond apologizing, too shattered to exhibit charm or cleverness of any kind. He could only grope for where the truth might lie.

'But you know her,' he said at last. There was resignation in his voice, for he was acknowledging what was becoming clear to me, too: that I was more powerful than he was, if I wanted to be.

I confirmed this for him. 'I know her well,' I said. 'She will do whatever I tell her, I'm sure.' This last was gratuitous. It was vengeful.

He was still a very sick man. I had come between his God and him. It was his turn to hang his head. 'Well,' he said, and there was a long pause, 'speak well of me, if you can.'

More than anything now, I wanted to rescue Mary Kathleen O'Looney from the ghastly life the dragons in her mind had forced her to lead. I knew where I could find her.

'I wonder if you could tell me,' I said to the broken Leen, 'where I could find a pair of shoes to fit me at this time of night?'

His voice came to me as though from the place where I was going next, the great cavern under Grand Central Station. 'No problem,' he said.

23

The next thing I knew, I, all alone, having made certain that no one was following me, was descending the iron stair-case into the cavern. Every few steps I called ahead, croon-ingly, comfortingly, 'It's Walter, Mary Kathleen. It's Walter here.'

How was I shod? I was wearing black patent leather even-ing slippers with little bows at the insteps. They had been given to me by the ten-year-old son of Arpad Leen, little Dexter. They were just my size. Dexter had been required to buy them for dancing school. He did not need them anymore. He had delivered his first successful ultimatum to his par-ents: He had told them that he would commit suicide if they insisted that he keep on going to dancing school. He hated dancing school that much.

What a dear boy he was – in his pyjamas and bathrobe after a swim in the living room. He was so sympathetic and con-cerned for me, for a little old man who had no shoes for his little feet. I might have been a kindly elf in a fairy tale, and he might have been a princeling, making a gift to the elf of a pair of magic dancing shoes.

What a beautiful boy he was. He had big brown eyes. His hair was a crown of black ringlets. I would have given a lot for a son like that. Then again, my own son, I imagine, would have given a lot for a father like Arpad Leen.

Fair is fair.

'It's Walter, Mary Kathleen,' I called again. 'It's Walter here.' At the bottom of the steps, I came across the first clue that all might not be well. It was a shopping bag from Bloom-ingdale's – lying on its side, vomiting rags and a doll's head and a copy of *Vogue*, a RAMJAC publication.

I straightened it up and stuffed things back into its mouth, pretending that that was all that needed to be done to put things right again. That is when I saw a spot of blood on the floor. That was something I couldn't put back where it belonged. There were many more farther on.

And I don't mean to draw out the suspense here to no purpose, to give readers a *frisson*, to let them suppose that I would find Mary Kathleen with her hands cut off, waving her bloody stumps at me. She had in fact been sideswiped by a Checker cab on Vanderbilt Avenue, and had refused medical attention, saying that she was fine, just fine.

But she was far from fine.

There was a possible irony here, one I am, however, unable to confirm. There was a very good chance that Mary Kathleen had been creamed by one of her own taxicabs.

Her nose was broken, which was where the blood had come from. There were worse things wrong with her. I cannot name them. No inventory was ever taken of everything that was broken in Mary Kathleen.

She had hidden herself in a toilet stall. The drops of blood showed me where to look. There could be no doubt as to who was in there. Her basketball shoes were visible beneath the door.

At least there was not a corpse in there. When I crooned my name and my harmlessness again, she unlatched the door and pulled it open. She was not using the toilet, but simply sitting on it. She might as well have been using it, her humiliation by life was now so complete. Her nosebleed had stopped, but it had left her with an Adolf Hitler moustache.

'Oh! You poor woman!' I cried.

She was unimpressed by her condition. 'I guess that's what I am,' she said. 'That's what my mother was.' Her mother, of course, had died of radium poisoning.

'What happened to you?' I said.

She told me about being hit by a taxi. She had just mailed a letter to Arpad Leen, confirming all the orders she had given to him on the telephone.

'I'll get an ambulance,' I said.

'No, no,' she said. 'Stay here, stay here.'

'But you need help!' I said.

'I'm past that,' she said.

'You don't even know what's wrong with you,' I said.

'I'm dying, Walter,' she said. 'That's enough to know.'

'Where there's life there's hope,' I said, and I prepared to run upstairs.

'Don't you dare leave me alone again!' she said.

'I'm going to save your life!' I said.

'You've got to hear what I have to say first!' she said. 'I've been sitting here thinking, "My God – after all I've gone through, after all I've worked for, there isn't going to be anybody to hear the last things I have to say." You get an ambulance, and there won't be anybody who understands English on that thing.'

'Can I make you more comfortable?' I said.

'I am comfortable,' she said. There was something to that claim. Her layers and layers of clothing were keeping her warm. Her little head was supported in a corner of the stall and cushioned against the metal by a pillow of rags.

There was meanwhile an occasional grumbling in the living rock around us. Something else was dying upstairs, which was the railroad system of the United States. Half-broken locomotives were dragging completely broken passenger cars in and out of the station.

'I know your secret,' I said.

'Which one?' she said. 'There are so many now.'

I expected it to be a moment of high drama when I told her that I knew she was the majority stockholder in RAM-JAC. It was a fizzle, of course. She had told me that already, and I had failed to hear.

'Are you going deaf, Walter?' she said.

'I hear you all right, now,' I said.

'On top of everything else,' she said, 'am I going to have to yell my last words?'

'No,' I said. 'But I don't want to listen to any more talk about last words. You're so rich, Mary Kathleen! You can take over a whole hospital, if you want to – and make them make you well again!'

'I hate this life,' she said. 'I've done everything I can to make it better for everybody, but there probably isn't that much that anybody can do. I've had enough of trying. I want to go to sleep now.'

'But you don't have to live this way!' I said. 'That's what I came here to tell you. I'll protect you, Mary Kathleen. We'll hire people we can trust absolutely. Howard Hughes hired Mormons – because they have such high moral standards. We'll hire Mormons, too.'

'Oh Lord, Walter,' she said, 'you think I haven't tried Mormons?'

'You have?' I said.

'I was up to my ears in Mormons one time,' she said, and she told me as gruesome a tale as I ever expect to hear.

It happened when she was still living expensively, still trying to find ways to enjoy her great wealth at least a little bit. She was a freak that many people would have liked to photograph or capture or torment in some way – or kill. People would have liked to kill her for her hands or her money, but also for revenge. RAMJAC had stolen or ruined many other businesses and had even had a hand in the toppling of governments in countries that were small and weak.

So she dared not reveal her true identity to anyone but her faithful Mormons, and she had to keep moving all the time. And so it came to pass that she was staying on the top floor of a RAMJAC hotel in Managua, Nicaragua. There were twenty luxury suites on the floor, and she hired them all. The two stairways from the floor below were blocked with brutal masonry, like the archway in the lobby of the Arapahoe. The controls on the elevators were set so that only one could reach the top, and that one was manned by a Mormon.

Not even the manager of the hotel, supposedly, knew who she really was. But everyone in Managua, surely, must have suspected who she really was.

Be that as it may: She rashly resolved to go out into the

city alone one day, to taste however briefly what she had not tasted for years – what it was like to be just another human being in the world. So out she went in a wig and dark glasses.

She befriended a middle-aged American woman whom she found weeping on a bench in a park. The woman was from St Louis. Her husband was a brewmaster in the Anheuser-Busch Division of RAMJAC. They had come to Nicaragua for a second honeymoon on the advice of a travel agent. The husband had died that morning of amoebic dysentery.

So Mary Kathleen took her back to the hotel and put her into one of the many unused suites she had, and told some of her Mormons to arrange to have the body and the widow flown to St Louis on a RAMJAC plane.

When Mary Kathleen went to tell her about the arrangements, she found the woman strangled with a cord from the draperies. This was the really horrible part, though: Whoever had done it had obviously believed the woman was Mary Kathleen. Her hands were cut off. They were never found.

Mary Kathleen went to New York City soon after that. She began to watch shopping-bag ladies through field glasses from her suite in the Waldorf Towers. General of the Armies Douglas MacArthur lived on the floor above her, incidentally.

She never went out, never had visitors, never called anyone. No hotel people were allowed in. The Mormons brought the food from downstairs, and made the beds, and did all the cleaning. But one day she received a threatening note, anyway. It was in a pink, scented envelope atop her most intimate lingerie. It said that the author knew who she was and held her responsible for the overthrow of the legitimate government of Guatemala. He was going to blow up the hotel.

Mary Kathleen could take it no more. She walked out on her Mormons, who were surely loyal, but unable to protect her. She began to protect herself with layers and layers of clothing she found in garbage cans.

'If your money made you so unhappy,' I said, 'why didn't you give it away?'

'I am!' she said. 'After I die, you look in my left shoe, Walter. You will find my will in there. I leave The RAMJAC Corporation to its rightful owners, the American people.' She smiled. It was harrowing to see such cosmic happiness expressed by gums and a rotten tooth or two.

I thought she had died. She had not.

'Mary Kathleen – ?' I said.

'I'm not dead yet,' she said.

'I really am going to get help now,' I said.

'If you do, I'll die,' she said. 'I can promise that now. I can die when I want to now. I can pick the time.'

'Nobody can do that,' I said.

'Shopping-bag ladies can,' she said. 'It's our special dispensation. We can't say when we will start dying. But once we do start, Walter, we can pick the exact time. Would you like me to die right now, at the count of ten?'

'Not now, not ever,' I said.

'Then stay here,' she said.

So I did. What else could I do?

'I want to thank you for hugging me,' she said.

'Any time,' I said.

'Once a day is enough,' she said. 'I've had my hug today.'

'You were the first woman I ever really made love to,' I said. 'Do you remember that?'

'I remember the hugs,' she said. 'I remember you said you loved me. No man had ever said that to me before. My mother used to say it to me a lot – before she died.'

I was starting to cry again.

'I know you never meant it,' she said.

'I did, I did,' I protested. 'Oh, my God – I did.'

'It's all right,' she said. 'You couldn't help it that you were born without a heart. At least you tried to believe what the people with hearts believed – so you were a good man just the same.'

She stopped breathing. She stopped blinking. She was dead.

Epilogue

There was more. There is always more.

It was nine o'clock in the evening of my first full day of freedom. I still had three hours to go. I went upstairs and told a policeman that there was a dead shopping-bag lady in the basement.

His duties had made him cynical. He said to me, 'So what else is new?'

So I stood by the body of my old friend in the basement until the ambulance attendants came, just as any other faithful animal would have done. It took a while, since it was known that she was dead. She was stiffening up when they got there. They commented on that. I had to ask them what they had just said, since they did not speak in English. It turned out that their first language was Urdu. They were both from Pakistan. Their English was primitive. If Mary Kathleen had died in their presence instead of mine, they would have said, I am sure, that she spoke gibberish at the end.

I inquired of them, in order to calm the sobs that were welling up inside me, to tell me a little about Urdu. They said it had a literature as great as any in the world, but that it had begun as a spare and ugly artificial language invented in the court of Genghis Khan. Its purpose in the beginning was military. It allowed his captains to give orders that were understood in every part of the Mongol Empire. Poets would later make it beautiful.

Live and learn.

I gave the police Mary Kathleen's maiden name. I gave them my true name as well. I was not about to be cute with the police. Neither was I ready to have anyone learn yet that Mrs Jack Graham was dead. The consequences of that announcement would surely be an avalanche of some kind.

I was the only person on the planet who could set it off. I was not ready to set it off yet. This was not cunning on my part, as some people have said. It was my natural awe of an avalanche.

I walked home, a harmless little elf in his magic dancing shoes, to the Hotel Arapahoe. Much straw had been spun into gold that day, and much gold had been spun into straw. And the spinning had just begun.

There was a new night clerk, naturally, since Israel Edel had been summoned to Arpad Leen's. This new man had been sent over to fill in on short notice. His regular post was behind the desk at the Carlyle, also a RAMJAC hotel. He was exquisitely dressed and groomed. He was mortified, having to deal with whores and people fresh out of jails and lunatic asylums and so on.

He had to tell me that: that he really belonged to the Carlyle, and that he was only filling in. This was not the real him.

When I told him my name, he said that there was a package for me, and a message, too.

The police had returned my shoes and had picked up the clarinet parts from my bureau. The message was from Arpad Leen. It was a holograph, like Mary Kathleen's will, which I had in the inner pocket of my suitcoat – along with my Doctor of Mixology degree. The pockets of my raincoat were stuffed with other materials from Mary Kathleen's shoes. They bulged like saddlebags.

Leen wrote that the letter was for my eyes only. He said that in the midst of the confusion at his penthouse he had never gotten around to offering a specific job to me. He suggested that I would be happy in his old division, which was Down Home Records. It now included *The New York Times* and Universal Pictures and Ringling Bros and Barnum & Bailey and Dell Publishing, among other things. There was also a catfood company, he said, which I needn't worry about. It was about to be transferred to the General Foods

Division. It had belonged to the *Times*.

'If this is not your cup of tea,' he wrote, 'we'll find something that is. I am absolutely thrilled to know that we will have an observer for Mrs Graham among us. Please give her my warmest regards.'

There was a postscript. He said that he had taken the liberty of making an appointment for me at eleven the next morning with someone named Morty Sills. There was an address. I assumed that Sills was a RAMJAC personnel director or something. It turned out that he was a tailor.

Once again a multimillionaire was sending Walter F. Starbuck to his own tailor, to be made into a convincing counterfeit of a perfect gentleman.

On the following morning I was still numbed by my dread of the avalanche. I was four thousand dollars richer and technically a thief. Mary Kathleen had had four one-thousand-dollar bills as insoles for her basketball shoes.

There was nothing in the papers about the death of Mary Kathleen. Why would there have been? Who cared? There was an obituary for the patient Sarah Clewes had lost – the woman with the bad heart. She left three children behind. Her husband had died in an automobile accident a month before, so the children were orphans now.

As I was being measured for a suit by Morty Sills, I found it unbearable to think of Mary Kathleen's not being claimed by anyone. Clyde Carter was there, too, fresh off the plane from Atlanta. He, too, was getting a brand-new wardrobe, even before Arpad Leen had seen him.

He was scared.

I told him not to be.

So I went to the morgue after lunch, and I claimed her. It was easily done. Who else would want that tiny body? It had no relatives. I was its only friend.

I had one last look at it. It was nothing. There was nobody in there anymore. 'Nobody home.'

I found a mortician only one block away. I had him pick up the body and embalm it and put it into a serviceable casket. There was no funeral. I did not even accompany it to the grave, which was a crypt in a great concrete honeycomb in Morristown, New Jersey. The cemetery had advertised in the *Times* that morning. Each crypt had a tasteful little bronze door on which the tenant's name was engraved.

Little did I dream that the man who did the engraving of the doors would be arrested for drunken driving about two years later, and would comment on what an unusual name the arresting officer had. He had come across it only once before – at his lugubrious place of work. The name of the officer, a Morris County deputy sheriff, actually, was Francis X. O'Looney.

O'Looney would become curious as to how the woman in the crypt was related to him.

O'Looney, using the sparse documents at the cemetery, would trace Mary Kathleen back to the morgue in New York City. There he would get a set of her fingerprints. On the outside chance that she had been arrested or had spent time in a mental institution, he would send the prints to the FBI.

Thus would RAMJAC be brought tumbling down.

There was a bizarre sidelight to the case. O'Looney, before he finally found out who Mary Kathleen really was, fell in love with his dream of her when she was young. He had it all wrong, incidentally. He dreamed that she was tall and buxom and black-haired, whereas she had been short and scrawny and red-haired. He dreamed that she was an immigrant who had gone to work for an eccentric millionaire in a spooky mansion, and that she had been both attracted and repelled by this man, and that he had abused her to the point of death.

All this came out in divorce proceedings brought against O'Looney by his wife of thirty-two years. It was front-page stuff in the tabloids for a week or more. O'Looney was already famous by then. The papers called him. 'The man who blew the whistle on RAMJAC,' or variations on that theme. Now his wife was claiming that his affections had been alienated by a ghost. He wouldn't sleep with her anymore. He stopped brushing his teeth. He was chronically late to work. He became a grandfather, and he didn't care. He wouldn't even look at the baby.

What was particularly sick about his behaviour was that, even after he found out what Mary Kathleen had really been like, he stayed in love with the original dream.

'Nobody can ever take that away from me,' he said. 'It's the most precious thing I own.'

He has been relieved of his duties, I hear. His wife is suing him again – this time for her share in the small fortune he got for the movie rights to his dream. The film is to be shot in a spooky old mansion in Morristown. If you can believe the gossip columns, there is to be a talent search for an actress to play the Irish immigrant girl. Al Pacino has already agreed to play Sheriff O'Looney, and Kevin McCarthy to play the eccentric millionaire.

So I dallied too long, and now I must go to prison again, they say. My high jinks with Mary Kathleen's remains were not crimes in and of themselves, since corpses have no more rights than do orts from last night's midnight snack. My actions were accessory, however, to the commission of a class E felony, which according to Section 190.30 of the Penal Law of New York State consists of unlawfully concealing a will.

I had entombed the will itself in a safe-deposit box of Manufacturers Hanover Trust Company, a division of RAMJAC.

I have tried to explain to my little dog that her master must go away for a while – because he violated Section 190.30. I have told her that laws are written to be obeyed. She under-

stands nothing. She loves my voice. All news from me is
good news. She wags her tail.

I lived very high. I bought a duplex with a low-interest
company loan. I cashed stock options for clothes and furniture. I became a fixture at the Metropolitan Opera and the
New York City Ballet, coming and going by limousine.

I gave intimate parties at my home for RAMJAC authors
and recording artists and movie actors and circus perform-
ers – Isaac Bashevis Singer, Mick Jagger, Jane Fonda, Günther
Gebel Williams, and the like. It was fun. After RAMJAC
acquired the Marlborough Gallery and Associated American
Artists, I had painters and sculptors to my parties, too.

How well did I do at RAMJAC? During my incumbency,
my division, including subsidiaries under its control, both
covert and overt, won eleven platinum records, forty-two gold
records, twenty-two Oscars, eleven National Book Awards,
two American League pennants, two National League pennants, two World Series, and fifty-three Grammies – and we
never failed to show a return on capital of less than 23 per
cent. I even engaged in corporate in-fighting, preventing the
transfer of the catfood company from my division to General
Foods. It was exciting. I got really mad.

We just missed getting another Nobel prize in literature
several times. But then we already had two: Saul Bellow and
Mr Singer.

I myself have made *Who's Who* for the first time in my
.life. This is a slightly tarnished triumph, admittedly, since my
own division controls Gulf & Western, which controls *Who's
Who*. I put it all in there, except for the prison term and the
name of my son: where I was born, where I went to college,
various jobs I've held, my wife's maiden name.

Did I invite my own son to my parties – to chat with so
many heroes and heroines of his? No. Did he quit the *Times*

when I became his superior there? No. Did he write or telephone greetings of any sort? No. Did I try to get in touch with him? Only once. I was in the basement apartment of Leland and Sarah Clewes. I had been drinking, something I don't enjoy and rarely do. And I was physically so close to my son. His apartment was only thirty feet above my head.

It was Sarah who had made me telephone him.

So I dialled my son's number. It was about eight o'clock at night. One of my little grandchildren answered, and I asked him his name.

'Juan,' he said.

'And your last name?' I said.

'Stankiewicz,' he said. In accordance with my wife's will, incidentally, Juan and his brother, Geraldo, were receiving reparations from West Germany for the confiscation of my wife's father's bookstore in Vienna by the Nazis after the *Anschluss*, Germany's annexation of Austria in Nineteen-hundred and Thirty-eight. My wife's will was an old one, written when Walter was a little boy. The lawyer had advised her to leave the money to her grandchildren so as to avoid one generation of taxes. She was trying to be smart about money. I was out of work at the time.

'Is your daddy home?' I said.

'He's at the movies,' he said.

I was so relieved. I did not leave my name. I said I would call back later.

As for what Arpad Leen suspected about me: Like anyone else, he was free to suspect as much or as little as he pleased. There were no more fingerprinted messages from Mrs Graham. The last one confirmed in writing that Clewes and I and Ubriaco and Edel and Lawes and Carter and Fender were to be made vice-presidents.

There was a deathly silence after that – but there had been deathly silences before. One lasted two years. Leen meanwhile operated under the mandate of a letter Mary Kathleen had sent him in Nineteen-hundred and Seventy-one, which said only this: 'acquire, acquire, acquire.'

She had certainly picked the right man for the job. Arpad Leen was born to acquire and acquire and acquire.

What was the biggest lie I told him? That I saw Mrs Graham once a week, and that she was happy and well and quite satisfied with the way things were going.

As I testified before a grand jury: He gave every evidence of believing me, no matter what I said about Mrs Graham.

I was in an extraordinary position theologically with respect to that man. I knew the answers to so many of the ultimate questions he might want to ask about that life of his.

Why did he have to go on acquiring and acquiring and acquiring? Because his deity wanted to give the wealth of the United States to the people of the United States. Where was his deity? In Morristown, New Jersey. Was she pleased with how he was doing his job? She was neither pleased nor displeased, since she was as dead as a doornail. What should he do next? Find another deity to serve.

I was in an extraordinary position theologically with respect to his millions of employees, too, of course, since he was a deity to them, and supposedly knew exactly what he wanted and why.

Well – it is all being sold off now by the federal government, which has hired twenty thousand new bureaucrats, half of them lawyers, to oversee the job. Many people assumed that RAMJAC owned everything in the country. It was something of an anticlimax, then, to discover that it owned only 19 per cent of it – not even one-fifth. Still – RAMJAC was enormous when compared with other conglomerates. The second largest conglomerate in the Free World was only half its size. The next five years after that, if combined, would have been only about two-thirds the size of RAMJAC.

There are plenty of dollars, it turns out, to buy all the

goodies the federal government has to sell. The President of the United States himself was astonished by how many dollars had been scattered over the world through the years. It was as though he had told everybody on the planet, 'Please rake your yard and send the leaves to me.'

There was a photograph on an inside page of the *Daily News* yesterday of a dock in Brooklyn. There was about an acre of bales that looked like cotton on the dock. These were actually bales of American currency from Saudi Arabia, cash on the barrelhead, so to speak, for the McDonald's Hamburgers Division of RAMJAC.

The headline said this: 'HOME AT LAST!'

Who is the lucky owner of all those bales? The people of the United States, according to the will of Mary Kathleen O'Looney.

What, in my opinion, was wrong with Mary Kathleen's scheme for a peaceful economic revolution? For one thing, the federal government was wholly unprepared to operate all the businesses of RAMJAC on behalf of the people. For another thing: Most of those businesses, rigged only to make profits, were as indifferent to the needs of the people as, say, thunderstorms. Mary Kathleen might as well have left one-fifth of the weather to the people. The businesses of RAMJAC, by their very nature, were as unaffected by the joys and tragedies of human beings as the rain that fell on the night that Madeiros and Sacco and Vanzetti died in an electric chair. It would have rained anyway.

The economy is a thoughtless weather system – and nothing more.

Some joke on the people, to give them such a thing.

There was a supper party given in my honour last week – a 'going away party,' you might say. It celebrated the completion of my last full day at the office. The host and hostess were Leland Clewes and his lovely wife Sarah. They have not moved out of their basement apartment in Tudor City, nor has Sarah given up private nursing, although Leland is now pulling down about one hundred thousand dollars a year at RAMJAC. Much of their money goes to the Foster Parents Programme, a scheme that allows them to support individual children in unfortunate circumstances in many parts of the world. They are supporting fifty children, I think they said. They have letters and photographs from several of them, which they passed around.

I am something of a hero to certain people, which is a novelty. I single-handedly extended the life of RAMJAC by two years and a little more. If I had not concealed the will of Mary Kathleen, those at the party would never have become vice-presidents of RAMJAC. I myself would have been thrown out on my ear – to become what I expect to be anyway, if I survive my new prison term, which is a shopping-bag man.

Am I broke again? Yes. My defence has been expensive. Also: My Watergate lawyers have caught up with me. I still owe them a lot for all they did for me.

Clyde Carter, my former guard in Georgia and now a vice-president of the Chrysler Air Temp Division of RAMJAC, was there with his lovely wife Claudia. He did a side-splitting imitation of his cousin the President, saying, 'I will never lie to you,' and promising to rebuild the South Bronx and so on.

Frank Ubriaco was there with his lovely new wife Marilyn, who is only seventeen. Frank is fifty-three. They met at a discotheque. They seem very happy. She said that what attracted her to him at first was that he wore a white glove on only one hand. She had to find out why. He told her at first that the hand had been burned by a Chinese communist flame thrower during the Korean War, but later admitted that he had done it to himself with a Fry-o-lator. They have started a collection of tropical fish. They have a coffee table that contains tropical fish.

Frank invented a new sort of cash register for the McDonald's Hamburgers Division. It was getting harder all the time to find employees who understood numbers well, so Frank took the numbers off the keys of the cash register and substituted pictures of hamburgers and milkshakes and French fries and Coca-Colas and so on. The person totting up a bill would simply punch the pictures of the various things a customer had ordered, and the cash register would add it up for him.

Frank got a big bonus for that.

My guess is that the Saudis will keep him on.

There was a telegram to me from Dr Robert Fender, still in prison in Georgia. Mary Kathleen had wanted RAMJAC to make him a vice-president, too, but there was no way to get him out of prison. Treason was just too serious a crime. Clyde Carter had written to him that I was going back to prison myself, and that there was going to be a party for me, and that he should send a telegram.

This was all it said: 'Ting-a-ling.'

That was from his science-fiction story about the judge from the planet Vicuna, of course, who had to find a new body to occupy, and who flew into my ear down there in Georgia, and found himself stuck to my feelings and destiny until I died.

According to the judge in the story, that was how they said both hello and good-bye on Vicuna: 'Ting-a-ling.'

'Ting-a-ling' was like the Hawaiian 'aloha,' which also means both hello and good-bye.

'Hello and good-bye.' What else is there to say? Our language is much larger than it needs to be.

I asked Clyde if he knew what Fender was working on now.

'A science-fiction novel about economics,' said Clyde.

'Did he say what pseudonym he's going to use?' I said.

' "Kilgore Trout," ' said Clyde.

*

My devoted secretary, Leora Borders, and her husband, Lance, were there. Lance was just getting over a radical mastectomy. He told me that one mastectomy in two hundred was performed on a man. Live and learn!

There were several other RAMJAC friends who should have been there, but dared not come. They feared that their reputations, and hence their futures as executives, might be tainted if it were known that they were friendly with me.

There were telegrams from other people I had had to my famous little parties – John Kenneth Galbraith and Salvador Dali and Erica Jong and Liv Ullmann and the Flying Farfans and on and on.

Robert Redford's telegram, I remember, said this: 'Hang tough.'

The telegrams were something less than spontaneous. As Sarah Clewes would admit under questioning, she had been soliciting them all week long.

Arpad Leen sent a spoken message through Sarah, which was meant for my ears alone: 'Good show.' That could be taken a million different ways.

He was no longer presiding over the dismemberment of RAMJAC, incidentally. He had been hired away by American Telephone and Telegraph Company, which had just been bought by a new company in Monaco named BIBEC. Nobody has been able to find out who or what BIBEC is, so far. Some people think it's the Russians.

At least I will have some real friends outside of prison this time.

There was a bowl of yellow tulips on the table for a centre-piece. It was April again.

It was raining outside. Nature sympathized.

I was seated at the place of honour – to the right of my hostess, of Sarah Clewes, the nurse. Of the four women I ever loved, she was always the easiest one to talk to. That may be because I had never promised her anything, and so had never let her down. Oh, Lord – the things I used to promise my mother and my poor wife and poor Mary Kathleen!

Young Israel Edel and his not-so-lovely wife Norma were there. I say that she was not-so-lovely for the simple reason that she has always hated me. I don't know why. I have never insulted her, and she is certainly as pleased as Punch with the upturn her husband's career has taken. He would still be a night clerk, if it weren't for me. The Edels are renovating a brownstone in Brooklyn Heights with all the money he makes. Still – every time she looks at me, I feel like something the cat dragged in. It is just one of those things. I think she may be slightly crazy. She miscarried twins about a year ago. That might have something to do with it. She may have some sort of chemical imbalance as a result of that. Who knows?

She wasn't seated next to me anyway, thank God. Another black woman was. That was Eucharist Lawes, the lovely wife of Cleveland Lawes, the former RAMJAC chauffeur. He is a vice-president of the Transico Division now. That is really his wife's name: Eucharist. It means *happy gratitude*, and I don't know why more people don't name their daughters that. Everybody calls her 'Ukey.'

Ukey was homesick for the South. She said the people were friendlier and more relaxed and more natural down there. She was after Cleveland to retire in or near Atlanta, especially now that the Transico Division had been bought by Playgrounds International, which everybody knows is a front for the Mafia. It just can't be proved.

My own division was being snapped up by I. G. Farben, a West German concern.

'It won't be the same old RAMJAC,' I said to Ukey. 'That's for sure.'

There were presents – some silly, some not. Israel Edel gave me a rubber ice-cream cone with a squeaker in it – a plaything for my little dog, who is a female Lhasa apso, a golden dust-mop without a handle. I could never have a dog when I was young, because Alexander Hamilton McCone hated dogs. So this is the only dog I have ever known at all well – and she sleeps with me. She snores. So did my wife.

I have never bred her, but now, according to the veterinarian, Dr Howard Padwee, she is experiencing a false pregnancy and believes the rubber ice-cream cone to be a puppy. She hides it in closets. She carries it up and down the stairs of my duplex. She is even secreting milk for it. She is getting shots to make her stop doing that.

I observe how profoundly serious Nature has made her about a rubber ice-cream cone – brown rubber cone, pink rubber ice cream. I have to wonder what equally ridiculous commitments to bits of trash I myself have made. Not that it matters at all. We are here for no purpose, unless we can invent one. Of that I am sure. The human condition in an exploding universe would not have been altered one iota if, rather than live as I have, I had done nothing but carry a rubber ice-cream cone from closet to closet for sixty years.

Clyde Carter and Leland Clewes chipped in on a far more expensive present, which is a chess-playing computer. It is about the size of a cigar box, but most of the space is taken up by a compartment for the playing pieces. The computer itself is not much bigger than a package of cigarettes. It is called 'Boris.' Boris has a long, narrow little window in which he announces his moves. He can even joke about the moves I make. 'Really?' he will say; or, 'Have you played this game before?' or, 'Is this a trap?' or, 'Spot me a queen.'

Those are standard chess jokes. Alexander Hamilton McCone and I exchanged those same tired jokes endlessly when, for the sake of a Harvard education in my future, I agreed to be his chess-playing machine. If Boris had existed in those days, I probably would have gone to Western Reserve, and then become a tax assessor or an office manager in a lumberyard, or an insurance salesman, or some such thing. Instead, I am the most disreputable Harvard graduate since Putzi Hänfstaengl, who was Hitler's favourite pianist.

At least I gave ten thousand dollars to Harvard before the lawyers came and took away all my money again.

It was time for me now at the party to respond to all the toasts that had been offered to me. I stood. I had not had a drop of alcohol.

'I am a recidivist,' I said. I defined the word as describing a person who habitually relapsed into crime or antisocial behaviour.

'A good word to know,' said Leland Clewes.

There was laughter all around.

'Our lovely hostess has promised two more surprises before the evening is over,' I said. These would turn out to be the trooping in of my son and his little human family from up-stairs, and the playing of a phonograph recording of part of my testimony before Congressman Richard M. Nixon of California and others so long ago. It had to be played at seventy-eight revolutions per minute. Imagine that. 'As though I hadn't had surprises enough!' I said.

'Not enough nice ones, old man,' said Cleveland Lawes.

'Say it in Chinese,' I said. He had, of course, been a prisoner of war of the Chinese for a while.

Lawes said something that certainly sounded like Chinese.

'How do we know he wasn't ordering sweet-and-sour pork?' said Sarah.

'You don't,' said Lawes.

We had begun our feast with oysters, so I announced that oysters were not the aphrodisiacs many people imagined them to be.

There were boos, and then Sarah Clewes beat me to the punch line of that particular joke. 'Walter ate twelve of them the other night,' she said, 'and only four of them worked!'

She had lost another patient the day before.

There was more laughter all around.

And I was suddenly offended and depressed by how silly we were. The news, after all, could hardly have been worse.

Foreigners and criminals and other endlessly greedy conglomerates were gobbling up RAMJAC. Mary Kathleen's legacy to the people was being converted to mountains of rapidly deteriorating currency, which were being squandered in turn on a huge new bureaucracy and on legal fees and consultants' fees, and on and on. What was left, it was said by the politicians, would help to pay the interest on the people's national debt, and would buy them more of the highways and public buildings and advanced weaponry they so richly deserved.

Also: I was about to go to jail again.

So I elected to complain about our levity. 'You know what is finally going to kill this planet?' I said.

'Cholesterol!' said Frank Ubriaco.

'A total lack of seriousness,' I said. 'Nobody gives a damn anymore about what's really going on, what's going to happen next, or how we ever got into such a mess in the first place.'

Israel Edel, with his doctor's degree in history, took this to be a suggestion that we become even sillier, if possible. So he began to make booping and beeping sounds. Others chimed in with their own *beeps* and *boops*. They were all imitating supposedly intelligent signals from outer space, which had been received by radio telescopes only the week before. They were the latest news sensation, and had in fact driven the RAMJAC story off the front pages. People were beeping and booping and laughing, not just at my party, but everywhere.

Nobody was prepared to guess what the signals meant. Scientists did say, though, that if the signals were coming from whence they appeared to come, they had to be a million years old or more. If Earth were to make a reply, it would be the start of a very slow conversation, indeed.

So I gave up on saying anything serious. I told another joke, and I sat down.

The party ended, as I say, with the arrival of my son and daughter-in-law and their two children, and with the playing

234

of a phonograph recording of the closing minutes of my testimony before a congressional committee in Nineteen-hundred and Forty-nine.

My daughter-in-law and my grandchildren found it natural and easy, seemingly, to accord me the honours due a grandfather who, when all was said and done, was a clean and dapper kindly old man. The model for what the children found to love in me, I suppose, was Santa Claus.

My son was a shock. He was such a homely and unhealthy and unhappy-looking young man. He was short like me, and nearly as fat as his poor mother had become toward the end. I still had most of my hair, but he was bald. The baldness must have been inherited from the Jewish side of his family.

He was a chain-smoker of unfiltered cigarettes. He coughed a lot. His suit was riddled with cigarette holes. I glanced at him while the record was playing, and I saw that he was so nervous that he had three cigarettes all going at one time.

He had shaken my hand with the correct wretchedness of a German general surrendering at Stalingrad, say. I was still a monster to him. He had been cajoled into coming against his better judgement – by his wife and Sarah Clewes.

Too bad.

The record changed nothing. The children, kept up long after their bedtime, squirmed and dozed.

The record was meant to honour me, to let people who might not know about it hear for themselves what an idealistic young man I had been. The part in which I accidentally betrayed Leland Clewes as a former communist was on another record, I presume. It was not played.

Only my very last sentences were of much interest to me. I had forgotten them.

Congressman Nixon had asked me why, as the son of immigrants who had been treated so well by Americans, as a man who had been treated like a son and been sent to Harvard by an American capitalist, I had been so ungrateful to the American economic system.

The answer I gave him was not original. Nothing about me

235

has ever been original. I repeated what my one-time hero, Kenneth Whistler, had said in reply to the same general sort of question long, long ago. Whistler had been a witness at a trial of strikers accused of violence. The judge had become curious about him, had asked him why such a well-educated man from such a good family would so immerse himself in the working class.

My stolen answer to Nixon was this: 'Why? The Sermon on the Mount, sir.'

There was polite applause when the people at the party realized that the phonograph record had ended.

Good-bye.

W.F.S.

Index